Dead Shot

By the same author

Loose Cannon
The Meddlers
Old Bones Buried Under
Countdown Murder

Dead Shot

June Drummond

ROBERT HALE · LONDON

ISBN 978-0-7090-9285-8

Robert Hale Limited
Clerkenwell House
Clerkenwell Green
London EC1R 0HT

www.halebooks.com

2 4 6 8 10 9 7 5 3 1

My thanks go to my agent Frances Bond, my editor Eileen Molver,
my publishers and all those colleagues and friends who have helped in
the production of this book

Typeset in 11/14½pt Sabon
Printed and bound in Great Britain by
Biddles Limited, King's Lynn

I

TREVOR CORNWALL LEFT the Savoy Hotel at twenty minutes past four on the first Friday in May, and drove eastward past the Royal Courts of Justice and St Paul's Cathedral. It wasn't the quickest route to follow, but he loved London and enjoyed idling through its history-laden streets.

He crossed the river at Blackfriars Bridge and skirted Southwark, heading for Greenwich. He owned a number of houses around the world, but Greenwich was home. The watchdog of England, he called it. From the heights overlooking the Isle of Dogs, men had seen the Norsemen's longships nose up the Thames, and the Nazi bombers converge on the heart of the City.

Greenwich was where East met West, no matter what Rudyard Kipling might have written.

He stopped in Bermondsey to buy wine. He had avoided alcohol at the luncheon. That was his practice when he had to make an important speech, and today's was important, not only because the victims of the Turkish earthquake desperately needed funds, but because today was the anniversary of Nerina's death. She'd been half Turkish. He'd met her in Istanbul, loved her at first sight and twenty years without her hadn't dimmed that love.

He'd built the house for her. She'd made it beautiful and comfortable. It stood on five acres of land, which included a strip of woodland. He smiled, remembering how she'd ignored the plants of indigenous-only buffs, and planted exotic trees all along their private access lane. There was a Canadian maple right opposite the gates to their driveway. In a few months the leaves would burn with a flame as red as Nerina's hair.

He turned from the tarred road into the lane, slowing to avoid a feral cat that fled into a roadside thicket. Reaching the wrought-iron gates, he saw that a motorbike had been propped against them. There was no sign of the owner. Gone into the woods, Cornwall thought. Trippers tended to treat them as a comfort zone.

Sighing, he climbed out of his car and crossed the road. The bike looked new and expensive, not the sort a careful owner would leave unguarded.

He was about to reach for its handlebars when the shot that killed him was fired. The bullet struck him in the back of the head, and the impact flung him forward against the gates. The sound of the shot was still echoing skywards as he slid to the ground.

Jumbo Barnes was not on the permanent staff of *The Sporting Monitor*. He didn't qualify, being as near as dammit intellectually challenged, but from time to time he was taken on to do work that others shunned.

On this afternoon, a team of workmen was engaged in digging up a broken sewage pipe that ran the length of *The Monitor*'s frontage. The pavement was blocked by piles of viscous mud and rubble, and only a plank bridge afforded access from the roadway to the entrance doors.

Jumbo's duties were twofold. First, he had to direct motor vehicles to the side lane that led to the paper's parking lot; and second, he had either to help pedestrians cross the malodorous trench, or take from them any envelopes they wished to deliver to the building. He was not permitted to waylay postmen, or to accept large packages that might contain bombs. These had to be sent to the back premises, to be checked by electronic scanners.

By ten minutes to six, the road team was gone, and pedestrians were giving the area a wide berth. Jumbo passed the time by watching the flow of rush hour traffic. He knew cars, trucks and motorbikes the way the experts in the building knew the shenanigans of the world of sport. At 6.30 he saw something that made him shift his shoulders from *The Monitor*'s wall, and advance across the plank bridge.

Twenty yards down the road, the traffic was halted at a red light, and in the nearside lane, a man sat astride a racing motorbike. Such bikes were not a common sight in the City, and this one was a Cougar III, newest model in a famous line; lean and light and strong, beautiful in Jumbo's eyes. The rider wore a sleek leather tracksuit, and his larger-than-normal helmet had a visor the tawny green of a highland stream. An oblong box was strapped to the carrier behind him.

The lights changed and the bike edged forward and stopped. In the rider's gloved hand was a brown business envelope. Jumbo seized his chance. Leaning forward, he called,

'Want that delivered, mate?'

The biker's head turned slowly. He did not speak, but seemed to consider the plank bridge, the cluttered pavement, and Jumbo's smiling face. He nodded and handed over the envelope. Jumbo carried it to the row of slots in *The Monitor*'s facade, and dropped it through the one marked 'Editorial Material'. He turned to wave to the biker, but the man ignored the signal and rode out into the westward-bound traffic.

His unfriendly attitude didn't disturb Jumbo. He never expected thanks. His mum always said that people who took out the rubbish or cleaned up dog sick were ministering angels who got their reward from Heaven. Jumbo wondered how many chores the biker had done to qualify for a Cougar III.

He wasn't to know that he'd just had a close encounter with the Angel of Death.

Rupert Hollings, editor of *The Monitor*, switched his attention from a report on the use of steroids by kickboxers, to the bespectacled man standing on the far side of his desk.

'What?' he said.

The man laid a sheet of paper on the desk.

'Sympathy notice,' he said, 'on the death of Trevor Cornwall. Delivered ten minutes ago.'

The editor stared. 'Don't talk crap, Rooney. Cornwall's alive and well. He's just been addressing a lunch at the Savoy, drumming up funds for the victims of the Turkish earthquake.'

'Yes,' Rooney agreed. 'Ted Jarvis covered it. I buzzed Ted and he told me Cornwall talked up a storm – the money poured in. Cornwall left to go home soon after four.'

The editor opened his mouth, shut it and picked up the sheet of paper. He read it, frowning.

'Don't we have our own obit. for Cornwall?' he asked.

'Umh. I wrote it myself.' Rooney had the task of preparing draft obituaries for the rich and famous, so that in the event of a sudden death, the paper could publish a prompt and suitable tribute.

Hollings tapped the desk. 'He's got his facts right, except that Cornwall's not dead.'

'Probably a hoax,' Rooney said. Thirty years as a journalist had convinced him that the world was full of nutters who'd do anything to see themselves in print.

Hollings scowled. He was no less cynical than Rooney, but he knew Trevor Cornwall as a good citizen who shouldn't be the target of cheap publicity-seekers. He referred to his electronic notebook, found the number of Cornwall's mobile phone and reached for the telephone. He tried the number, listened briefly then shook his head.

'Not answering. He's probably driving.'

'Try Liz,' Rooney suggested.

Liz Cupar was Cornwall's daughter and also his publicity agent. She was well known to *The Monitor*'s staff, not only for her press handouts, but as a horsewoman of note. There were photos in the files of Liz soaring over fences, or clutching trophies. Two years back, she'd given up competitive riding, and concentrated on helping to train Cornwall's string of racehorses.

Hollings called her work and home numbers and received the recorded message that she was not available.

He leaned back in his chair, staring at the paper on his desk. Reason said it was a hoax, but unreason touched cold fingers to the nape of his neck.

'It doesn't feel right,' he muttered.

Rooney wanted to catch a train to Chelmsford and spend the weekend in his garden. 'Try again later,' he offered, but Hollings ignored him. He was consulting a list of London's police stations.

This time his call was answered at once. He said, 'My name is Rupert Hollings. I'm the editor of *The Sporting Monitor*. I've received what may be a threatening message.... No, not to myself, to Mr Trevor Cornwall, the industrialist.... Yes.... What? Yes, I'll hold.' Waiting, he scowled at Rooney.

'How was this thing delivered?'

'Editorial postbox,' Rooney said.

'Who's on door duty?'

'El Thicko. Jumbo Barnes.'

The receiver quacked, and Hollings said, 'Yes, I'm here. Yes, that's right. It's in the form of an obituary notice. Yes, Trevor Cornwall.... What? Christ, no, he was talking at the Savoy just a ... yes, it was delivered fifteen minutes ago.... No, of course, I understand.... Yes, I'll tell our security to bring you straight to my office.... Yes.... Right.... Goodbye.'

He replaced the receiver with a clumsy hand, staring blank-eyed at Rooney.

'Cornwall's dead,' he said. 'Shot at the gates of his property in Greenwich. The cops are sending a couple of men to collect this ... thing ... and ask questions. Warn the security man that they'll be here shortly. I'll see them directly. And get Jumbo Barnes up here, now. Don't tell him why, we'll let the cops handle that. Come back here yourself. They'll want to hear your side of the story.'

As Rooney hurried from the room, Hollings reached for the intercom. He spoke to the news editor and told him that Trevor Cornwall had been shot at his home in Greenwich.

'Send your best man and a photographer,' he directed. 'We'll have to work fast. I'll talk to you later. Right now I'm expecting a visit from the police.'

Hollings studied the sheet of paper on his desk. Cornwall's death by murder would hit the headlines around the world. By tomorrow every media outlet would be competing for details of the story.

The Monitor, so far as he knew, was the sole possessor of the obituary under his hand. Later he would have to question who had sent it to him, and why. Right now, it offered him the rare opportunity of putting *The Monitor* in the forefront of the news-breakers.

He read it through carefully. It was short, apparently accurate and as cold as polar ice. It professed to be a notice of sympathy, but it was not.

'The people of this country,' it said, 'and indeed of the world will be saddened to learn of the untimely death of Mr Trevor Cornwall. He was an industrialist of international repute, head of the massive chain of companies known as Cornwall Electronics. He was a well-known sportsman, played polo for England and donated large sums to sporting interests. He owned a racing stable which ranks with the best in Europe, and only last week he bought the champion horse, French Toast, by Here's How out of Mademoiselle Gigi. An admirer of the Arab breed of horse, he helped to introduce the strain into local blood lines.

'Mr Cornwall is survived by his daughter Mrs Elizabeth Cupar and his grandson Steven Cupar.'

Hollings heard the lift ascending. The police were about to arrive. He used the office machine to make a copy of the obituary, which he locked in his wall safe.

II

AS JOHN THORNEYCROFT drove through the gates of his home, he heard the hall telephone ringing off the hook.

By the laughter, shrieks and frenzied barks coming from the swimming pool in the back garden, he knew that Claudia, Luke and the dog, Gatsby, were not going to answer the call. He left the car on the driveway, let himself into the house and picked up the receiver in time to hear sobs and garbled words.

He said loudly, 'Who is this?'

The sobs ceased on a shuddering intake of breath. A voice quavered, 'John?' and he answered.

'John Thorneycroft. How can I help you?'

'John ... thank God. It's Liz. Liz Cupar. My dad's dead. He's been shot. I found ... oh God ... I can't....'

'Liz my dear, I'm listening, just tell me.'

'I can't believe ... I found him lying by the gate. Shot. His head. Can you come John? I don't know what to ... anything.'

'Of course I'll come. Have you called the police?'

'Yes.' She drew a steadier breath. 'They're everywhere. I'm waiting for someone to tell me what to do.'

'Are the Mitchells there?' The Mitchells were Trevor Cornwall's live-in housekeeper and her handyman son.

'Yes. Will's with the police and Molly's putting Stevie to bed. I haven't told him. He's only five.'

'Have you called your doctor, Liz?'

'No. He's away in Spain. The police doctor spoke to me. He left me some pills. I don't want pills.' Her voice rose. 'I don't want to be doped, I want to talk, I want to know—'

'I'm coming right now,' Thorneycroft told her. 'We'll talk, Liz. Just stay quiet, and in a little while we'll talk.'

'Yes. Thank you. I'll wait.'

As he replaced the receiver, the back door was flung open and three figures erupted into the hallway. Claudia, three months pregnant, clutched a towel around her. Luke wore nothing at all and Gatsby drizzled water from every hair on his large body.

Claudia caught sight of Thorneycroft's face and the smile died on her lips.

'What's happened?' she said. She gave Luke a pat on the shoulder and waved him towards the kitchen. 'Get Gatsby's towel from the yard, darling, and rub him nicely.' As boy and dog headed for the kitchen door, she turned back to her husband.

He said, 'Liz Cupar called. Trevor's dead. She says he's been shot.'

Claudia stared, shaking her head, and he put an arm round her. 'I've said I'll go to her. She's obviously in deep shock, and her doctor's away.'

'I'll go with you,' Claudia said quickly. 'The neighbours will look after Luke.'

'No. Stay here and get the spare room ready. I'll bring her and Stevie back with me, but it may be a while. The police are at the scene. There'll be questions, delays.'

Claudia pressed a hand to her neck. 'I can't believe it. Poor Liz. I don't suppose it's any use telling Bruce.'

'None at all,' said Thorneycroft flatly. A cheating, abusive and divorced husband was not going to provide any comfort for Liz.

He reached for the telephone and punched in a number. Chief Superintendent Buxton was an old friend and a man of influence in the south London police establishment. From him, Thorneycroft obtained the name of the officer currently investigating Cornwall's death.

'DCI Iain Dysart,' Buxton told him. 'I'll have a word with him, tell him you're on your way to see Mrs Cupar, in your capacity as a psychiatrist. He's a good man, he'll go far, just don't offer him advice unless he asks for it.'

'I just want to help Liz,' Thorneycroft said.

'So does Dysart,' Buxton answered. 'So all I'm saying, laddie, is keep your tongue between your teeth.'

Thorneycroft followed the tarred road to the point where it fed the private lane serving Cornwall's property. He found that access to the lane was prevented by yellow police tape. A uniformed constable bent to the window of the car.

'Dr Thorneycroft? This is scene-of-crime, sir. DCI Dysart says you should go another hundred yards on the tar, and you'll find the back gate. You'll be let through there. It takes you right to the house.'

Thorneycroft followed the instructions.

From the paved track, he could see across manicured lawns to where the police were at work. Lights shone on the closed gates and the area beyond them. From time to time, a photographer's flash glinted, and elf-lights flickered in the belt of trees on the far side of the lane.

Men would be searching there, in case the killer was still hidden in the shadows. They would also be looking for traces he might have left ... footprints, a dropped cigarette butt, an expelled cartridge case.

Thorneycroft told himself that he had no part to bear in that work. His job was to sustain Liz Cupar in her dire distress. The dead man had been a loved friend, but his own grief for Trevor, his anger at the manner of his death, had to be disregarded. Only Liz's feelings must occupy his mind.

A policeman admitted him to the building, and housekeeper Molly Mitchell came to meet him. Her eyes were red and swollen, but her appearance was as neat as ever, and she greeted him calmly.

'Dr John, I'm glad you could come. She's in a bad way, poor lamb. I lit the fire in the lounge, she can't shop shivering. I tried to get her to take a hot drink, but she won't touch anything. She says she just wants to be alone. At first she wouldn't let go of Stevie, just held him so tight it frightened him. Then she let me put him to bed. She said I must sit with him, in case he wakes.'

'You've done the right things,' Thorneycroft said. 'Will you make some fresh tea for her, now? I'll see she drinks it.'

Mrs Mitchell hurried away, and Thorneycroft walked to the door of the living room. He remembered it as Trevor's favourite space, redolent of his personality. The rosy floor tiles were covered with hand-woven rugs, the furnishings were a miscellany of antique and modern. A glass-fronted cabinet held sporting trophies, a photograph of Trevor and Prince Charles between chukkas and a bronze model of a stallion. There were three pictures on the rear wall: a Modigliani, a Grandma Moses and a pastel sketch of Trevor's late wife, Nerina. Silence and semi dark-ness gave the room the feeling of a shrine, and Thorneycroft pressed a switch and flooded it with light.

Liz Cupar was in an armchair close to the fireplace. She sat crouched forward, her head almost touching her knees, but at Thorneycroft's approach she rose slowly to her feet. He put his arms round her and for a moment she leaned against him.

'Thank you for coming.' Her voice was flat. 'I shouldn't have burdened you. You can't do anything.'

'I can, Liz.' He drew her to a sofa and sat down at her side. 'Claudia and I want you and Stevie to come to us for the night.'

She shook her head. 'I can't leave. Iain Dysart said he would want to talk to me again when they've … finished, down there.'

'We'll see what he says. Do you know him?'

She shrugged listlessly. 'He likes horses. He comes to some of the meetings.' She raised her gaze to his face. 'Why would anyone do this? Dad never harmed a soul.'

Thorneycroft took her hand. It was ice cold and he rubbed it gently. 'It will be for the police to find out. I'm told Dysart's a good man. Have you talked to him?'

'Yes. He questioned me. I couldn't tell him much. I stayed at The Savoy after the luncheon, to tidy up the donations. Make lists. I wasn't with Dad.' Her voice rose. 'Someone must have been waiting in the woods. Watching.' Horror flooded her face and Thorneycroft sought to distract her from the pictures in her mind.

'Was there any trouble at the luncheon?'

'No. Everything went smoothly, there were lots of big dona-tions.' She drew a long breath. 'I've been wondering if this could have been terrorists. The people in the Middle East are so divided. There's so much hate, and violence.'

'It's a line that'll be followed, I'm sure.'

Footsteps sounded in the corridor, and Molly Mitchell appeared with a tray of tea. She set it on the table, patted Liz's shoulder and went away. Thorneycroft poured tea into a cup, added milk and plenty of sugar and handed it to Liz.

'Drink up,' he said, and she drained the cup, eyes closed.

Thorneycroft smiled at her. 'Good. What time did you leave the hotel?'

She answered with certainty. 'At 5.30.'

'Did you drive straight home?'

'Yes. I didn't want to waste any time. We were going to spend the weekend at Penwold.' This was Cornwall's racing stable on the North Downs. 'We were all packed and ready.' A thought came to her and she frowned. 'Dad called me from Bermondsey. He stopped to buy wine in Bermondsey.'

'Can you remember what time he called?'

'It was at ten to five. I was still at the hotel.'

And Trevor was still alive, Thorneycroft thought. That infor-mation would help to establish the time of his death. He prompted, 'You drove home, Liz, to the front gates....'

She nodded. 'Yes. It was still light. I saw Dad's car in the lane, and then I saw him lying by the gates. I thought he must have fallen, and I got out of my car and went across to him. I knelt down and turned him over. I saw his face. It was broken, just blood and bone. His body was ... he was gone. I held him, and I looked about. There was nobody. Just birds coming in to roost.'

She fell silent, staring into space.

'You called the police, didn't you?'

'Yes. I called Iain Dysart. They came very quickly. Iain asked me questions. I couldn't tell him much. I told him that when I arrived, Dad was already dead.'

'Did you notice the time, Liz?'

She glanced at him, blank-faced.

He repeated, 'What time did you reach home?' and she frowned, wrapping her arms about her body. 'I think ... it was just after half past six. Iain told me that I called him at twenty minutes to seven.'

'And you called me at seven.'

She said wearily, 'The times are important, aren't they?'

'They may help to nail the person who did it.'

'I want him caught,' she said passionately, 'I want him to burn in hell.' She beat her fists on the cushions of the sofa, and the heat of her rage seemed to melt the ice of shock. She wept, the tears running down her face. Thorneycroft waited and in a few minutes she grew quiet, found a handkerchief and mopped her face. She turned to face him, gripping his arm.

'I want you to be part of the investigation. On the team.'

'That's not for me to decide, Liz. I can act as your advisor, your friend, but unless the police choose to call me in as a consultant....'

'They must,' she said. 'I'll talk to Iain. I'll tell him I want you in.'

Before he could answer, there came a tap at the open door, and two men walked into the room. Both of them were in plain clothes. Thorneycroft rose and went to meet them.

'I'm John Thorneycroft,' he said. 'I'm a friend of Mrs Cupar. She asked me to come.'

The larger of the two men nodded. 'Superintendent Buxton told me, Dr Thorneycroft. I'm DCI Dysart and this is DS Mick Clay.' Dysart's voice was measured, with a Scots intonation. His eyes measured Thorneycroft. 'You're a forensic psychiatrist. I followed the Bonbouche case.'

Liz cut in sharply. 'I want John to help find the man who shot my father. I'll pay his fee if that's a problem.'

Dysart seemed to turn the idea over in his mind. He said, 'It's not my decision. I'll see if it can be arranged.' He turned back to Thorneycroft, fixing him with the dispassionate stare of the career policeman. He was a tall man, thickset, but his stance suggested that he could move quickly. His eyes were dark blue under heavy brows, and his thick black hair, cut short, showed a tendency to curl.

'Would you be prepared to act as a consultant, Doctor?'

'Certainly. I'm on your books. I'll act pro bono if money's a problem.'

'If Mrs Cupar wants you, we'll try to oblige.' Again Dysart glanced at Liz, and Thorneycroft saw the softening in the hard blue eyes. Dysart, he thought, might be fond of horses, but he was a great deal fonder of Elizabeth Cupar.

Thorneycroft made for safer ground. 'My wife and I would like to have Liz and Stevie to stay the night … longer if she wants. She's concerned about leaving the Mitchells to cope here.'

'No need to worry,' Dysart said. 'They'll be quite safe. I'll have a man in the house, and we'll be watching the grounds. We'll make a full search of the woods at first light tomorrow. I'll need to talk to Mrs Cupar again, in the morning.'

'Of course. I'll bring her back here, or to the station if you prefer.'

'I'll let you know,' Dysart said. He leaned towards Liz, who was watching him closely. 'Go and pack what you need,' he said.

She rose unsteadily. 'It will be better for Stevie, away from here.'

'Yes it will. Off you go.'

She headed for the door, and halfway there stopped and stared at her outstretched arms. The sleeves of her jacket were caked with blood. She quickened her pace, holding her arms away from her body. Reaching the corridor, she broke into a run.

When she had gone, Dysart said abruptly, 'I'd like a few words with you, Dr Thorneycroft, if you don't mind.' He motioned Thorneycroft to a chair and took his place on the sofa. DS Clay sat next to him.

'You've talked to Mrs Cupar,' Dysart said. 'I'd be grateful if you'd tell me exactly what she said to you.'

They settled to talk. DS Clay pulled a notebook from his

pocket, but at a sign from Dysart put it away again. The interview was apparently to be off the record.

Dysart's opening remark was a statement, not a question. 'You were a friend of Mr Cornwall.'

'Yes,' Thorneycroft answered. 'He engaged me some years ago to counsel members of his staff who'd been traumatized by a bomb attack on one of his factories. We remained friends.'

'And with Mrs Cupar?'

'She and my wife were at school together.'

Dysart appeared to approve these credentials. 'To come to the present,' he said, 'Mrs Cupar called me at 6.40 p.m. to tell me her father had been shot dead at the gates of this house. I arrived here with my squad about fifteen minutes later. Mrs Cupar was kneeling by the gates, holding her father. He was dead. The bullet that killed him had penetrated his head and was lying in the grass verge, next to the left hand gatepost. The gates were locked. They operate electronically.

'Mrs Cupar confirmed that the dead man was her father. The centre of his face was destroyed, but she identified his clothes, a birthmark on his right wrist, and the keys and wallet in his pockets. The remote control for the gates was on his keyring.'

'So the killer didn't try to enter the property? Cornwall's wallet, keys and car weren't stolen.'

'No. It doesn't look as if robbery was the motive, but maybe the perp didn't have time, or was disturbed.' Dysart hunched his heavy shoulders. 'Mrs. Cupar was in a very distressed state. I asked her a few basic questions, and she did her best to answer, but it was plain she had to have time to recover. She told me she wanted to talk to you. She called you from the scene of the crime.'

'Yes. She told me Trevor had been shot dead.' Thorneycroft read the question in Dysart's eyes, and answered it. 'Liz knew he'd been shot. She's a countrywoman, she's seen what bullets do, the entry and exit wounds they make.'

'And she asked you to come here?'

'Yes. She said she needed to talk.'

'That's unusual, isn't it? For someone in shock to want to talk?'

'Most people in shock find talk difficult or impossible, but there are some – Liz is one of them – who need to vocalize their feelings … horror, grief, whatever. It's their way of dealing with denial. The mind says, "it hasn't happened, I refuse to believe it," but a second voice says, "it has happened, get help, get someone to help you face it." Talk can be a catalyst, a reaching for acceptance and eventual recovery.'

'You came at once.'

'I spoke to Superintendent Buxton first. I didn't want to intrude on your territory.'

'The super told me.' Dysart smiled faintly. 'I'm familiar with your work. You're an accredited consultant on forensic psychiatry, you've had some successes. Mrs Cupar wants you on this case, but you know that would have to be sanctioned by the top brass.'

'It would,' Thorneycroft said mildly, 'but you're entitled to make the call.'

'I am, and I will. There's a good chance it'll succeed. Cornwall was an important man with international links. That may have made him the target for some lunatic.'

'Liz suggested it might be a terrorist act … Turkish separatists, or one of the extremist factions. Trevor had links with the Middle East. His wife was half Turkish.'

'It's too early to guess at motives.'

Thorneycroft remembered Buxton's warning against treading on Dysart's toes, and decided to ignore it.

'You recovered the bullet,' he said. 'What did it tell you?'

Dysart took his time answering. 'I assume you're capable of treating what I say as confidential?'

'Absolutely.'

'It was a rifle bullet, accelerator type, probably of German make. It tore up Cornwall's head. We'll search for the sabot at first light.'

Thorneycroft felt cold. A teflon-coated accelerator bullet wasn't everyday ammunition. The bullet itself was enclosed in a plastic sabot. As the projectile travelled through the rifle barrel at a rate of over 4,000 feet a second, only the sabot would be scarred by the lands and grooves of the barrel, making it more difficult for the ballistics experts to identify the firearm that despatched it. Moreover, an accelerator bullet had a hollow-point construction with a raised central point. When it entered a body, hydrostatic pressure made its peripheral rim flare open like the calyx of a flower. The metal petals did terrible injury to bone and soft tissue.

'Did you find the cartridge case?' he asked, and Dysart shook his head.

'I don't think we will. The perp had prepared a firing site. He'd cut away some green branches in the wood, to give himself a clear view of the gates. We've searched the area, and we'll broaden the search tomorrow, but I think we're dealing with a professional. He prepared the site, he used an accelerator bullet, he'd have been careful to retrieve the cartridge case. We may find the sabot. It could have travelled some distance from the firing point. The perp didn't have time to look for it. He must have left fast.'

'The preparation of a firing site confirms premeditation,' Thorneycroft said. 'The killer must have gained access to the woods well before the killing; picked a site, pruned branches, cleared away the cuttings. And how did he get into the wood? It's private land. There must be a fence.'

'There is, with a padlocked gate. The perp cut the padlock chain.'

'He took a chance. Someone might have seen him.'

'We're questioning the locals, but the ground beyond the wood is virtually wasteland. It's earmarked for municipal development, and there's a legal squabble going on, about tenders. People don't go there much.'

'Did anyone hear the shot?'

'We haven't found anyone, so far. The Cornwall gates are a good distance from the highway. Folks in the neighbourhood would probably dismiss a shot as someone after a rabbit, or a vehicle backfiring. Molly and Will Mitchell were in their quarters at the back of the house, watching a gangster movie. Bangs all the time.'

'Do you have an estimated time of death?'

'The medical officer thinks Cornwall had been dead about an hour, when he made his examination. Rigor hadn't set in. The autopsy will tell us more.'

'Trevor was alive at ten to five,' Thorneycroft said. 'Liz told me he phoned her from a wine shop in Bermondsey at that time. She was still at The Savoy.'

Dysart's eyes brightened. 'That gives us some sort of time frame. If he was in Bermondsey at 4.50, he could have reached here in about twenty minutes.'

'Where was his car?'

'Parked on the left side of the lane, opposite the gates.'

'So he must have left the car and crossed over to the gates. He had the remote in his pocket. Why didn't he just use it and drive through the gates?'

'I think he crossed the lane to move an obstacle,' Dysart said. 'We found the tracks of a motorbike next to the left-hand gate. Cornwall came to move it, and put himself in the killer's sights.'

'Careful planning and execution,' Thorneycroft mused. 'A pro, or someone who's a very good shot and knows where to obtain unconventional ammunition. He didn't steal the car. He must have used the bike as transport. It may have been noticed in the vicinity.'

'We're checking on that. Highway patrol are on the lookout. It's also possible he left a car or van somewhere nearby, put the bike into it and drove away, just another vehicle in the evening rush hour.' Dysart sighed. 'At least we have some sort of timetable.' He counted on his fingers.

'At 4.20, Cornwall left The Savoy. Stopped in Bermondsey around 4.50 and called Mrs Cupar, who was still at the hotel. He drove to his home, could have reached the gates by a quarter past five. He saw the bike blocking the entrance, went across to move it and the perp shot him. The perp didn't rob him or steal his car, didn't attempt to enter the grounds. He left the crime scene at once.'

'You can't be sure of that,' Thorneycroft said. 'Admittedly a professional hit man doesn't hang around to watch the sunset, but he could have spent a little time looking for the sabot.'

Dysart fixed Thorneycroft with a measuring stare. He seemed to be debating something in his mind. At last he said, 'He left at once. I'm sure of that because at 6.30, well before Mrs Cupar called me to say her father had been killed, I was informed by our City division that a man on a Cougar III motorbike had stopped at the premises of *The Sporting Monitor*, in Fleet Street, and delivered a document. It was in the form of an obituary notice. It stated that Trevor Cornwall was dead.'

It was Thorneycroft's turn to stare. 'You heard about the death before Liz discovered his body?'

'Yes. The editor of the paper, Rupert Hollings, was given the obit. just before six o'clock. He spent a few minutes trying to get in touch with Cornwall or Mrs Cupar, and failed. At 6.05 he phoned the City Police and told them about the obit. They sent men to talk to Hollings and collect the document. They took it seriously enough to fax it through to me, and to suggest I check that Cornwall was okay. Before I could do that, Liz phoned to say he'd been shot. A Cougar III bike could have made the tracks at Cornwall's gates.'

Thorneycroft did mental sums. 'If the killer and the Cougar III messenger are one and the same, he must have moved fast to get from Greenwich to Fleet Street.'

'A bike can weave through traffic, take short cuts.'

'There's no way of stopping a story like that,' Thorneycroft said sombrely. 'The news will be across the world by tomorrow.'

'Yes. Let's hope it puts people on the alert. He may be planning other hits.'

'Yes. Did *The Monitor* give any description of the biker?'

'He was wearing a leather jumpsuit, and a helmet that effectively concealed his face. Medium height and build. Never spoke, just handed over an envelope and drove off. We got the description from the kid on duty at the doors of the building. He's a bit slow, but he gave an exact description of the Cougar bike and he detailed its capabilities. That's an expensive model. Still, there are a few thousand around. We'll check on owners. It could have been stolen for the job.'

'The lad who saw the biker may be at risk.'

'He's been warned not to brag of the encounter. We'll keep an eye on him.'

'What made the perp choose a small publication like *The Sporting Monitor?*'

'Hollings had links with the Cornwalls. Trevor was a patron of sport and the paper supported his fund-raising campaigns, and from time to time they published articles Liz wrote.'

Dysart halted, as if his use of Liz's Christian name caused him embarrassment. After a moment he said, 'There's something I want to ask you. Mrs Cupar's divorce was a messy one. There was a fight over the custody of the boy.'

'There was,' said Thorneycroft grimly. 'Bruce Cupar didn't care a damn for Steven. He married Liz for her money, was grossly unfaithful to her and used the custody claim to pressure Trevor into buying him off.'

'Did Cornwall do so?'

'Yes. There was an out-of-court settlement, Liz was given sole custody. Cupar tried a couple of times to buck the rules, and Liz obtained a court order prohibiting him from approaching her or Steven. He hasn't troubled them since. If you're wondering if he might have killed Trevor, my answer is, "I don't think so". For one thing, he hasn't the guts or the brains to carry out an assassination, and for another he couldn't hit a haystack at three paces.'

'He could have paid someone to shoot Cornwall.'

'And kill the goose that laid the golden egg? I don't think so.'

Dysart looked relieved. 'Then we're looking for a killer outside of the family circle.'

'It's hard to believe anyone had a motive to kill Trevor. He was tremendously popular, a man of goodwill, apolitical, kind and tolerant of others.'

'The Devil hates that sort,' Dysart said. Before he could enlarge on this unexpected remark, Liz and Steven appeared in the doorway, Liz carrying an overnight bag, and Steven a dog-eared picture book. Both of them looked exhausted, and Thorneycroft lost no time in installing them on the back seat of his car.

Dysart stooped to the driver's window.

'I've warned Molly and Will Mitchell not to take any calls, and not to tell anyone at all where Mrs Cupar and Steven are. I'll call her tomorrow to make an appointment for an interview.' He stepped back to allow the car to move away. He did not stay to watch it leave the property, but hurried to the distant gates, where the lights of the searchers still shone.

Thorneycroft stopped at the end of the lane to phone Claudia and tell her he was bringing Liz and Steven to stay. A glance in the rearview mirror showed him that Steven was already asleep, and Liz lying back with her eyes closed.

He took the ring road, avoiding the fast lane. He needed time to make his own adjustment to the day's events. He would be drawn into this investigation, he knew. Not only did Liz need his and Claudia's companionship at this time, but she believed that he could help to nail her father's killer.

DCI Dysart's readiness to involve him was harder to explain. Why would a policeman who disliked intruders on his turf want to share the investigation with an outsider?

Superintendent Buxton had hinted that Dysart was an ambitious man, destined for promotion. Such men played their cards close to their chest. Yet Dysart had chosen to tell Thorneycroft about the message delivered to *The Sporting Monitor*, a decision that might be seen as an indiscretion deserving censure.

It could be Dysart had strong feelings for Liz and wished to please her. Or did he feel that having a forensic psychiatrist on board would increase his chances of success?

Thorneycroft sighed. Time would reveal Dysart's thought processes. Meanwhile, the task in hand was to care for Liz and Steven.

In Wimbledon, Claudia greeted them with comforting arms, warm food and drink, beds turned down. Liz spoke little until the meal was over, and Steven tucked into bed. Then she said wearily that she must make some phone calls.

'Dad's lawyers, and Hamish Freeman our London CEO,' she said. 'They can't just learn the news from the papers.'

'Let me call them,' Thorneycroft said. 'I'll arrange for them to talk to you tomorrow, if you wish. They can take whatever steps are necessary to deal with Trevor's business affairs. Dysart has told Will and Molly not to give anyone your address or phone number, and believe me, that's wise, because if that information leaks, the press and the sensation-seekers will be here, thicker than ants on a honey-jar.'

She gave him a list of names with their contact numbers, and then accepted Claudia's offer of a sleeping tablet, and went to bed.

Thorneycroft made the required calls which were met with shock, outrage and immediate offers of help. He impressed on everyone the need for keeping Liz's whereabouts secret, and fixed tentative appointments for them to call on her the following afternoon.

At last he was able to sit and talk to Claudia. She listened to his account of Trevor's murder, and at the end said quietly, 'You're already involved, aren't you John?'

He shrugged. 'Nothing's certain yet. Liz wants me to act as a consultant. She needs us both, Clo. She has no close family.'

Claudia poured coffee into a mug and passed it to him. 'Are Liz and Stevie in danger?' she said.

Thorneycroft knew that she was thinking that by harbouring Trevor's kin, they might be attracting a killer to their own home. She was concerned for Luke and their unborn child, and she was right to be concerned.

He said slowly, 'The man who shot Trevor could have gained access to the house by using the remote on Trevor's key ring, but he didn't. He didn't lie in wait for Liz to come home. DCI Dysart has set a guard on the property, and I'm sure they'll keep an eye on our house, too.'

Claudia said uncertainly, 'I want to help, but....'

He reached for her hand. 'I've been thinking that in a few days, when Liz has had time to take stock, she and Steven should go to Penwold.'

'Penwold! That's just a village. Why would they be safer there?'

'Because it has better security than any house I know. After last year's attempt to steal Ship Ahoy, Trevor had his experts work on the stables and the grounds. The place has electric fences, laser beams, every security device known to man, and it's set in the middle of miles of open land. The manager is ex-army, and the staff and grooms are used to protecting millions of pounds worth of horseflesh. What's more important, Liz and Stevie love it. Being there will be good for them. It's not far from London. We can visit them often. But for the next few days, they're best off here, with us. The police have to question Liz, and there'll be an inquest. She may have to attend that.'

'Must she? It'll bring it all back to her.'

'You know Liz. She won't rest until the man's identified and jailed.'

Claudia got to her feet. 'Of course they must stay with us as long as they want. You can work from your office here, and we can employ a security guard at night. We'll be fine.'

On their way to bed they stopped to listen at the spare room door, but there was no sound from within.

Gatsby, conscious of human anxiety, left his basket in the kitchen and spent the night stretched out at the head of the stairs.

Thorneycroft found himself reverting to the uneasy sleep of his combat days. He got out of bed several times during the night to peer through the curtains at the street. Once he saw a car opposite his gate. It might be there on Dysart's orders. It might be a reveller sleeping off too much beer at the pub. It might be a killer with a telescopic rifle.

He resolved that first thing in the morning he would engage round-the-clock security guards.

III

DAWN BROUGHT A murky sky slashed with daggers of rain. Thorneycroft showered, dressed and put through a call to a security agency. A guard, he was assured, would report for duty at eight o'clock.

He took Gatsby into the garden. There was little passing traffic. The parked car was gone. A Rastafarian in a caftan was sitting in the bus shelter ten yards from the gate. He took no notice of Thorneycroft and didn't appear to be fully awake.

Thorneycroft returned to the house. As he stepped into the hall, the telephone rang. It was Dysart, calling from the Greenwich police station.

'I wanted to let you know,' he said, 'we're keeping an eye on your property.'

'Dreadlocks and a caftan?' Thorneycroft asked, and Dysart grunted.

'He's not as silly as he looks. Tell your people to stay indoors as much as possible.'

'I will, and I've arranged for security guards to be on site, until we have a better idea of what we're dealing with. The Bladen Agency.'

'Good. They're reliable.' Dysart cleared his throat. 'Er … we have to get a full statement from Mrs Cupar. I don't want to bring her to the nick, there's press all over the place. We could come to your home. Do you think she's up to it?'

'I'll talk to her. I'll let you know if she can't face it. Can you throw off the newshounds? It won't do for them to follow you here.'

'We'll arrange for them to chase wild geese,' Dysart said.

'Right. Then let's say, be here at ten o'clock, unless I call you back.'

Sounds from the kitchen proved to be Claudia putting together a full English breakfast, and Luke and Steven banging on a Kiddies Keyboard.

'Liz is awake,' Claudia said. 'She insists on coming down.'

Thorneycroft nodded. 'I'm going for the papers,' he said. 'Dysart's put a watch on this house – the Rasta sitting in the bus shelter. Don't try to speak to him, and stay indoors, all of you. There'll be a man from Bladen's arriving at eight. I'll be back before then.'

He jogged to the corner where a newspaper stall operated, and bought *The Sporting Monitor*, and several other papers. *The Monitor*'s front page screamed RACING TYCOON SLAIN and the story ran on to page three. There was a photograph of Trevor and Liz, taken in the owners' enclosure at Ascot, and one of Cornwall's home ... a file copy, no sign of a body or a police presence. Dysart must have kept the media at bay.

What Dysart had described as an obituary notice occupied a black-edged panel on page one, and Thorneycroft studied it with care. It made him think that either the killer had known Trevor personally, or had made a study of his curriculum vitae. The short passage carried the very recent information that Trevor had acquired the stallion, French Toast. That story had not, to Thorneycroft's knowledge, appeared in the British press.

The police were in possession of the original obit. They'd subject it to forensic examination; identify the paper it was printed on and the type of machine that had produced it. It would be tested for fingerprints and trace material. Sweat, saliva or a stray hair could supply samples of DNA. Thorneycroft doubted if much would come of these labours. So far, the killer had marked himself as a professional who knew the pitfalls, worked to a plan and left no clues to his identity.

What he did leave was traces of his character. It was these that Thorneycroft must study: the killer's modus operandi, his choice of weapon, his skills and weaknesses, his personal idiosyncrasies would help to define the criminal's mind, and allow the profiler to interpret its twisted processes and to predict what actions they were likely to trigger.

The choices made by a killer gave insight to the mind that made them. Why, for instance, would a man intent on murder choose such a flamboyant vehicle as a Cougar III? Was that his normal mode of transport? Had he chosen the Cougar in a deliberate move to gain publicity for his crime? Was he laying a false trail for the police to follow?

The bike, as much as the rifle and ammunition used by the killer, must be investigated. The police must establish where the Cougar was manufactured and sold. Buyers and owners must be identified. Within days, thousands of people around the globe would be poring over pictures and descriptions of the bike. Innocent Cougar owners would be fingered by self-appointed whistle-blowers, and questioned by the police. It was unlikely that would lead to the identification of the killer; by now he was probably far away from England, and the bike lying at the bottom of a salt marsh.

The Monitor was the only paper to mention the obituary message, but all the papers Thorneycroft had bought carried the news of the murder.

The Sun, lacking factual meat, filled its space with speculation. It suggested that terrorists or robbers might have killed Trevor Cornwall. He was known, said *The Sun*, to have business interests in the Middle East, and his collection of pictures and artefacts was worth millions.

A reporter from *The Gazette* had spoken to Will and Molly Mitchell, and gained little from them save lamentation over the loss of a loved employer.

The Independent published a genuine and glowing obituary of the dead man, and displayed a photograph of him leading in one of his recent winners.

Thorneycroft wondered how long it would be before the media learned that Liz was staying with friends in Wimbledon. In a few hours the phone might be ringing non-stop – this house might be a target for the paparazzi or a murderer.

He stashed the papers in the living room. Better to keep them away from Liz until he'd had time to warn her that Trevor's death was in the public domain.

The guard from Bladen's arrived promptly at eight. Thorneycroft explained the reason for employing him, and stressed the need to keep Liz's whereabouts secret.

Liz herself came down the stairs as the guard was starting a circuit of the house and grounds.

'Who was that?' she demanded.

'A watchdog,' Thorneycroft answered. 'We don't want you bothered by morbid onlookers.'

She met his eyes. 'Is that your real reason, John? Do you think he may come here?'

'I think we have to cover all the possibilities.'

She grimaced. 'We shouldn't be putting you and Clo and Luke in danger.'

'I doubt there's any risk. We simply have to take proper precautions. We like having you here, believe it.'

She started to argue, but he took her arm and steered her towards the kitchen.

'Breakfast's ready, we can talk and eat. DCI Dysart phoned to know if you're up to giving him a full statement this morning. If you're not, I'll let him know, otherwise he'll be here at ten.'

'I'm all right. Let them come. Did you speak to Hamish and the lawyers?'

'Yes. I made provisional appointments for Hamish at two o'clock, and your lawyers at four. They won't keep you long and if you decide to cancel, they'll understand.'

She said fiercely, 'I won't cancel. They're the proper people to take control, and the sooner they do, the better it will be for all of us.'

The interview with Dysart and Sergeant Clay produced nothing new. At Dysart's invitation, Thorneycroft sat quietly in the bay window of the study while Liz gave her account of the events of the previous day. She described the fund-raising luncheon, her supervision of the counting and banking of the donations, the call she'd received from her father in Bermondsey and her drive to Greenwich. She insisted that there'd been no untoward incidents at The Savoy, and no one had followed her on her journey home.

She confirmed that she'd arrived there at 6.30. 'St Cyprian's bell was ringing for evening service as I turned off the motorway.' Her voice faltered when she described how she'd found her father's body, but she recovered her calm and gave her report clearly.

That done, Dysart took her through the procedures that follow a violent death. The autopsy, he said, was being performed as he spoke, and the results would be delivered quickly. There would be an inquest, and unless an early arrest was made, a verdict of murder by person or persons unknown would be returned.

Liz made an impatient gesture. 'I know there has to be all this legal stuff, but when will you start looking for the man?'

'The search has already started,' Dysart answered.

She gave him a hostile look. 'Molly Mitchell told me you questioned her and Will, last night. You can't possibly suspect them. They adored Dad. They would never have done anything to harm him. Never.'

Dysart said patiently, 'We question everyone, Mrs Cupar. We can't exonerate the Mitchells on your say-so. We need to build a picture of what's happened, not just yesterday, but in the weeks and months before that. Our inquiries may take us into places you don't want us to go, but in our work, uncomfortable questions often lead us to the truth. Will and Molly were close to your father. Questioning them may provide us with valuable answers.'

Liz sank back in her chair. 'Yes. Of course. I know you'll do your best. I'm glad you're in charge. Dad always trusted your judgement.'

Dysart brushed the compliment aside and began to ask her about Trevor Cornwall's recent past, the people he'd met in his daily round, in particular the people concerned in the fund-raiser. He made a note of the names of the organizers, and of the people in Turkey who would take charge of the funds and transfer them to the earthquake victims.

'You told Dr Thorneycroft that you thought the shooting might have been the work of Turkish separatists,' he said. 'Do you have any particular group in mind? And facts to support what you said?'

'No. I just spoke without thinking. It seemed so impossible that any ... any normal person could want to hurt Dad. He just didn't have any enemies.'

'It's possible for a man to have enemies he doesn't deserve. Your father may have had rivals in the business world, or in the racing world. He was a big winner. There could be owners, trainers, gamblers, jockeys with private scores to settle.'

Liz seemed puzzled by the idea. 'Dad ploughed his race winnings back into racing,' she said. 'He sponsored races and prizes, he founded jockey academies. He imported great blood stock. He supported the whole industry.'

'How about his own trainer and riders? Was there any trouble from them?'

She frowned. 'There were arguments, sometimes. Differences about how a horse should be trained, or raced, and about who should get the rides. That's normal. The people at Penwold know they're lucky to work there. They're well paid, they have good living conditions for themselves and their families. They get great racing opportunities.'

Dysart ended the interview, saying he'd be in touch when he had information about the autopsy and the inquest. Liz went away to be with Steven, and Thorneycroft accompanied the policemen to their car. He had a question for Dysart.

'Have you spoken to Kaminsky?'

Dysart rolled his shoulders. 'Yeah. I called him last night. He said he knew of no terrorist threat against Trevor Cornwall. He said I should apply to the proper authorities.'

Thorneycroft blinked. Huw Kaminsky was a third-generation Welshman of Polish extraction whose grandfather had died in one of Stalin's gulags. He had joined the police force at the age of eighteen, and against all expectations had graduated to the Special Branch of the Metropolitan Police.

Kaminsky was not only highly intelligent, he had the memory of an elephant and the thick hide of a rhinoceros. He had developed an extraordinary knowledge of the criminal circuits of the world, and forged links with key people in its intelligence and security units. "Ask Kaminsky" had become a catchword for investigators, and Kaminsky was usually quick to supply answers, despite his superiors' preference for silence.

The fact that he was clamming up on the facts surrounding Cornwall's murder suggested that someone at a very high level had ordered him to zip his lip.

As Dysart was about to climb into the waiting car, he paused to make one of his seemingly irrelevant remarks.

'That Cougar bike,' he said. 'I asked the head of our transport division. He said a Cougar III will set you back at least nine thousand quid.'

Thorneycroft answered the implication rather than the words. 'He could have stolen it.'

'Difficult. The new model has a built-in tracker system. None of the tracker companies has had a complaint of theft.'

'So maybe he owns the bike himself, or someone's sponsored him.'

'Looks that way.'

When the police had left, Thorneycroft spent time in his study, mulling over questions that rose in his mind. Was the killer rich enough to own a Cougar III? Did he have a rich backer? A backer rich enough to hire a professional hit man? And who was powerful enough to muzzle Kaminsky?'

Dysart was already carrying out the routine procedures of a murder investigation. Thorneycroft's job was to add lateral thinking to the mix; to probe the shadowy distances that seemed to surround this murder.

At one o'clock, Claudia tapped on the door.

'Lunch is ready,' she said. 'After lunch, will you set up the train set in the attic?'

'What?'

'For the children,' Claudia explained. 'It's stopped raining, and if I'm to keep them indoors, I'm going to need a powerful inducement.'

IV

THE HORNBY TRAIN set occupied half the attic floor and Claudia had filled the space between the winding rails with a model farm.

Luke, used to his afternoon nap, soon fell asleep on a pile of dust covers, but Steven shunted and halted the engine, and loaded and unloaded its miniature goods trucks with unflagging enjoyment.

At four o'clock Thorneycroft went down to the living room to see if Liz had ended the meeting with her lawyers. He found that they had been joined by the London CEO of Cornwall Electronics, and the group was deep in discussion.

As he closed the door on them, he heard Gatsby's furious bark in the front garden, and went out to see what caused it. The mastiff was hurling himself at the gate at the foot of the driveway, and Bladen's guard was grappling with a sandy-haired man who was trying to climb over the gate. As Thorneycroft approached the fracas, the man turned his head and screeched, 'Call off this thug and your bloody mongrel. I'm here to see my wife.'

The guard said fiercely, 'I caught this person trying to sneak over the gate, sir. I told him he couldn't come in and he punched me in the face.'

Thorneycroft nodded. 'I know him. I'll handle him. There's tea and cake in the kitchen, go and have a cuppa.'

'He may take a swing at you,' the guard warned, and Thorneycroft smiled.

'I hope he does. I'd welcome the excuse.'

The guard moved away. Thorneycroft placed a calming hand

on Gatsby's ruff, and the dog sank, grumbling, to a crouch. Thorneycroft eyed the interloper. 'You're breaking the law, Cupar. The court states that you are not to come within a hundred yards of Liz or Steven.'

'The law's an ass.' Bruce Cupar put up a shaking hand to smooth back lank strands of hair. 'Liz's father has been murdered,' he said. 'It's only right I should come to express my sympathy.'

'I'll convey your sympathy to her, but she's made it plain she doesn't want to see you. Not now, not ever.'

'That's for her to say, not you. I know she's here. It wasn't hard to guess she'd run to you and Claudia. I demand to see my wife and child.'

Thorneycroft felt rage rise in his throat. 'Liz is not your wife,' he said. 'The reason she divorced you was that you abused Stevie. You hit him with a cricket stump, you shut him in a broom cupboard, you left him in a locked car, in the middle of a heat wave. Luckily a passer-by broke the car window and got him to a doctor.'

'I was ill. I popped into a chemist....'

'You popped into a bar two blocks away.'

'I only had one drink.'

'You were too drunk to stand.'

'It was Liz's job to look after the fucking kid, not mine.'

'That last time, Liz was in hospital because you broke her nose.' Thorneycroft stepped nearer to the gate, staring at Cupar, noting the sweating face, the pinpoint pupils and twitching jaw muscles.

'What are you on now?' he said. 'Is it still coke, or have you advanced to something more trendy? Ecstacy, or heroin?'

Cupar drew in a hissing breath. 'I have a right to talk to her.'

'You have no right. No legal right and no human right. Get the hell out of here. Live your miserable little life, and let her live hers.'

Cupar clenched both fists and raised them high. 'I signed a settlement. I want to know if that still holds.'

'Ah. I see. You're concerned about money. Trevor did indeed settle money on you, more than enough to keep you in the comfort you don't deserve.'

'He was a multi-millionaire, what he gave me was peanuts compared to what he owned. Houses, companies, horses, stuff all over the world. He was filthy rich, filthy rich, and he wanted me to live on a pittance.'

'I know what Trevor awarded you. It was a very handsome sum; you can live on it comfortably for the rest of your days, provided you quit drugs and liquor and greedy women.'

'I can't come out on it. You hear me? I can't come out on it!' Cupar's voice rose to a scream. 'I'm not going to let a witch doctor like you cheat me out of what's due to me.'

'If you've wasted the fortune that Trevor gave you, then there's only one thing for it. You'll have to change your lifestyle.' Thorneycroft glanced at the gleaming Cadillac parked against the kerb. 'Sell your car, move out of your Chelsea penthouse, book yourself into a rehab and get a job.'

Cupar's face worked. He jabbed a finger at the house. 'She's the fat cat now,' he said. 'She's news, too. I could get a hundred thousand, easy, for telling people where she's hiding.'

Thorneycroft reached across the gate, caught Cupar's flailing wrists, and slammed them down hard on the top bar of the gate.

'Listen to me,' he said softly. 'Listen carefully. If you want to stay out of jail, leave Liz alone and don't say a word about her to anyone.'

'I'm not afraid of jail. No court could blame me for coming here on an errand of sympathy.'

'I'm not talking about the court order,' Thorneycroft said. 'I'm talking about Trevor's murder. There are plenty of us who remember how you bad-mouthed him at the time of the divorce. You spouted insults in clubs, at parties and in the divorce court. You said a number of times that you hated him. I'm warning you, if the police hear that you're trying to screw more money out of Liz, they'll wonder if perhaps you had a motive for putting Trevor out of your way.'

Cupar stopped trying to free himself from Thorneycroft's grasp and stared at him blankly. 'That's ridiculous,' he said. 'I'm not a murderer.'

'You're a punk, a drug addict, a child- and wife-beater, you could become a murder suspect without the slightest difficulty.' Thorneycroft released Cupar's wrists and thrust him backwards. 'Get out of here,' he said. 'Stay out of the police eye and keep your fat mouth shut. And if you have any sense, get yourself into a good rehabilitation centre.'

He turned, whistled to Gatsby and walked towards the house. He heard the Cadillac start and saw it glide away towards the river road. By nightfall Bruce Cupar would be back in his comfort zone, high on some illegal substance.

He was a man without morals or compassion, a drug addict who lacked the ready cash for the fix of his choice. Had he approached Trevor for money and been refused? Did he believe that with Trevor out of the way, Liz would be a soft touch? Desperation could have made Cupar a killer; and even if that wasn't the case, he was still malicious enough to lead the media to Liz's hiding place.

Thorneycroft reached for his mobile phone and sent an SMS to Dysart: 'Bruce Cupar tried 2 gatecrash. Need to talk. Come for beer this eve. JT.'

The answer came quickly. 'OK 6.30. Your job agreed bringing docs for you and Mrs Cupar to sign. Dysart.'

Liz's guests left at five. Thorneycroft found her sitting in the living room, as if she hadn't the will to move. She said tiredly, 'They were all so kind, so helpful. Tony Mason explained the terms of Dad's will, and dear Hamish is already seeing to it that the company here and abroad will run the way Dad would have wanted.'

She paused, biting her lip. 'It's Penwold I worry about. They seem to think I'll want to sell it, but I don't. I can't just dump the people who work there, and the horses. It's kind of … Dad's monument. Stevie loves it, too. I think I should move in and make it my job. I have to go back to Grasmere, to sort things out, but I don't think I can ever live there again.'

'I've been thinking about Penwold, myself,' Thorneycroft said. 'It has great security, and you'd be more private there. But there's no need to make hasty decisions. Take your time.' He hesitated, wondering if he should tell her about her ex-husband's visit, and decided he should.

'Bruce was here this afternoon,' he said, 'demanding to talk to you. I sent him packing, but there's no guarantee he won't haunt this place.'

'What did he want? Money?'

'Yes. He's afraid you'll cut him off.'

Liz's mouth tightened. 'I won't let him starve, but I won't have him near me or Stevie.' She sighed. 'I have to find a way to tell Stevie. He keeps asking about his things at Grasmere. I thought I'd take him over there, tomorrow, collect his books and toys, and while we're there, tell him what happened. I must talk to Will and Molly, too, ask them if they want to come to Penwold or stay where they are.'

'I'll drive you and Stevie over, tomorrow,' Thorneycroft said. He glanced at his watch. 'Iain Dysart will be here at 6.30. He's going to sign me on as a consultant.'

Liz's face brightened. 'Oh, that is good news. I can't ask for more than to have you and Iain on the case.'

Dysart arrived on time, accepted a tankard of ale and handed Thorneycroft an envelope. 'Read, digest and sign,' he said. 'Make it soon. We can do with some unorthodox thinking.'

Thorneycroft grinned. Police procedure was painstaking, invaluable, and at times monumentally boring.

'How's it going?' he asked.

'No obvious leads,' Dysart answered. 'Nobody except Jumbo Barnes has reported seeing the bike. Nobody witnessed anyone breaking into Cornwall's private wood. We found no prints or trace material at the crime scene, though we did find the sabot. Forensics think it's a Russian make, but that doesn't mean much. Arms and ammo move around the world. If you know where to shop you can buy whatever you want.'

'Maybe you don't even need to shop,' Thorneycroft said. 'Thieves steal weapons, soldiers pick them up on battlefields, ordinary citizens collect souvenirs.'

'We're building a list of possible assailants: shooters with priors, ex-army snipers, known terrorists, hit men. It's a long, long list, and it may turn out that our man doesn't figure on it. We're applying to the US and to Wiesbaden for specific MOs of known assassins who use guns.' He took a pull at his tankard, watching Thorneycroft over the rim. 'What did Cupar want?'

'Money,' Thorneycroft answered. 'I warned him off, but he's a user. He may get high and try again. I told him to be careful not to act in a way that might suggest he killed Trevor. That really seemed to scare him.'

'I'll keep up the good work,' Dysart promised. There was a sparkle in his eye that suggested he'd enjoy scaring Cupar.

Thorneycroft leaned back in his chair. 'I've been doing some lateral thinking.'

'And?'

'Kaminsky. It takes a lot to muzzle him, but someone has.'

'Yes, and I'd like to know why. Cornwall wasn't into politics, he wasn't a security risk. So why is his death off limits?'

'Another point,' Thorneycroft continued. 'You say that the Cougar III has a built-in tracker system. That means it's unlikely to have been stolen. Someone owns it legitimately, and some tracker firm knows where it is, either in the UK or possibly further afield. So who owns the tracker firm?'

'We don't know. None of the established firms in Britain has reported a Cougar III stolen. None of them can tell us if one of their listed machines was in the vicinity of Cornwall's property when he was killed.' Dysart rubbed a hand over his eyes. 'I asked one of our lads to check how fast a biker could get from Grasmere to *The Monitor*'s premises. He rode the course three times on a Cougar III, and made it in the same time as the perp, but he told me it required skill and nerve. It seems the perp knows how to handle his bike, as well as his rifle.'

'What if the bike was bought in some other country, and listed with a tracking company that isn't legally registered?'

'An illegal tracker?' Dysart thought about it. 'I suppose it's possible in the short term. It couldn't operate for long. You think someone was keeping tabs on the perp?'

'It did occur to me. Let's suppose that an organization has the motive and the hard cash to arrange a hit on Trevor. The hit man is provided with whatever he needs ... rifle, ammo, bike, safe house. The bike is fitted with a tracker device, which ensures that the hirer can check at any time that the hit man is where he's supposed to be. The planting of an obituary notice could be a signal from the perp to the hirer that the job's been done, and the fee should be paid into his numbered account in the Cayman Islands or wherever.'

'Why such an elaborate system? Professional killers have much quieter and more effective ways of communicating with their paymasters.'

'Perhaps this hit man isn't a pro.'

'A contradiction in terms, laddie. There's no such thing as an amateur hit man.'

'Let's lose the word hit man. Let's envisage an individual who's hired by backers to kill another individual. He's not a professional killer, but he has a strong motive for making this particular kill. The backers employ him because he has the know-how and the opportunity to do the job ... and because they can control him with more certainty than would be possible with a pro.'

'Who do you think's backing him?'

'I have no idea. Some rogue organization. Mafia, a terrorist group.'

'That's a bit too lateral for me.' Dysart set down his tankard and waved away the offer of a refill. His voice betrayed the edginess of twenty-four hours without sleep, and Thorneycroft changed the subject.

'Liz wants to leave London and go to Penwold.'

'Why not? The security's better there than here, and the staff will look after her. Anyway, if she's made up her mind to go, you won't dissuade her.'

'You've known her a while, haven't you?'

Dysart gave him a bleak glance, but he answered the question. 'Fourteen years,' he said. 'My father was a masseur; he looked after athletes' injuries. There was this small Hungarian circus, when it came to England, they'd hire him. I used to go with him on his visits. I loved the horses. There was every breed, from Shetland ponies to Percherons.

'One day, Liz visited the stable lines. The stablemaster had special skills – he could turn a rogue horse into a star performer. He taught Liz how to break a racehorse of its bad habits and make him a champion.

'Liz and I got friendly. She was just a kid. I knew there was no future in it. My father warned me Liz could look forward to a great future, and I couldn't compete in her circles. I knew he was right. So ... well ... the circus left town.'

'She's glad you're on the case.'

'And that's where I stay, on the case.' Dysart reached for his briefcase. 'I have her statement here, for signature. If you'll ask her to join us, we can finish the paperwork now, before I leave.'

Liz was summoned and signed the statement and Thorneycroft put his name to a contract as forensic psychiatrist. As Dysart gathered up the papers, Liz said,

'Is it all right if I take Stevie over to Grasmere tomorrow? John will drive us.'

Dysart looked up sharply. 'No, it's not all right. The press are watching the property like hawks. If they see you they'll follow you back here.'

'But Stevie wants his books and toys.'

'Make a list of what he wants and I'll see he gets them.' Dysart saw her face pucker and his voice softened. 'It's just not wise.'

'Why don't I go for the stuff,' Thorneycroft suggested. 'I can bring it to the nick, not directly back here.'

Dysart nodded. He was still watching Liz. 'I hear you're thinking of moving to Penwold,' he said. 'That's an excellent idea. I have to visit the stables myself, within a day or two. We need to talk to the people there about your father's racing business.'

She said stiffly, 'Of course, you have to talk to everyone. I'll write the list for John at once.'

When she'd left the room, Thorneycroft said, 'Do you think Trevor's murder is connected to his racing interests?'

'Frankly, no,' Dysart answered, 'but we have to study them. Maybe we'll learn something useful.'

'Straight from the horse's mouth,' Thorneycroft said. It was a remark he was to remember in the days to come.

V

WATCHING DYSART'S CAR drive away, Liz said, 'Iain and I were friends, once.'

'I know,' Thorneycroft said. 'He told me.'

'He dumped me.'

'His father told him not to get too fond of you.'

'Because of my money.'

'Because your lifestyle was different from theirs.'

'That's the money, isn't it? I'm used to that. Money closes as many doors as it opens. I wasn't given a chance to say what I thought. I believe Dad was glad that Iain left me alone. He wouldn't have tried to make me break my friendship with Iain, but he was glad that it broke.'

'You were very young. Trevor was protecting you.'

'I know. It was long ago. Now Iain calls me "Mrs Cupar".'

'He's in charge of the case, Liz. He can't seem to show any bias towards you. He gives you your proper title.'

'"Mrs Cupar". I got over Iain and married Bruce. There's irony for you.' She sighed. 'Dad always put me first, you see. Before his companies, his giant projects, he always put me first. It was a strain, sometimes, knowing how much he loved me. Now I don't know how I'll survive without him.'

'You'll survive. You'll come through this.'

'Without him.'

'But with Stevie.'

'Yes. Thank God for him.' She turned towards the house. 'I'll tell him now. I can't let him hear about it from anyone else.'

*

Thorneycroft drove over to Grasmere early the next day. He found Will and Molly waiting for him at the front door. Together they worked to fill two tea chests with Steven's possessions. Thorneycroft told them that Liz planned to move to Penwold, and Molly nodded. 'We'll go wherever she goes,' she said. 'This house isn't the same. He's gone and his space can't be filled. Now it's up to her, where we live. We'll just take things one day at a time, until things settle down.'

The packing completed, Thorneycroft walked down to the gate where Trevor had died. A policeman was still on duty there, and police tape was stretched across the path that led into the wood. Thorneycroft identified himself, and walked a short way down the lane.

He found the marker that had been set where the sabot from the bullet had been found. Linking that to the patch of cut branches in the wood, he calculated that the sabot had travelled about thirty feet from the firing point. The distance between that point and the gate was short – less than fifteen yards. Thorneycroft felt the hair rise on his neck, in the old atavistic horror at cold-blooded murder. Trevor had stood no chance of survival.

He returned to examine the gate. It had been cleaned of blood and brain matter, but the iron itself seemed to cry out. Thorneycroft forced himself to think not of Trevor dead, but Trevor alive. The motive for killing a man was usually linked to the man's character. A good man could be martyred for his goodness as easily as a bad man could be killed for his sins.

He remembered Trevor as a man big in build and personality. In the polo field his size had demanded the strongest of ponies.

In the boardroom his size and rich voice had often dominated debate. But his mind, too, was large. He was clever, inventive, far seeing, and those qualities, allied to his integrity, had taken him to the top of his profession.

And his defects? Hard to name. Some might think him straight-laced. He was a devout Christian and went regularly to church.

He cherished an old-fashioned patriotism that might have grated on some people. He disliked folk who criticized their fellows but did nothing themselves to better the world. Freeloaders, he'd called them.

Sometimes one might be irritated by Trevor's absolute disciplines; but let him see your irritation, and at once he would seek to overcome it, he would apologize, listen, search for an understanding.

He should not have died. The world had need of his kind.

At Greenwich police station, Dysart assembled his investigating team to meet Thorneycroft. They were DI Kevin Roberts (grey at the temples, overweight, but sure-footed on the slippery slopes of the law); DS Ivans (computer skills and irreverent black eyes); DS Simcox (young, quiet-spoken and probably a good man in a fight); and DS Frank (young Sri Lankan woman, science degrees, a disquietingly grim mouth); and of course prime observer, DS Clay. Dysart handed Thorneycroft a stack of reports covering the work done so far; the extensive questioning of the people who lived in the vicinity of Grasmere, of Cornwall's lawyers and business reps of the organizers of the fund-raiser Cornwall had addressed on the day of his death and of the traffic police who had been on duty along the routes the Cougar biker could have taken on the Friday of the murder.

A separate file contained the statements made by Liz Cupar, and Will and Molly Mitchell.

Also filed separately were the reports describing the part played by *The Sporting Monitor*'s staff. Jumbo Barnes was the only person who had seen the biker, and could say only that he was slender, and had hidden his face behind a dark perspex visor. 'He never spoke,' Jumbo insisted, 'never even said "ta", just stared at me and buggered off.'

Thorneycroft, asked to give an opinion of the killer, said that it was too early to draw a profile; 'But there are certain things we do know. The killer's an excellent shot and a competent rider of a Cougar bike. Which raises questions. Where did he learn to shoot?

In the armed forces, in a terrorist group, or simply as an amateur interested in marksmanship? Where did he learn to handle a racing bike? Was he trained as a combatant, a policeman, or was he just a member of Hells' Angels?

'It seems likely,' Thorneycroft continued, 'that he knows London, and has studied maps to plan the quickest route from the crime scene at Grasmere, to the premises of *The Sporting Monitor*. He's a careful planner. He planned entry to Cornwall's private wood, he prepared a firing site, he was equipped with a rifle, ammunition and motorbike that are beyond the reach of ordinary citizens.

'We don't have many facts, but the ones we do have shed some light on the character of the perpetrator. He's a cold-blooded killer, callous and possibly vindictive. It's worth remembering that professional hit men don't feel a personal desire to kill a victim. To them, murder is just a job they're paid to do.

'However, I have the feeling that this man did have a strong personal reason to kill Cornwall. He took risks that a professional wouldn't take. He risked being seen near Grasmere. He risked being stopped at *The Monitor*. It could be that he's used to taking risks. Maybe risk turns him on.

'The dropping off the obituary notice is puzzling. I've suggested that it could be an arranged signal, informing a paymaster that the job's been done, but frankly I don't credit such a weird action. The obit. could also be a red herring, left by a pro hit man to suggest that the killing's the work of a madman.'

'And is he mad?' demanded DI Franks.

'As I said, it's too early to reach conclusions,' Thorneycroft answered. 'My guess is he's psychotic, but not a typical serial killer. I feel he's killing to protect his own interests, or possibly to avenge some action that's caused him damage.'

DI Franks's small mouth grew smaller. 'That's just your guess?'

'For the moment, yes.'

DS Simcox intervened. 'He's got plenty of cash. The bike, the weapon, the ammo, those don't come cheap.'

'Money, or a rich backer,' said DI Roberts, 'and whether he's a pro or an amateur, he could still kill again.'

'Yes,' Thorneycroft agreed, 'and our only chance of stopping him is to keep up the good work of following the facts. We need to trace the provenance of the bike, the source of the weapon and ammo.' He turned to Ivans. 'You've been checking records. Have you found any previous case where there was this modus operandi?'

Ivans shook his head. 'Not in this country. There've been plenty of cases where the killer used a gun, but nothing as ... as fancy as this. This bastard is clever and cruel. He's playing some kind of game. He makes my skin crawl. Maybe some other country has him on record, but for now, well, he's one of a kind.'

When the discussion ended, Thorneycroft asked to see the autopsy and forensic reports. Dysart produced a file and a pack of photographs.

'Our local pathologist is a woman,' he said. 'She's good, and careful, and best of all she's modest. She asked for Prout of Concorde Street to assist at the autopsy, which he did. The coroner will be satisfied that the post-mortem results are in order.'

Thorneycroft read the written report first, then listened to the tape recording made by the two doctors as they conducted the autopsy. It was detailed, exact and chilling.

The photographs, displayed on a computer screen, made terrible viewing. Looking at Trevor's shattered head, Dysart said grimly, 'He made sure of Trevor, didn't he?'

'Yes,' said Thorneycroft softly, 'and we'll make sure of him.'

VI

THE INQUEST INTO the death of Trevor Cornwall took place on Wednesday, in the courthouse adjacent to the municipal offices. By nine o'clock a sizeable crowd had gathered there, and when the doors were opened the public and press seats were quickly filled.

Dysart and Thorneycroft stationed themselves in the foyer to watch the people filing into the courtroom. Rupert Hollings and Jumbo Barnes were early arrivals, and the media were very present. Thorneycroft recognized a number of Liz Cupar's friends, but Bruce Cupar didn't show his face.

Liz herself came in company with her lawyer and Will and Molly Mitchell. Liz was very pale, but she had herself well in hand, and spoke quietly to the policewoman who ushered her to the witnesses' waiting room.

As the doors of the courtroom were closing, Dysart and Thorneycroft moved to the seats reserved for them. Dysart scanned the faces round them. Thorneycroft knew he was thinking the killer might be in the building.

'He won't come,' he said. 'He's too disciplined.'

Dysart sniffed. 'He's a chancer. He might have been seen, breaking into Cornwall's grounds, or stashing the bike at the gate. Like you said, he takes risks.'

'Yes, but he plans them. He's cold and methodical, which is why I don't think Cupar's the killer.'

'The top brass don't agree with you. They like him as a suspect.'

'Do they now? Perhaps they're looking for a whipping-boy.'

Before Dysart could reply, the usher signalled the 'all rise' and the coroner took his place on the bench.

Dysart was called to the witness stand, and gave his testimony crisply. Dr Prout made his report on the autopsy, which could be summed up in a sentence: Trevor Cornwall had been a man in sound health who died when a bullet blew his head apart.

There was a murmur of sympathy from the public benches when Liz described how she had found her father lying dead at the gates of Grasmere, and a sharpening of attention in the press area when Jumbo Barnes and Rupert Hollings spoke about the biker who had delivered a fake obituary notice to *The Sporting Monitor*.

The case already had those elements of the grotesque that capture public attention. Was that also part of the killer's plan?

The coroner duly delivered his verdict: Trevor Cornwall was the victim of murder by person or persons unknown.

The hearing concluded, Thorneycroft joined Dysart on the front steps of the building. Rupert Hollings, lingering at the back of the crowd, tapped Dysart on the arm.

'I'd like a private word with you, Chief Inspector.'

Dysart smiled. 'Dr Thorneycroft's engaged as a consultant in this investigation. You can say what you like in front of him.'

The editor looked embarrassed, but complied. 'Very well. I was approached this morning by Mr Bruce Cupar. He said he had a story to sell me, concerning you and Mrs Cupar. He said you had an affair with her when she was fifteen, and her father found out about it and warned you off. Cupar claims you had a furious row with Mr Cornwall, and that you've "had it in" for him ever since.'

Dysart's face reddened, but he said quietly, 'Thank you for telling me. Bruce Cupar is a drug addict, and he's never had a regard for the truth. Liz Cupar and I were friends, no more. She was sixteen, not fifteen and there was no affair. It was my father, not hers, who "warned me off", and I remained on good terms with Mr Cornwall.'

Hollings nodded. 'That's what I thought. I told Cupar we don't publish dirt, and he'd be well advised to avoid making slanderous statements. He tried to argue and I showed him the door. In my book, he's a malicious little prick. I think he may try to peddle his malice elsewhere. I thought I should warn you.'

'Thank you. I'm grateful. I'll deal with it.'

Hollings moved away and Dysart drew a hissing breath. 'I don't need Cupar suggesting I'd reason to kill Cornwall.'

'That's just Cupar crap,' Thorneycroft said. 'No one in his right mind will listen to what he says.'

Dysart hunched his shoulders. 'It's not that simple, John. A man heading a murder investigation can't have his name linked to anyone who benefits from the crime. Liz and I were close, once, and now she's due to inherit a vast fortune. The paparazzi could make a meal of Cupar's crap. I could be taken off the case, and I don't want that, for Liz's sake or mine.'

'My advice is, pre-empt the paparazzi. Tell your chief about Cupar's approach to Hollings, and ask Liz's lawyers to impress on Cupar that if he hopes to keep feeding at the Cornwall trough, he'd better mind his mouth.'

'Yeah. I'll do that, but I tell you straight, there's something about this case that gets up my nose. There's too much string-pulling, and I don't know who's the puller, or why.'

Thorneycroft didn't argue the point. He shared Dysart's view that someone in authority was attempting to set the limits of the investigation.

What could be the motive for such intervention? Come to that, what was the motive for the killing itself?

Most murders were committed on impulse, in the heat of domestic violence, gang warfare, a clash between criminals and the police. This murder didn't seem to fall into any of those categories. It had been meticulously planned, carried out with cold savagery and the killer's motive remained a mystery.

The man who had gunned down Trevor Cornwall didn't appear to have been driven by primitive rage, or greed, or thwarted passion.

It was true that some perverts killed for the pleasure of it, but that was the mark of sadistic insanity, and the definition didn't quite fit this case. The killer knew exactly what he was doing; he was smart enough to leave no clue to his identity, he gave no indication of what might be his future actions.

So far, the only people who stood to gain by the murder were Liz, the Mitchells and a bunch of blameless charities. It was hard to believe that the killer came from those ranks.

Someone had wanted Trevor dead. Something in his life had prompted that fixed intention; something he'd done or planned to do, something he'd known, had made him the victim of a killer.

Thorneycroft reflected on the difficulties of probing every aspect of a man's life. Trevor had been a tycoon, a noted sportsman, a husband and father, a convinced Christian. In any of those areas could lie an incident that had triggered murder in a disordered mind. How many events great and small must be examined to find the one that had led to Trevor's murder?

He returned to the puzzle of the obituary. Bizarre as it seemed, it expressed the killer's thoughts. It shed light on his dark persona.

And why had the killer mentioned Trevor's acquisition of a horse? Why that particular horse, and what significance did it have for the killer, or for Trevor? The provenance and history of French Toast must be carefully studied.

Thorneycroft walked slowly to his car.

There were so many questions, so few answers.

Perhaps a start could be made at Penwold Racing Stables, which Trevor had created and brought to prominence in the racing world. French Toast occupied one of its stalls.

Liz was leaving tomorrow, going to Penwold with Steven and the Mitchells. Dysart and Clay planned to go there on Saturday, to question stable manager Bunny Rourke, and the staff, jockeys and grooms that worked with him.

Go with the flow, Thorneycroft decided. Take Claudia and Luke to spend the weekend at Penwold. See if some of the daunting questions could be answered there.

VII

THORNEYCROFT, CLAUDIA AND Luke travelled to Penwold village on Friday afternoon. They had enjoyed other visits, sharing time in the country with loved friends. This journey was heavy with the sense of a friend lost, his companionship, skills and virtues gone for ever.

The racing stables lay on the outskirts of a hamlet that had escaped the long arm of tourism. Trevor had chosen the site for its geography, a flat plain given over for centuries to wheat and barley farms. There were few trees, and the surrounding hills were low and rounded. Good roads led to Epsom, Ascot, the large towns east and west and north to London.

Circling the village, Thorneycroft remembered that at the outset he'd judged Trevor's racing ambitions to be just a rich man's foible, but time had proved him wrong. Trevor quickly gained recognition as a man of sincere commitment, whose horses ran good races and achieved significant results. He won a place in the echelon of successful racehorse owners.

Three years ago, a gang had attempted to steal a horse that was fancied for the Derby. Trevor set his electronic whizz kids to making Penwold Stables thief-proof.

The property consisted of three concentric circles. The outermost ring was formed by the original farmlands. Electrified fencing marked the boundary, and the access gates were manned by armed guards. Within that area was an inner enclave containing a practice racecourse, and tan and grass gallops. Thorneycroft's measuring eye judged that the enclave would be out of range for a sniper stationed beyond the outer fence.

At the heart of the property lay three stable-yards, the owner's and manager's houses and the cottages, canteen and leisure rooms provided for the staff, jockeys and grooms who lived on the Penwold estate.

Liz's house stood close to the yards. The original farmhouse had been extended and modernized, and at its west end Trevor had added a tower from which he could see his horses at exercise, and which was the core of the security system. As the car drew up on the parking ground, Thorneycroft saw that two men were on duty in the tower, keeping the surrounding country under observation.

Liz and her trainer-manager Bunny Rourke came forward to meet the car. Liz looked tired, but less strained than she'd been in London. She swept Claudia and Luke into the house, leaving Thorneycroft alone with Rourke.

The trainer was small and wiry, his hair cropped close to his skull, his face seamed with wrinkles. He had the sharp bright gaze of a ferret, and Thorneycroft knew him to be impatient of fools. Critics described Rourke as a jumped-up jockey, but this was far from the truth. He had done honourable service as a cavalryman, and when time made warhorses redundant, he had worked first as a trainer of police horses, and then as trainer of the string of race-horses belonging to a well-known British woman. On her death he was hired by Trevor Cornwall, and helped to create Penwold Stables. His devotion to Trevor showed not only in the black band on his sleeve, but in the grim set of his features.

'I told Liz I needed a word with you,' he said. 'Tomorrow the cops will be here, taking up my time, and I maybe won't have a chance to tell you what's on my mind.'

'So tell me now,' Thorneycroft said.

Rourke made a sweeping gesture. 'You can see that since the boss died, I've made some changes here. Brought in extra guards, lads I know can be trusted. We're training the horses inside the fence, now, not out on the hills. No visitors are allowed, not even people we know. I'm not sure that's enough.' He met Thorneycroft's eyes. 'I don't know if this is the best place for Liz and Stevie to be.'

'Why not? The security's great. She's safer here than at Grasmere, or in my house.'

'She's only safe if she does what she's told and stays inside the boundary fence,' Rourke said flatly. 'She's set on riding out on the hills. I've told her that's too risky. Do you agree?'

'Yes I do. I hope to God she and Stevie aren't targets, but we can't take any chances.'

Rourke nodded vehemently. 'She's been giving me a big argument. I told her flat, you have to think of your boy. He's lost his grandad, he can't be losing his mam as well. Liz saw my point, but you know how she is, she hates restrictions. I'm hoping the bastard that killed the boss will be caught fast. Liz says this Inspector Dysart is a good cop, but is he good enough? That's what I'd like to know.'

'He's very good,' Thorneycroft said slowly, 'but to be honest, I don't know if anyone can achieve an early arrest. This case isn't straightforward.'

'Then,' said Rourke, 'you'd best warn the inspector that Liz has entered horses for some big races, and she'll be straining her gut to go and watch them run.' He ran a hand over his stubbled skull. 'I wonder would you care to take a stroll round the place with me, see if you can suggest any improvements in the security?'

They made the tour of the complex, and it confirmed Thorneycroft's view that Penwold was the safest place for Liz and Steven to be. He assured Rourke that he would impress on her the need to stay within its boundaries.

They ended their tour in the stable yards, and Thorneycroft broached the question on his mind.

'I'd like to know more about the horse Trevor bought,' he said. 'Is French Toast stabled here?'

Rourke's mouth twisted. 'Yes, he's here. I saw he was mentioned in that shit *The Sporting Monitor* printed.'

Thorneycroft nodded. 'And I'd like to know how the killer got to hear about the horse. I don't recall seeing anything about it in the press. Dysart's team hasn't found any reference to it, either, but the killer knew about it.'

'He didn't hear about French Toast from me,' Rourke said, 'but let's face it, one of the lads here might have talked in the pub, or in a letter home. The news could have leaked in spite of what Trevor wanted.'

'He didn't want the acquisition to be made public, did he?'

'No. He didn't want any publicity until we had a chance to see how good French Toast is. He looks a picture, and he's had some wins, but that doesn't make him a champion.'

'Do you have the details of his breeding, where he was foaled, past owners, past performance?'

'Sure. There's a file in my office, I'll give it to you to read. Liz can likely tell you more than I can. Trevor talked to her a lot. They were very close.'

'What do you think of French Toasts's prospects?'

Rourke pursed his lips. 'Hard to say. He's got some bad habits. Maybe we can cure him of them.' He sighed. 'Trevor was over the moon about him. He said to me, "Next year's going to be our best ever." Now he's gone. He was the heart and soul of this place. I don't know how we'll do without him.' He glanced at the stable clock. 'I must be about my work. See you at evening rounds.'

Thorneycroft made his way into the house. Luke and Steven were sitting on the stairs, playing with a set of mini cars. Passing them, Thorneycroft knew that they and Claudia had to be protected as closely as Liz; kept within safe bounds, watched over day and night. The miasma of murder threatened them all.

Liz met him in the upper corridor, and he repeated Rourke's warnings about not leaving the Penwold property. She pulled a wry face, but said, 'I know. I'll do as I'm told. I admit I feel safer here than I did in London.'

He took the chance to ask the question that had been on his mind.

'Rourke said Trevor didn't want publicity about French Toast until he was sure of his abilities. Why did Trevor buy him, if he didn't know how he'd perform?'

Liz hesitated. 'The fact is, Dad didn't buy French Toast. He was a gift.' She smiled at Thorneycroft's look of surprise. 'Dad was in

Istanbul in April. A cousin of my mother is building a luxury hotel there, and he engaged our company to provide and install all the electronic equipment ... not just the computers, but the communication systems, the laser beams, the alarm networks. It's specialist work, and Dad went to Istanbul himself to see it was properly done. He stayed with Cousin Salim for two weeks. He said Salim was family and must be treated as such. He gave Salim marvellous terms for the job.'

'Salim who?'

'Salim Jadwat. He's a financier, very rich, a big man in Turkey. When the work on the hotel was nearly complete, he said he wanted to express his gratitude by giving Dad French Toast.'

'A lavish gift.'

'Yes, though I don't think Salim was remotely interested in owning a racehorse – especially one he described as "naughty". When Dad told him naughty horses could be trained to be good ones, Salim promptly sealed the offer.'

'What's the horse's history?'

'He was bred in France, by Here's How out of Mademoiselle Gigi. Jules Lafayette owned him, but sold him as a colt to one of Salim's rich pals. The man died owing Salim money, and his widow gave French Toast to Salim. He's won some good races, but he's failed in others he should have won.'

'What do you think is his potential?'

'He can be a great champion.' Liz spoke with conviction, and Thorneycroft smiled.

'Are you working with him yourself?'

'Yes, and he's already responding. He's been badly exploited. Lafayette never troubled to develop him, said he was just another showy chestnut, and the man who had him from Lafayette hired jockeys who never tried to bring him to his best. They just took him to the front of every race, and he got the idea that he mustn't be passed. He tries to lead all the way. I'm teaching him that something has to be saved for a great finish, and he's learning fast. He loves to race. Next year, he'll do great things, I promise.'

Thorneycroft raised the point that troubled him. 'Trevor didn't want the public to know about French Toast. Yet the obituary left at *The Sporting Monitor* mentioned him by name. Rourke thinks the story may have been leaked by someone at Penwold.'

'I suppose that's possible,' Liz answered, 'but I think it's much more likely that the leak happened between Turkey and England.'

'Why do you think Trevor was so keen on secrecy?'

For the first time in the conversation, Liz looked unsure of herself. 'I don't know,' she said slowly. 'He never discussed his reasons with me. Perhaps, as Rourke says, he wasn't sure if French Toast was a star or a dud. Perhaps he was scared that someone would try to steal him, or nobble him.'

At that moment, the dinner gong sounded, and Molly Mitchell appeared at the foot of the stairs to announce that the meal was ready.

That afternoon, Thorneycroft put through a call to Dysart. He told him the story of Trevor's acquisition of French Toast, and asked Dysart to find out what he could about Salim Jadwat.

'There's something odd about the deal,' he said. 'Jadwat made Trevor the gift of a horse with an uncertain record, and it seems Trevor welcomed it. That wasn't like him. He was a shrewd businessman, he never made dubious investments. And how did the killer get to hear about French Toast? Why did he mention him in the obit.?'

'Secrets leak,' Dysart said.

'They do, but there's the possibility this one didn't leak through stable gossip. Somehow the perp had inside information. Maybe he was told by Salim Jadwat, or someone close to him. We need to know more about Jadwat and his gift horse.'

'I'll see to it,' Dysart said, 'but I tend to agree with Rourke. Give a man a few beers and he'll forget to mind his tongue.' He heaved a sigh. 'Any fresh lead is welcome. We'll discuss Jadwat tomorrow.'

VIII

THORNEYCROFT ROSE AT six on Saturday morning, dressed and made his way to the largest of the three stable yards. Several horses were already leaving it, headed for the practice course, their riders perched on racing saddles. At the far end of the yard Liz, Rourke and a jockey were in close consultation next to a magnificent chestnut horse. Liz caught sight of Thorneycroft and beckoned him over.

'Meet French Toast,' she said. 'Beautiful, isn't he?'

Thorneycroft nodded. Even an amateur could admire the embodiment of power, grace and energy in this glossy animal, see the spirit that glowed in the splendid eyes. French Toast looked ready to soar like Pegasus into the sky. Liz reached up to pat the arching red-gold neck.

'We're going to try him on the main circuit,' she said, 'see how he shapes up against the best in our stables. We'll be watching from the tower. Would you like to join us?'

'Very much,' Thorneycroft said. He was interested in French Toast not as an equine phenomenon, but as a factor in a murder investigation: the horse might shed some light on the motive of a murderer. Moreover, a visit to the tower would allow him to judge how safe the Penwold estate was against an attack by an expert sniper.

He stood back while the jockey was thrown up into the saddle, and watched horse and rider move down the track that led to the practice course. Liz led the way along the back of the house to a door that gave access to the tower, and a lift carried them to its third storey.

Thorneycroft saw that since his last visit to Penwold, the electronic equipment in the tower had been upgraded. Two operators faced a bank of computers, cameras and video screens and a third, who was evidently the man in charge, was scanning the practice course through binoculars. He turned to greet Liz.

'All quiet,' he said. 'There've been a couple of Mr Filbrow's trucks come past, and Dr Maytom's car. Nothing we couldn't identify.' He handed the binoculars to Thorneycroft, and went back to the communications area.

Thorneycroft followed Liz and Rourke to a row of swivel chairs that overlooked the course. The horses had reached the holding ring next to the line of electrically-operated starting-stalls. Trevor Cornwall had spent some of his billions on creating what was, in fact, a model racecourse.

The horses were being walked round quietly. Thorneycroft focused on French Toast. He seemed to be dancing, neck arched, hoofs as light as feathers on the springy turf ... imbued like all great athletes with a love of the game and a hunger for victory.

The handlers began moving the horses into the starting stalls. French Toast took his place calmly. All the stalls filled, the gates sprang open and the thirteen runners surged forward in a line that first bunched and then narrowed, moving at speed towards the first right hand bend of the course.

French Toast was lying fifth, going steadily. The jockey had him well in hand. The four leading horses were close-packed. It was a real race ... except for the silence. There was no watching crowd to stand at the rails and yell their triumph or despair.

At Thorneycroft's left, Rourke watched the race stony-faced. The stopwatch he held clicked at regular intervals. When the field reached the six-furlong post, he leaned forward in his chair, as if he was willing French Toast to fly.

French Toast was moving up, first to fourth place, then to third, but he still had ground to make up. His jockey shifted him away from the rail. Thorneycroft wondered, why. Wasn't the rail the shortest route to the winning post?

The field rounded the final bend and entered the finishing

straight. French Toast's jockey was urging him now with knees and voice and swinging arm, and French Toast was responding, becoming longer, lighter, passing the leaders, flying like a red-gold arrow to win by a length.

Rourke was on his feet, fists raised, and Thorneycroft turned to congratulate him.

'That was great, wasn't it? He's a star.'

Rourke lowered his arms and said flatly, 'Next year he'll meet the topnotchers that know all the tricks of the trade. But yes, he knows now he must keep something for the finish, and do what the jock tells him.'

Liz leaned over to hug Rourke. 'He's a champ, Bunny, and you know it. We must ease him into the big time, plan his future. That's what Dad would have done.'

Thorneycroft left them analyzing the evidence of Rourke's stopwatch, and crossed to the windows that faced the distant perimeter fence. The flat plain beyond it looked empty, quiet under the early sun. The only vehicle on the road was an ancient motorcycle with sidecar. The driver was red-faced and obese, and the passenger in the sidecar was a border collie.

The head operator came to stand beside Thorneycroft. 'That's old Pinkerton,' he said. 'He lives in the village, but he rides over to his daughter's home every day. That's ten miles west of here. We have that stretch of road covered.' He indicated one of the computer screens that showed Pinkerton's vehicle vanishing westward.

'Are you in touch with Inspector Dysart?' Thorneycroft asked, and the man nodded. 'Yes. Their car will reach the village in about an hour. I'll buzz your mobile when they're close.'

Thorneycroft thanked him. He knew the value of electronic security, but an atavistic sense warned him not to relax his vigilance. The man who killed Trevor had managed to evade the security measures at Grasmere and *The Sporting Monitor*. Evidently he understood security systems. Certainly he was familiar with Trevor's CV. He knew about the hush-hush acquisition of French Toast. He was clever, organized, ready to take risks, and he was driven by a powerful but unidentified motive. Like the trapdoor spider he had gone to ground, but he was no less poisonous for being out of sight.

Liz interrupted his thoughts. 'Rourke and Jack will see to French Toast,' she said. 'We must have breakfast before the police arrive.'

The police team arrived at the outer gates forty minutes later, and Liz and Thorneycroft went out to the parking circle to meet them. Dysart, Clay and a tall bespectacled woman stepped out of the car, and Liz moved quickly to greet Dysart.

'Iain, thank you for coming,' she said. 'Is there any news?'

He put a hand on her shoulder. 'We're making progress.' He turned to indicate the woman behind him. 'This is Detective Inspector Robarts. She's assisting with our financial investigations.'

Liz frowned. 'I don't understand. What financial investigations?'

'We have to examine your father's financial records. It's an enormous job, as you can imagine. He had holdings in so many parts of the world. His accountants have supplied us with a mass of information. DI Robarts is here to check the business records held at Penwold.'

Liz's face reddened. 'There's nothing to question. We don't keep two sets of books. You know my father was totally honest, he declared every penny, I don't see why—'

Dysart held up a hand. 'Wait, wait. Trevor's integrity is not in question, but we are trying to discover why he was killed. There may be someone in Cornwall Electronics or his other holdings who had reason to want him out of the way. Someone could have been working a scam, or looking for personal advancement.'

Liz subsided. 'Oh. Yes, I see. So what do you want us to do? How can we help?'

'Clay and I need to talk to everyone on the Penwold payroll,' Dysart said. 'Is there a room where we can conduct interviews?'

'Of course. You can use the morning room – it's on the stables side of the building.' She turned to DI Robarts. 'Perhaps you'd like to use the records room? Mr Rourke, our manager, can show you where everything is.'

Dysart said, 'We'll start by interviewing Mr Rourke. After that he'll be free to help DI Robarts check your files, and see what can be examined here and what must be taken to London.'

As Liz led the way back to the house, Dysart lingered to hand Thorneycroft a sheaf of papers.

'Prelims on Salim Jadwat,' he said. 'There'll be a lot more stuff, but you can make a start. On the face of it, he's clean. A shrewd entrepreneur with international holdings. No known links to terrorists or drug cartels. A good Muslim, good family man, gives generously to charity.'

'He gave away a horse that looks like being a champion,' Thorneycroft said. 'Is that shrewd business, or a big mistake?'

'Could be he doesn't like horses, doesn't gamble, was happy to be rid of a useless encumbrance. Middle Eastern potentates think nothing of giving lavish gifts to people who've done them favours. Why do you think French Toast is so important?'

'Because the perp knew about him. He was supposed to be a well kept secret. Cornwall warned everyone at Penwold not to gossip about the horse, but somehow the perp knew it was here, and mentioned it in the obituary.'

'Maybe he just wanted to give the obit. authenticity,' Dysart said. 'The fact that the horse was mentioned has made you focus on it. Why would a killer draw attention to himself in that way? Surely he knows we'll investigate the French Toast deal? It may help us to identify the killer. Why would he invite that?'

'Because he's not normal,' Thorneycroft answered. 'He may be legally sane, but he's certainly mentally disturbed. It could be that he's challenging us. Some killers see themselves as waging a mental conflict with the police. They take incredible risks because they see themselves as invincible. There's also the possibility that this man wants to be stopped. Deep down, he may feel that his compulsion to kill can only be stopped by his being arrested. He places clues that will bring that about.'

'Then he's crazy, never mind what the law says.'

'Abnormal, as I said.'

While Dysart set up the interviews with the Penwold personnel, Thorneycroft read the notes on Salim Jadwat. As Dysart had told him, they gave only a surface picture of a man whose wealth and spread of influence was very great.

It would take months to amass and sift the salient facts of Jadwat's life. Dysart didn't have the manpower or the time to devote to what could be a dead-end search. Jadwat must be left to satellite investigators around the world. The reasonable course would be to leave Sadwat and French Toast to them, and concentrate on routine targets.

Thorneycroft scowled. He had earned the reputation, in certain quarters, of being inclined to stray from the path of reason.

IX

DYSART'S INTERVIEW WITH Bunny Rourke proved unexpectedly difficult. Rourke was pugnacious, saying bluntly that Penwold Stables was a well run establishment as the records would show, that no one there had ever wished Trevor Cornwall ill or failed to obey his orders and that the police were wasting everyone's time trying to prove otherwise.

When Dysart asked if Cornwall had ever been involved in any controversy in the racing world, Rourke's answer was vehement.

'Certainly not! Mr Cornwall kept out of the wheeling and dealing. He was a straight talker and an honest dealer and he expected others to be the same.'

Dysart persisted. 'There are controversies that arise from illegal activities in the racing fraternity. Horses are pulled to prevent them from winning, owners form dicey cartels. Sometimes a good horse is replaced by a ringer which loses and costs the backers and bookies a lot of money. Did Mr Cornwall remain silent about such things, or did he speak out about them?'

Rourke made an impatient gesture. 'If he thought he should speak out, he did, but he tried not to get involved with the shenanigans of the dirty-tricks brigade.'

Dysart let that one lie. 'In racing circles,' he suggested, 'owners have to make decisions. Nothing illegal, just decisions about when to give a horse an easy run, and when to go for a win. Decisions like that can cost backers and bookies big money. Even an honest owner can make enemies.'

Rourke's lips protruded. 'Bookies and gamblers take risks and they know it. They know which jocks can be bought and which can't, they know who runs honest races and who doesn't. Trevor was never a fixer. He was trusted.'

'So I've been told, but my point is that an honest man can make enemies. Mr Cornwall may have been the target of someone who lost money and blamed him.'

Rourke shrugged. 'I can't speculate about that.'

'Did Mr Cornwall take you into his confidence at all times?'

'We discussed things that concerned me. We talked about every race where we entered a horse, every rider we chose, every result, win or lose. That was my job, and I was always in his confidence there. When it came to his private life ... well ... he kept himself to himself. I respected that.'

'Did he talk bout his acquisition of French Toast?'

Rourke's gaze flickered. 'He didn't want a lot of talk about that. He told us to hold our tongues, and we did.'

'You must have been involved in bringing the horse into this country, weren't you?'

'That, of course. You don't just import a racehorse like a crate of bananas. There's a lot of paperwork, health tests, laws to be kept. You'll find it all on our files in the records room.'

Dysart glanced at Thorneycroft. 'I expect you'll want to join DI Robarts there?'

'Later,' Thorneycroft agreed. 'First, I want to listen to what the security staff have to tell you.'

Dysart nodded and turned back to Rourke. 'You're the man who watches the watchers. What's your opinion of the security staff?'

Rourke said unhesitatingly, 'It's as good as it gets, anywhere in the world.'

'And the jockeys, grooms, cleaners?'

'They're rock solid. I handpick them myself.'

'Human beings have their off moments. Did one of your people here leak information, or maybe sell it to the media, or to a competitor?'

Rourke dismissed the suggestion with contempt. By his account, the personnel of Penwold Stables was, without exception, discreet, loyal and devoted to duty. 'They know if they put a foot wrong, they're out,' he said. 'They've got plum jobs here and they don't want to lose them.'

When Rourke at last departed, Dysart growled, 'band of ruddy saints, according to him. Nobody's that perfect. Someone must have passed the word the horse was here.'

But subsequent interviews with the security staff and yard workers confirmed Rourke's views. Penwold Stables appeared to be a happy and well-disciplined community, genuinely distressed by Cornwall's death.

At noon, Thorneycroft left the morning room and moved to the office where the records were housed. DI Robarts was seated at a long table in the middle of the room, surrounded by orderly stacks of files. She greeted Thorneycroft with a brisk nod.

'Are you an accountant, Doctor?'

Thorneycroft smiled. 'No, I'm a forensic psychiatrist and I'm interested in a horse named French Toast.'

'Has it committed a crime, or does it need psychiatric assessment?'

'Neither, to my knowledge. It was mentioned in the obituary notice the killer delivered to *The Sporting Monitor*.'

'Ah. I read about that. An anomaly, certainly. Though one could describe anything unusual as an anomaly, a departure from the rules. Is this man insane?'

'Mentally disturbed, at the least. He's also clever and methodical. He made deliberate mention of French Toast in the obituary. I want to know why.' Thorneycroft glanced about him. 'Mr Rourke says the files on the horse are stored here. Do you mind if I look for them?'

'Do. I imagine they're in that section.' She indicated a bank of filing cabinets at the far end of the room. 'All the stuff about blood lines and pedigrees and race statistics is there. There are a lot of photographs, too.'

'Will you need those?'

'No. Cornwall's lawyers and accountants have already given us the facts and figures relating to these stables. I'm just here to make an on-site assessment.'

'So you're looking for anomalies?'

Her mouth creased in a smile. 'If you like, yes. So far, I've found nothing but apple-pie order. I wish you better luck.'

Thorneycroft found two files bearing French Toast's name, carried them to the far end of the table and settled down to study them.

The first file contained sparse details of the horse's history. The French breeder, Jules Lafayette, had had little faith in the colt, and had sold him as a 2-year-old to a noted Arab playboy who raced his horses at Dubai. The playboy went broke, and died soon after. His widow settled his obligation to Salim Jadwat with the gift of French Toast.

The horse was a gelding. He would never earn fees by standing at stud. To become a good investment he had to win races, and his record there was uncertain.

Trevor Cornwall had gone to trouble and expense when he brought French Toast to England. The file listed the results of various tests required by law; permits, guarantees and insurance documents; and the transport arrangements covering the journey from Dubai to Penwold.

The file shed no light on why Trevor had insisted on secrecy, nor on how the killer had breached that barrier of silence. One point interested Thorneycroft; in his fake obit. the killer had inferred that Trevor bought the horse, but according to Liz there was no sale, merely a free gift.

The second file was devoted to photographs of French Toast. A large envelope contained pictures taken by a professional photographer in Dubai. Each picture bore a stamp of the studio's name, PHOTOXIM, and an address and telephone number.

The photos had been taken to show off the horse's points, and pinned to the envelope was a description of his physical characteristics; colour, markings, blood and DNA test results, information that would be important to an owner, and to race officials who had to be sure that an entrant to a race was the genuine article and not a ringer.

The records said that French Toast was who he claimed to be. No trickery there.

There were a number of informal shots of the horse. One of them showed him winning a race. He occupied most of the foreground. No other horse seemed to be in camera range. A flying finish?

Thorneycroft peered more closely. The crowd on the rail appeared to be yelling their heads off. He studied the edges of the photograph. They were not symmetrical. The four outer edges had been trimmed off. On the back of the photo was scrawled the single word 'Dubai'. Hard to guess who wrote it.

Trevor had been an ardent photographer, he'd owned several marvellous cameras. Could he have taken this shot with a wide-angle lens, and trimmed away all but the central portion of the positive?

DI Robarts broke in on his thoughts. 'You found something you like?'

'Could be,' he acknowledged. 'Is it all right for me to remove the photographs?'

She lifted a shoulder. 'Ask Dysart, ask the owner. Photos are not my territory. I'm here to look at figures.'

He took her advice and spoke to Dysart, who looked briefly at the photos, then nodded. 'Take them. We'll check the studio in Dubai. Maybe that's where the story leaked. Sign the pics out in your name and return them to our files.'

Thorneycroft next went in search of Liz. She was in the kitchen with Claudia and Molly Mitchell, fixing lunch for the children. Thorneycroft showed her the shot of French Toast in the Dubai race.

'Do you know who took this picture?' he asked.

'I never saw it before.' She turned it over. 'That could be Dad's writing. If he did take it, why did he cut off the edges?'

Molly Mitchell put down the salad dressing bottle and said, 'He did take it, in Dubai on that last trip. After Mr Jadwat said he was to have French Toast, he went to Dubai to see it run, and he took the picture. He showed it to Will and me before he cut it smaller.'

'Molly,' said Thorneycroft urgently, 'did he keep the pieces he cut off?'

She shook her head. 'No, he threw them in the rubbish bin.'

'But the negatives? Did he keep the negatives?'

She pursed her lips. 'That I can't say. Will would know, he looked after all Mr Cornwall's cameras and photos. He's out in the barn helping to stack hay and stuff.'

Thorneycroft detached Will from his labours and showed him the photograph. Will turned it in his thick fingers.

'Aye, Mr Cornwall took that, just for the horse. French Toast won by lengths, he said, and he didn't want that news to get about. It'd affect the weights he'd be given.'

'Molly told us Trevor cut the edges off the picture and threw them away,' Thorneycroft said. 'Did he keep the negatives?'

Will frowned. 'I'd say so. He never threw negs away. A great one for keeping things, he was, there's drawers full of things he never looked at again.'

'Where did he keep them, Will?'

'In his study at Grasmere. I could find the negs for you, if you want.'

'I'd be grateful. We'll be going back to London tomorrow. Can you come with us and help me look through Trevor's collection?'

'I can come, but the cops have locked up everything in the house. Only their people can go inside.'

'They'll let us in, don't worry.'

Will looked earnestly at Thorneycroft. 'Is the photo going to help you find who killed him?'

'It might.'

'Might's good enough for me. I'll be ready whenever you say.'

'Thank you.' Thorneycroft returned the photo to its envelope. A thought occurred to him.

'When did Trevor show you and Molly the picture?'

Will pondered. 'That'd be at Grasmere, two days after he came back from Istanbul,' he said. 'Ma and me were in the kitchen. He came and showed us the picture. He said, "The horse is called French Toast. He'll be at Penwold next week".'

'He trimmed the photo at that time?'

'Yes, and chucked the pieces in the bin.'

'Why did he do that, Will?'

'I don't know. He didn't say.'

'Did he say anything at all about the horse?'

'No.' Will gulped, and his eyes filled with tears. 'He just said he was glad to be home again, with us all.'

Dysart, Clay and DI Robarts completed their work by seven o'clock on Saturday evening and left at once for London, taking with them a box of documents from the Penwold records room.

The Thorneycrofts remained at Penwold for the night. After supper Thorneycroft sought a quiet talk with Liz. They strolled together round the stable yards, and he questioned her about Trevor's last visit to the Middle East. She repeated what he had already learned from Rourke, and ended by saying, 'He was away for two weeks. He enjoyed himself. He liked Salim and his family, and found the work at the hotel interesting. It was kind of a working holiday for him.'

Thorneycroft did figures in his head. 'He must have left for Istanbul early in April?'

'He left here on April 9th, and came back on April 24th.'

'And when did French Toast make his journey?'

'On April 15th. Dad and Salim had already made all the arrangements at the Dubai end, and Dad pulled strings to get him here fast. Tiger Rattigan, our head groom, went over to collect him, and travelled to Penwold with him.'

Thorneycroft produced the truncated photograph.

'This was taken in Dubai, probably by Trevor. Did he break his stay in Istanbul to go there?'

'Just for one day. He wanted to see French Toast run. He phoned me to say he'd been given a horse, and he wanted to see if it was worth bringing it back here.'

'He didn't look his gift horse in the mouth. He brought it here, fast.'

Thorneycroft found Tiger Rattigan, the head groom, in the main tack room, and questioned him about his journey with French Toast. He learned nothing new, and Rattigan insisted that the story of the horse had not been leaked by anyone attached to Penwold.

'I was with that hoss every inch of the way from Dubai to here,' he said. 'I let no one near him, save for the vet and the immigration officers. I've had dealings with them many's the time, and they don't gossip. You can bet your boots the news was leaked by one of those furriners. Do anything for cash, some of 'em.'

Shown the photograph of the Dubai race, Rattigan studied it with interest. 'The boss never showed me that,' he said, 'but I heard about that win when I collected French Toast. Won in a canter, they told me, and I believe them. I've seen what he can do. Give him the nod and he'll go into overdrive and nothing can catch him. Sad the boss isn't here to see him. Bloody sad, that is.'

The Thorneycrofts, with Will Mitchell, returned to London after lunch on Sunday. In Wimbledon they received a rapturous welcome from Gatsby, and a report from Bladen's man that no one had tried to invade the premises.

Thorneycroft left Claudia and Luke at home and drove to Grasmere with Will. The main gates to the property were locked, but the policeman on guard at the back gate let them through and travelled with them to the house.

'The DCI said you can go where you want,' he said. 'I'm to sign out anything you take away from here.'

As they walked along the passage to Trevor's study, Thorneycroft had the sense of being watched by silent ghosts. The place was full of memories of Trevor; chatting before a fireplace, hosting a formal reception, showing Steven how to flick a marble from his thumb. The memories were overlaid by the chilling reality of murder.

There was already a film of dust on Trevor's desk, and Will ran a finger through it, shaking his head. 'We must get back here,' he muttered. 'Can't let things drift. Life must go on.'

He produced a key from his pocket and unlocked the steel door at the rear of the study. 'He kept all his cameras and photos in here,' he said. 'His dark room's to the right of the safe. He liked to develop his own photos. If he was too busy, he sent them to Chiltern's in Greenwich.'

'Did they develop this one?' Thorneycroft held up the Dubai photo, and Will shook his head.

'No, he did that lot himself. He came home on the Saturday and developed the whole reel on the Sunday.'

Will selected the last of a row of cardboard boxes, and carried it through to a table in the study. Opening the box, he lifted out a folder. Its left-hand pocket contained negatives, its right, positives. Most of these were postcard size, but three had been enlarged to portrait size.

Thorneycroft picked up the topmost negative and held it to the light. 'This looks like the first in a series,' he said. 'It's the start of the Dubai race.' He examined several more. 'This one's the negative of the photo from Penwold. French Toast is running well clear of a bunch of horses. You can see their heads and necks on the left of the negative. Trevor trimmed them off the developed picture, which was an enlargement.'

The final photo was of French Toast passing the winning-post. There was no other horse in the picture. Trevor had recorded a magnificent win by his gift horse. The edges of the photo had been removed. A viewer could see the moment of victory, but not the ease with which victory had been won.

The horse might indeed prove to be a champion. Did Trevor fear that Salim Jadwat might want to reclaim his present? That didn't fit with what Thorneycroft knew of Trevor. His nature was over-trusting, not suspicious. It was more likely he'd realized that, left in Dubai, French Toast would be exploited, not schooled to become a world-beater. The sadness was that Trevor hadn't lived to lead his horse into more winners' stalls.

Thorneycroft shook himself. Trevor was gone. The task now was to nail his killer. He turned to Will.

'Can I see the camera Trevor used?'

Will produced it, a German model that could no doubt do wonderful things in the right hands. Thorneycroft replaced it in its sling bag and turned to the waiting policeman.

'I'd like to take the camera and all the material in the folder, to DCI Dysart. Will you sign them out to me?'

The goods were bagged, tagged and handed over. Thorneycroft and Will headed back to Wimbledon. To the land of the living, Thorneycroft thought. Will was right. Life had to go on.

X

ON MONDAY MORNING, Thorneycroft displayed the trophies to Dysart, and said he'd like some enlargements made. Dysart told him to consult DS Nosey Turner. Nosey pursued two interests: photography and gossip. He was probably the most inquisitive man in Britain. Everything was grist to his mill, from the mega-plots of international villains, to the private lives of his friends and colleagues.

Shown the photos of the Dubai race, he shot Thorneycroft a sidelong glance.

'Is this the gee that Trevor Cornwall owned? I read about it in *The Monitor*. Odd story, made me wonder.' He slid the photo Thorneycroft selected under a magnifier. 'Wide angle lens, the proof's been cut to exclude the edges. What's in the sling bag?'

'Negatives, positives and Trevor's camera.' Thorneycroft placed the bag on Nosey's desk, and watched him lift the camera out and turn it in his hands.

Nosey purred. 'Yerss. Very nice. Precision, economy and some special tricks, if you know how to use it. So many amateurs buy a pricey camera, point it and bang it off. Did Cornwall take these pics?'

'He did, and he developed the film. I'd like enlargements, Nosey.' Thorneycroft handed over two packs. 'These three to poster size, the rest of the set to portrait size. Can you do it?'

'Not to do them justice. I'll send them over to Concorde Street. They'll see you get 'em good and big, without losing the fine detail.' Nosey studied the negatives. 'Cornwall knew his job. Why did he trim down that photo?'

'I don't know,' Thorneycroft said.

Nosey tilted his head. 'And why did the perp mention the horse in the obit.?'

'I don't know, but it's a good question. How soon can we have the enlargements?'

'Depends on the laboratory. They're behind schedule, right now. I'll ask them to do it as fast as they can.'

And then, Thorneycroft thought, maybe that side alley will be closed, and we'll be able to rule French Toast out of the equation.

As he stepped into the corridor he saw Dysart and Clay hurrying towards him. Dysart caught him by the arm and towed him towards the door that led to the parking garage.

'There's been another hit,' he said. 'Julian Bakstein, you've heard of him. He was shot dead at his property in Poulton Lane early this morning. The prime minister's already bashing the super's ear. Bakstein was a big wheel in nuclear physics.'

Bakstein was indeed a world figure, a leading scientist at a hush-hush, lavishly-endowed research centre in the Wye valley. A few years back he'd been nominated for a Nobel Prize. His life had made headlines, and his murder would do the same.

As they climbed into Clay's car, Thorneycroft said, 'Poulton Lane's in Chelsea. Not your bailiwick. Why are you called in?'

'It should be DI Blount's case, but the super's convinced it's the same perp as killed Cornwall. He's pushing for a regional team to work both cases.'

'The fact that both victims were shot doesn't mean there was a single killer. Was it the same MO? Did the killer leave an obit.?'

Dysart spread his hands. 'There are similarities. Bakstein was shot twice in the head and once in the heart. The weapon was a pistol and the shooter knew how to use it. There was a poem pinned to Bakstein's shirt.'

Thorneycroft blinked. 'What poem?'

'*Ozymandias*,' Dysart said. 'You heard of him?'

'Um.' Thorneycroft mumbled, trying to recall schoolday knowledge. 'Shelley, isn't it?'

Dysart shook his head. 'You tell me.'

Thorneycroft quoted:

'I met a traveller from an antique land
Who said, "two vast and trunkless legs of stone
Stand in the desert".'

Dysart grunted. 'Poulton Lane's no desert. What's this Ozzy man got to do with Bakstein?'

'In the poem,' Thorneycroft said, 'the poet describes the broken statue of a colossus – a face with "wrinkled lip and sneer of cold command".' The inscription on the remains of the statue reads, "My name is Ozymandias, king of kings. Look on my works, ye mighty, and despair". Only there aren't any works to see. Just the broken statue and the empty desert. It illustrates the futility of tyranny.'

'And does that refer to Bakstein?'

'Maybe.' Thorneycroft hesitated. 'It doesn't sound much like the Cornwall obit. That was almost complimentary. This poem paints the picture of an unlovable despot.'

'Well, they both of them had their heads blown off. As you say, that doesn't mean it was the same killer. Could be a copycat. I don't know why the super's so sure we need a regional team.'

'Maybe he knows something we don't,' Thorneycroft said.

Dysart squinted at him. 'Secret agendas? If there's something going down, I wish to hell they'd tell me.'

He spent the rest of the journey making and answering phonecalls, none of which afforded him visible satisfaction. Reaching Poulton Lane, they found it lined with police vehicles. They were waved through an electronic gateway into a flagged drive, and Clay parked behind a scene-of-crime van.

The house facing them was modern, blue-tiled with a lot of picture windows. Trees lined the hedges on all sides, so it was impossible to see the neighbouring buildings. Dysart led the way along a path to their left, to a garden where a group of men were gathered on a stretch of lawn. One of them advanced towards Dysart.

'DI Blount,' Dysart murmured. 'Due to retire in a month's time. I doubt he wants the case.'

Reaching them, Blount shook hands with Dysart and exchanged nods with Clay and Thorneycroft. He drew Dysart aside and they fell into close conversation. Clay and Thorneycroft headed for the group on the lawn.

The body of Julius Bakstein lay on its back, one arm outflung, the other bent across the belly. A sheet of paper was pinned to the shirt, above the bloody circle over the heart. On the far side of the body, a man in a white jumpsuit was sliding a sample of brain matter into a plastic container. Glancing up, he saw Thorneycroft and raised a hand in greeting.

'Hullo, John. You on this case?'

'If it's linked to the Cornwall murder, I am.'

'Huh! Be like old times, eh?'

Dr Prout ruled the forensic roost at the police laboratories in Concorde Street. His presence at the primary examination of this corpse suggested that it was already the subject of a priority investigation.

Prout seemed to read Thorneycroft's thoughts. 'Bakstein was a national asset,' he said. 'Someone came in and shot him in the head and heart. Shot his dog, too.' He gestured towards the body of a brindled bull terrier that lay a few paces away. 'The poor brute must have spotted the killer, and got a bullet in the brain. The killer's an excellent shot. Both bullets fired at Bakstein struck vital areas. He was dead before he hit the ground.'

'Did any of the neighbours report hearing shots fired?'

'Blount says not. Mind you, people aren't keen on getting out of a warm bed at six a.m.'

'Was that the time of death?'

'It fits with my estimate. Seems that Bakstein was in the habit of bringing the dog out at six, come rain come shine. The autopsy will give us something more precise.'

Thorneycroft remembered Trevor's killer, an experienced shot, perhaps a professional hit man.

'He may have used a silencer,' he suggested.

'Very probably. He tidied up nicely, didn't leave any cartridge cases.'

Prout got to his feet and signalled to the waiting murder team to get on with their work. A photographer moved in to take pictures of the area and, after him, a woman in overalls transferred the contents of the dead man's pockets to plastic containers, labelling each with meticulous care. It was a mundane collection of articles: a clean handkerchief, house and car keys, a small wallet holding various credit cards. No diary or mobile phone.

The woman stretched a hand to the paper pinned to Bakstein's bloodstained shirt, and Thorneycroft said quickly, 'Wait, please. I'd like to see that.'

Prout nodded consent, and Thorneycroft stooped to scan the sheet of paper. It was not typescript, but a printed sheet torn from a small book, perhaps a paperback. Thorneycroft straightened to face Prout.

'You'll try to establish where it came from?'

Prout smiled wryly. 'Of course, but the poem's a classic; it appears in thousands of editions, from school primers to gilt-edged anthologies.' He stripped off the thin rubber gloves he wore and dropped them into a disposal bag. Thorneycroft offered one more question.

'Is Liam Connor at Concorde Street?'

'No. He's in Sweden, helping to break a child pornography ring.' Picking up his pathologist's bag, Prout spoke almost under his breath. 'We'll keep you informed, John.' He walked away, Thorneycroft sighed. He felt it was becoming clear that the need-to-know level of this case was set very high indeed.

Clay, who had been walking round the perimeter of the garden, came to join Thorneycroft.

'The lads say the perp stood over there.' He pointed to the shrubbery that bordered the lane. Midway along it was a gazebo, almost shrouded in banks of wisteria and jasmine. It lay within the police tapes that marked the scene of the crime.

Thorneycroft would have liked to get a closer look at the place, but he knew that would be frowned upon. Evidence could be destroyed by the trampling of too many feet.

'We'd better get back to the boss,' he said.

As they trod across the grass, they passed the body of the dog. There was a handsome red leather collar round its neck, and the name tag attached to it looked like solid gold. The dog, like its master, had died instantly. A dead shot, this murderer, though the messages he'd left on his victims differed greatly. Trevor had received a respectful obituary; Bakstein a contemptuous poem. Both were dead, but for different reasons.

'Did the dog bark?' Thorneycroft asked, and Clay frowned. 'Nobody heard barking, but an attack dog doesn't always give warning. Sometimes he just comes at you.'

They found Dysart standing alone, Blount having joined the team on the lawn. Dysart was scanning the trees and rooftops that surrounded them.

'Bakstein was a loner,' he said. 'According to Blount, the neighbours hardly knew him. He spent most of his time at Clunbury Research Centre; only came to London when he retired at the end of last year. He was unfriendly, refused to join the neighbourhood watch committee. He didn't employ resident staff, just called in cleaners, caterers, gardeners whenever he needed. He hated old houses, called them fleapits. He tore down his granddad's house on this site, and built this one, used it for the occasional weekend or holiday break.'

'Well-heeled, by the sound of it,' Thorneycroft said, and Dysart smiled sourly. 'Loaded. Millions from his father who was a merchant banker, but refused to give a farthing to our widows' and orphans' fund. The group he gave cash to was The Sons of England. Wouldn't support any Jewish charity, although he was a Jew by birth. He wasn't much liked hereabouts.'

'Ozymandias,' Thorneycroft murmured. 'Was there forced entry to the property?'

'Seems not. The car gate was open when Blount's team arrived, and there's no sign of forced entry to the house. I'd say the perp just walked in while it was still dark, and took up his position over there in that summer house. There are signs that someone stood there, and smoothed over the soil in the flowerbed, after he'd left. He must have waited until Bakstein came out at six o'clock, with the dog, and shot them both.'

'Meaning he knew Bakstein's habitual behaviour. Though if it's a gossippy neighbourhood, it wouldn't be hard for an observer to learn at what times Bakstein was vulnerable.'

'The dog didn't bark. Perhaps it recognized the killer.'

'That's what I think. I think the perp knew Bakstein. I think he's a trained marksman who used a pro's pistol fitted with a silencer. He also has access to a sniper's rifle, accelerator bullets, a racing motorbike and plenty of cash to buy whatever he wants.'

'I agree,' Thorneycroft said. 'He knew Bakstein and hated him. He killed the dog not because it attacked him, but because it recognized him. Who found the body?'

'A lady who lives across the square. She walks her toy pom early every morning. She came up the lane and saw the gate was open, which surprised her. She expected to see the bull terrier. It knew her, she said, and always came to the gate when she passed because she carried dog treats in her pocket. When it didn't appear, she stepped into the driveway, and saw Bakstein and the dog on the lawn, both shot. She ran back into the lane and called the nick on her mobile.'

'Did she see anyone on the property?'

'No. She told Blount the property seemed deserted. She gave the time she was at the gate as ten minutes past seven. I'd say the killer was long gone by then.'

'Were there any other reports from witnesses?'

'Just one. A refuse removal van stopped near the mouth of the lane soon after six. One of the team saw a jogger leave the lane. He was wearing a black tracksuit with the hood up. His face was hidden, but the witness said he had a full beard, black and grey coloured. You can buy false beards at a novelty shop … or grow the real thing.'

Clay spoke. 'The lady with the pom knew the dog, but did she know Bakstein?'

'Seems not. She says he avoided speaking to people. A curmudgeon, she called him, with a rude manner.'

Thorneycroft voiced the question on all their minds. 'Are we on the case?'

'We will be, by noon,' Dysart said grimly. 'Blount doesn't want it and I can see why. The way things look, we'll have the PM, Intelligence, and all the nuclear bigshots breathing down our necks.'

As he spoke, the mobile phone in his pocket jangled. He listened without moving, eyes fixed on Thorneycroft. Cutting the connection, he said:

'We're on the case. I'm to go back to Greenwich at once, to talk to the super about setting up the joint investigation unit. Kevin Roberts will probably be management officer. I'll be in command and you're appointed as consultant, John. Prout will do the autopsy, and Blount and his team will carry on with the search-and-recovery work here ... fingerprinting, records, accounts, the usual routine. The super's briefing Blount.' Dysart glanced towards the lane. 'The media will be swarming any minute. Make sure that no press or spin-doctors set foot on the property – it's all scene-of-crime area. Tell them a statement will be made shortly.'

'If Blount's doing the work here,' Thorneycroft said, 'there won't be much for Clay and me to do.'

Dysart smiled. 'That won't last, I promise. Meanwhile, you're to observe, feel the vibes, think out of the box, look for anything that may shed light on why Bakstein was killed. There was no mobile or diary on his body. If those aren't found in the house, it suggests that the perp removed them, to destroy any record of communication between himself and Bakstein.'

'You think he came by appointment, sir?' Clay asked.

'May have done. Let's say the dog didn't bark because it knew the killer. Bakstein owned the property, but until he retired last year, he hardly ever stayed here. If the dog recognized and tolerated the killer, it may well have been because he met the person frequently in some other place.'

'Someone he worked with?' Clay suggested.

'Exactly. We'll be going to Clunbury to question the people employed there.'

'Did Bakstein have a personal computer?' Thorneycroft said.

'There's one in the house, but it must be accessed by experts who know something about nuclear physics, as well as computer programmes. You and Clay must concentrate on Bakstein as a person. What was his lifestyle? What made him a target for this perp? Why did the perp liken him to a power-crazy tyrant?'

A uniformed driver appeared on the driveway and signalled to Dysart that the car was ready for him. He walked away towards the lane, and Thorneycroft and Clay entered the house.

XI

DI BLOUNT MET them in the hallway. He indicated the security keyboard set in the wall next to the front door. 'The alarm wasn't activated,' he said, 'and when we got here, this door was closed but not locked. Bakstein wasn't expecting an attack. All the house keys were on a ring beside his bed.'

'And no signs of breaking and entering?' Thorneycroft said.

'Nary a one. Doors, windows, roof tiles, untouched. There's a beautiful Jag in the garage, clean as a whistle. No one except Bakstein himself's laid a finger on it. Robbery doesn't seem to be the motive. The perp came, he killed and he left.'

Which, reflected Thorneycroft, seemed to be the modus operandi of this killer.

Blount's team was hard at work in the living room of the house. Two men were testing every available surface for fingerprints. A third man in a jumpsuit was operating a miniature vacuum cleaner on a section of the tiled floor, and Blount's sergeant was going through the drawers and pigeonholes of a desk in a corner of the room. Blount went across to speak to him. Thorneycroft and Clay, mindful of Dysart's orders, stayed in the background and observed their surroundings.

The room was air-conditioned, the Italian tiles underfoot warm to the touch, as if heating beneath them had only recently been switched off. Bakstein, thought Thorneycroft, hadn't expected much of the English summer.

The furnishings were splendid, the rugs scattered about hand-woven, the chairs and sofas upholstered in natural leather and piled with brilliantly-coloured cushions. The pictures were all by

British artists: Constable, Flint, Seago. If they were originals they were worth tidy sum. A china-cabinet displayed the art of Chelsea, Spode and Royal Albert and the opened bottle of whiskey on the small bar-counter was a ten-year-old Glenfiddich.

There was nothing in the room to suggest that Bakstein's fame and evident fortune derived from his work as a nuclear physicist. No photographs, no framed citations graced the walls. There was no bookcase, and no music centre, but a vast flatscreen television dominated the west wall, and facing it in splendid isolation stood a Relaxa chair, with, beside it, a dogbasket lined with red wool blankets.

The man, who avoided human company, had shared his solitude with his dog.

Thorneycroft's circuit brought him to the desk, and Blount pointed to the meagre pile of documents at the sergeant's elbow.

'There's not much of a paper trail,' he said. 'There's a few telephone accounts, calls made online from his bedside phone. I'd say he used his PC to pay bills and fix appointments, and he may have used a mobile for most of his calls. I've faxed the accounts to DCI Dysart – he wanted to check them at once.'

'Did you find a mobile phone or a diary in the house?' Thorneycroft asked.

'No. Maybe the perp took them from Bakstein's body. Finlay's coming over from Concorde Street to access the computer. Checking its contents could be a long job.' Blount hesitated. 'What d'you make of this house?'

'Buy British,' Thorneycroft answered, and Blount nodded. 'That's right. The furniture, the fittings, the food in the kitchen, it's all British. Where he couldn't get a local product, like with spices, he bought from British firms. There's a wine rack full of stuff from the Dominions, nothing French or German or Italian. That looks obsessive to me. I always thought of Julian Bakstein as a nuclear physicist, but here he looks ... well, kind of different. I'd like you to see his bedroom, see what you make of it.'

He led the way along the broad corridor that served the back of the building. The first room they entered was a spare bedroom, here the furniture was Quaker-plain: a bed covered with a patch-work quilt, a wardrobe and table of natural oak and a brown fitted carpet. The connecting bathroom displayed no towels on the rails, no soap or tissues on the handbasin. Bakstein had not planned to entertain guests.

The master bedroom at the end of the passage was very different. Immense and full of light, it overlooked a patio and a swimming pool. The bathroom boasted a circular sauna, and two marble-topped cabinets crammed with expensive aftershaves, oils and soaps. The bathsheets on the rail smelled faintly of sandal-wood.

Stooping, Clay wrinkled his nose. 'Liked to live soft, didn't he?'

Thorneycroft wasn't listening. He was wondering if the finger-print powder on the gleaming surfaces spoke only of Bakstein's presence, or if some other person had shared the luxury. The bed was a fourposter, elaborately carved and gilded, but only one set of the silken pillows had been slept on. At the bedside was a dog-basket with a wool blanket.

The bookcase next to the bed held nothing but scientific tomes in English, French and German. One book lay on the folded-back duvet and Thorneycroft studied its title: *The Omega Essays 2009*. Not light reading. That yearly collection included writings from the eggiest of eggheads, speaking a language unknown to ordinary mortals.

Julian Bakstein was one of a select number. He might have lacked social skills, but he certainly hadn't lacked knowledge. There must have been a wealth of information hidden away in his brain before it was destroyed by the killer's bullet. Which gave Thorneycroft pause.

People were murdered for divers reasons ... for what they owned, what they did, what they were or what they knew. Both Cornwall and Bakstein had died of a bullet to the head. Had the killer felt a subconscious desire to wipe out what his victims knew?

Blount interrupted his thoughts, beckoning him towards the rank of cupboards that stretched from floor to roof along the right-hand wall. As Thorneycroft and Clay approached, he flung wide the double doors furthest away. Behind them was a deep and wide recess, in which stood a computer, a colour printer and a tall column of drawers.

Blount jabbed a finger at the drawers. 'Files,' he said. 'I've not touched them, that's Finlay's job. What I want to show you is these.'

He opened the next pair of doors, exposing clothes. Thorneycroft stared at them in silence. Nearest him was a selection of formal western gear. A rack of suits, Armani by the look of them, casual trousers, shirts, two leather jackets and shelves of T-shirts and cardigans. Everything looked immaculate; enviable stuff, part of Bakstein's public image.

More interesting were the garments that crowded a long rail; full-length caftans of silk or cashmere wool, some of them heavily embroidered in silver or gold; wide-wristed jackets buttoned to the throat; several Japanese kimonos, their broad sashes ending in toggles of carved ivory or jade.

'Not British,' Thorneycroft murmured, and Blount nodded agreement.

'Looks to me like women's stuff,' he said. 'Could be he was a cross-dresser. Men have been killed for that.'

Thorneycroft shook his head. 'The styles are eastern, but they could have been made in Britain, to comply with Bakstein's dislike of foreign goods. Can you see where he bought them?'

Blount examined the necklines of the garments. 'The plain stuff came from Harrods',' he said, 'and the pretty stuff came from somewhere called Roxanne's, which I've never heard of.'

'I know where it is,' Clay said. 'It's in Sloane Street, there's always just the one outfit in the window, and no price tag. The moguls shop there, and I'd say it costs them.'

Clay's knowledge of the streets of London was extensive, and Blount shrugged.

'Well, you'll want to check it out, but we'll have to rely on his computer to tell us more about him. We have to know if there are any relatives, who are his lawyers, where his heirs are.'

'The Research Centre at Clunbury will be able to give us that information,' Thorneycroft said. He continued to contemplate the contents of the cupboard. In Clunbury Bakstein was known as the nuclear physicist, but here, it seemed, he'd lived like a solitary sultan. He was a man of two personalities, but which of the two was Ozymandias? In which of these two identities lay the motive for his murder?

They completed their tour of the house. In a state-of-the art kitchen they inspected a deep-freeze stacked with delicacies. They had been selected for healthiness as well as pleasure. Bakstein the sybarite had kept a wary eye on his cholesterol levels.

Returning to the living room, Thorneycroft spoke to Blount. 'I feel that Clay and I aren't needed here. You have everything well in hand. I'd like to visit Roxanne's and talk to the owner. Dress designers get to know a lot about their customers. If it's okay with you, I'll clear it with Dysart.'

He put through a call to Greenwich. Dysart queried the change of plan, and Thorneycroft said, 'Bakstein's an enigma. I suppose he had to be secretive in his job, but he seems to have continued that way in retirement. There are no photographs in this house, no trace of connections with colleagues, family or friends. His tailor may throw a bit of light on him.'

'Guessing, aren't you?'

'You advised me to think outside of the box.'

'All right.' Dysart was rustling papers. 'Blount sent me Bakstein's online telephone accounts. One he made two days ago was to Roxanne's. Find out what it was about if you can, but don't muddy the waters.'

'We'll tread carefully.'

'Ask Blount to give you authorization, and get back here as soon as possible. There's a flood of info coming through about Bakstein, from all over the world. We have to set up ways to make the most of it.'

XII

ROXANNE'S BLACK GLASS door bore a CLOSED sign, but Clay kept a finger on the doorbell.

'Someone's in there, watching us,' he said.

As he spoke, the door was inched open and a face peered round it, a spiky face, pointed nose and chin framed by black hair cut short and waxed into thorns. The voice that spoke matched the hair.

'We're closed. Can't you read?'

'Police, ma'am,' Clay said. He held up his identity token. 'We need to ask you a few questions.'

'What about?'

'Mr Julian Bakstein. You'll have heard ...'

'Yes, I've heard, he was murdered this morning and I don't know a thing about it.'

Thorneycroft intervened. 'If we may come inside for a short while? It can't help your business to have the cops standing on your doorstep.'

Sharp teeth chewed the question and decided not to spit it out. The door swung wide and Thorneycroft and Clay stepped through it. Roxanne's certainly looked closed. No fashionwear was in sight, and the mirrored doors of all the cupboards were shut.

Thorneycroft said mildly, 'I'm Dr Thorneycroft and this is Detective Sergeant Clay. Are you the owner of these premises?'

Black eyes glinted behind gold-rimmed spectacles. 'No I am not. I'm the treasurer, stroke secretary, stroke dogsbody.'

'And your name is?'

'Maisie Banning. Why are you here?'

'Clay and I are helping with the investigation into the death of Dr Bakstein. He was one of your customers, I understand.'

'Yes, a good one. Paid on the nail, and sent us business. We saw the news on the lunch-time telly.'

'We?'

'Me and Mrs Hopewell. She owns the shop and designs the eastern lines. Mr Bakstein went for that in a big way.'

'Is Mrs Hopewell here?'

'No, she's not and she sent all the girls home.'

'But not you?'

'I chose to stay. I have work to do.'

'Was Mrs Hopewell very upset by the news?'

There was some lipchewing and the sharp eyes measured Thorneycroft.

'She took it badly. Very badly. Shook all over, said she couldn't bear it and she was going home.'

'Where is that?'

'She has a cottage near Colchester. I reminded her we have a show at The Belgrave Hotel a week from now, and she said, "Bugger that, you cancel it!" And off she went.'

It was Thorneycroft's turn to stare. A mannequin parade at The Belgrave must be the cherry on the top for any fashion designer. To cancel it would require nerves of steel, or perhaps a total nervous collapse.

He tested the water. 'A murder is a very distressing thing, particularly if the victim is someone one knows.'

Maisie shrugged, and Thorneycroft read her expression. Fury was there, and cold determination, but no compassion.

'Did you phone The Belgrave?'

'Yes, I did, and I told the manager Mrs Hopewell was taken ill, and I'll be handling the show instead of her. He wasn't too pleased, but he agreed in the end.'

'Can you deliver on the promise? Will the show take place?'

'Yes, it will. Hazel and Clem and the girls and me will see it does.'

'Can you give me Mrs Hopewell's home address and telephone?'

Maisie reached into a pocket and produced a card. 'We're all on that. She's at the top.'

'Does she not have a London address?'

'There's a flat upstairs, but it's just for the odd nights she stays in London. She does a lot of her designs at the cottage, keeps in touch by computer. When she's ready to cut, or wants to see to the sewing and beadwork, she spends more time in London, but it's not her home.'

'Does she have family in London?'

'She doesn't have family anywhere. She was married, back in the dark ages, but he died. Not that she cared much. She only married him to get citizenship. She was a seamstress then a cutter, then she set up this shop. That was fifteen years ago.'

Thorneycroft tilted his head. 'Where did she learn to make caftans and kimonos? Not in England, surely?'

'Learned it at her mama's knee, I'd say, on the road to Mandalay.'

'Where was she born?'

'She never would say. Gave us a different answer every time.'

'Do you have a photograph of her, by any chance?'

'No. She didn't like pictures of herself. Can't say I blame her. She has a pudding face with slitty eyes, and her skin's kind of dark and waxy.'

The telephone rang sharply, and Maisie turned to answer it. She spoke for some minutes, evidently about the vaunted mannequin parade. Ending the conversation, she squinted up at Thorneycroft.

'That's all I have time for, gentlemen.'

Thorneycroft ignored the brushoff.

'One more point, Ms Banning. Did Dr Bakstein phone Mrs Hopewell, two days ago?'

Maisie scowled. 'Yes, he did. He wanted to have a caftan cleaned, and asked for the name of a good dry-cleaner. She told him to go to Hilliers, in Knightsbridge. They only spoke for a couple of minutes.'

'Did Mrs Hopewell seem disturbed by the call?'

'She was annoyed, being asked a silly question like that.'

'Was she fond of Dr Bakstein?'

'God no. All she's fond of is hard cash. She makes fancy clothes and sells them to the highest bidder.'

It was clear that they'd get nothing more from Maisie. Thorneycroft thanked her for her cooperation and wished her good luck with The Belgrave show. She answered with a sardonic twist of the mouth. As Thorneycroft and Clay stepped into the street, she was already turning over the fashion sketches on her desk.

'She's a hard case,' Clay said. 'D'you think she was telling the truth?'

'Why wouldn't she?' Thorneycroft asked. 'She's the sort of woman who says what she thinks or keeps quiet.'

'She doesn't like Mrs Hopewell.'

'No. That's not a criminal offence, but we'll need to take a close look at Roxanne and Company.'

They drove to Hilliers in Knightsbridge and spoke to the manager. Like Maisie, he knew of Bakstein's murder, but his reaction was more urbane and less informative. He said Dr Bakstein had not brought any article for cleaning. His death was a great loss to the nation. It was to be hoped that the police would make an early arrest of the killer.

Thorneycroft put through a call to Dysart. 'We're heading back now,' he said, 'and we've plenty to tell you. In the meantime will you put through a request to the Colchester division to check if Mrs Rosa Hopewell is back in her cottage? By what her secretary Maisie Banning told us, Mrs Hopewell's running scared. I think we need to get to her before she does a bolt.'

He gave Dysart Mrs Hopewell's address and telephone number, and settled back in the passenger seat to make a mental list of the questions he'd like to ask the lady … if they found her.

XIII

ARRIVING AT GREENWICH station, they went straight to Dysart's office. They found him handing piles of documents to a policewoman.

'Bakstein's life and times,' he said as the woman departed. 'It's coming from international authorities, the press, the Internet and God knows who else. Phoebe will sort it and see it's indexed and analyzed. Sit down, I want to hear how you got on at Poulton Lane.'

Thorneycroft described their inspection of Bakstein's house, and Dysart listened, frowning.

'Sounds as if he lived a double life,' he said.

Thorneycroft answered slowly. 'Not precisely. I'd say that on retirement he chose to indulge his taste for comfort and British excellence. He didn't do any harm by dressing like an eastern potentate.'

'If he was homosexual, that could have got him killed by some fanatic.'

'There's no proof he was gay. It's more likely he wasn't interested in sex. The people at Clunbury will be able to enlighten us on that point. But homosexuality certainly didn't get Trevor Cornwall murdered. What strikes me about this case is the vast difference between the two victims.'

'How d'you mean?'

'A typical serial killer chooses a certain category of victim. He kills prostitutes, or drifters, or clergymen, or children. His choice of victim is rooted in a fixed aberration in his mind, and he doesn't alter that choice. I can find no way to place Bakstein and Cornwall in a single category.

'Trevor was an extrovert. He liked people and they liked him. He had many personal relationships, with family, friends and colleagues. He was involved in massive outreach business deals, in religious observance, in social concerns and celebrations. The obituary the killer wrote for Trevor virtually acknowledged that this was a good man. It's as if the killer felt his death was a necessity, but took no pleasure in it.

'With Bakstein, the situation was different. He was introverted, a loner. I think the killer knew him, and hated him. Hence the label left on Bakstein's body: *Ozymandias*, a tyrant, devoid of human virtue.

'I'm also struck by the victims' style of residence. Trevor's house was a home. It was furnished and maintained to make people feel welcome and comfortable. He enjoyed entertaining and often invited people to stay.

'Bakstein's house is not welcoming, and the comfort was designed for one man and his dog.'

Dysart grimaced. 'What you say may be true, John, but it doesn't provide the facts on which we can base a prosecution.'

'We must find the facts, to back the supposition,' Thorneycroft insisted. 'The key to this case is finding the reason for the murder of two such different men. Somewhere, somehow, they had something in common, something that made them a threat to the killer. Until we know what that was, we won't be able to make an arrest.'

'All they had in common, so far as I can see, was a distant connection with the Middle East. Cornwall married a Turkish girl and had Turkish relations by marriage. One of them gave him a racehorse. Bakstein liked to wear Eastern clothes. I can't build a case on that.'

Thorneycroft said flatly, 'Cornwall and Bakstein were killed because of something they had in common. We can approach this case from east or west, whichever you prefer. The solution lies at longitude nought, where Cornwall and Bakstein meet.'

The telephone at Dysart's elbow buzzed and he took the call, listened in silence to a rumbling voice, thanked the caller and replaced the receiver.

'Colchester', he said. 'They sent someone over to Mrs Hopewell's place, but it's deserted. The local plod will keep an eye on the property and Colchester will put out feelers in case she's holed up somewhere in the neighbourhood.'

'Running scared,' Clay said, and Dysart nodded. 'Could be. Stay on it, Mick, see if you can find any other associates who might be giving her shelter.'

As Clay left the office, Dysart said, 'He's the best man at looking for needles in haystacks. If she's holed up somewhere, I'd like to know why. She wouldn't jettison a show at The Belgrave without good reason.'

He reached for a sheet of paper on his desk. 'The list of calls made on Bakstein's latest telephone account,' he said. 'There weren't many over the past month, but the call to Roxanne's is verified. It was made two days ago, and lasted a minute and a half. By what you tell me, Bakstein asked Mrs Hopewell for the name of a good dry-cleaner, she gave him Hillier's name, but they say he never showed there.

'He made another call the same day, to our Foreign Office. He asked to speak to Mr Jeremy Cousins. He was in the habit of phoning Cousins when he wanted information about nuclear projects in foreign countries.

'He was told that Cousins is on vacation in America. Bakstein refused to speak to anyone else; said he'd wait until Cousins is back from leave, which should be in three days' time.'

Dysart dropped the paper into a drawer of his desk. 'The FO have no idea why Bakstein wanted to speak to Cousins. Every lead we get runs into the sand. Tomorrow we'll go down to Clunbury and see what the boffins have to tell us.'

'I'd like to look at the information that's come in on Bakstein,' Thorneycroft said.

'Feel free. Speak to Phoebe.'

Thorneycroft collected a batch of material from Phoebe and a pie from the canteen, and spent the next four hours learning about Julian Bakstein. His standing as a scientist was described by peers and proletariat as being of national and international importance. His degrees, citations and awards were impressive. Thorneycroft decided that Bakstein's immense achievements would have to be assessed by people who understood nuclear physics. He selected the material that referred not to his work but to his personal life.

A point that quickly became clear was that Bakstein had been extremely rich. He had inherited a fortune from his banker father, and added fat amounts from his own earnings and investments. It seemed he had never married, had no living relatives, and no children.

His character was a strange mix of the conservative and the eccentric. On the one hand he was a model citizen, scrupulously honest in financial and scientific matters and intensely patriotic ... to the point, some said, of fanaticism. He made handsome donations to causes he favoured; the arts, Olympic athletic teams, and the armed forces of Great Britain.

On the other hand, he refused to give a cent to any applicant who fell outside of his set preferences. He had no religious faith. The grandson of a Hungarian Jew, he had, at the age of twenty, renounced all ethnic and religious loyalties, stating that religion was a dummy for babies to suck. One commentator had written of him, 'Julian Bakstein thinks he's God, and resents any prior claim to that role.'

Given the name Jacob by his parents, he had changed it by deed poll to Julian. No doubt that had earned him criticism in some quarters, but it could hardly provide a motive for his murder some forty years later.

Nor, in Thorneycroft's view, should it have earned him the title of Ozymandias.

As Thorneycroft was about to leave for home, Dysart waylaid him. 'Clunbury's fixed for tomorrow,' he said. 'We'll talk to Bakstein's workmates, see if we can smell out any enemies among them. The super's pinning his hopes on them.'

He hesitated, rubbing a hand over the back of his neck. 'For your ears only, I asked the super why top brass is being so cagey.

He didn't give me a straight answer, which means he knows something we don't.'

'Politics?' Thorneycroft murmured.

'Sure, but whose?'

Thorneycroft knew what Dysart meant. Pressures on police work came from many quarters, from national and international governments, from religious and social groups and of course from criminal organizations.

Dysart grinned. 'Don't worry, the super's in our corner, I can tell by the look in his eye. He'll give troublemakers the finger when the time's right. He's arranged for a chopper to take us to Clunbury. We'll pick you up at eight tomorrow, take to the air at 8.30.'

Thorneycroft fixed supper for himself and Gatsby, then put through a call to Claudia. She spoke about the small events of the day.

'Luke claimed he'd found a cow's egg in one of the mangers. Stevie explained that cows don't lay eggs, and it must have been a hen. Luke was inclined to argue until I said he could have the egg for his supper. He loves the life here, but he asked me when you were coming to see us.'

'I wish I could,' Thorneycroft said. 'We're going to Clunbury tomorrow, to Bakstein's research centre.'

'We've been following the case on the news. It upset Liz terribly to hear of a second murder, but at least it's convinced her that she must stay inside the security limits. John, what struck me is that neither Trevor nor Dr Bakstein seemed to expect an attack. Is that common? An unknown enemy?'

'An unsuspected enemy, rather. You're right, though, that is one resemblance between the two murders.'

Thorneycroft spoke briefly to Liz, asking her if she knew of any link between her father and Bakstein.

'No, none,' she said. 'I've been thinking about that, and I'm sure Dad never spoke of him. It's not likely their paths ever crossed. Dad wasn't into nuclear physics.'

'And Bakstein wasn't a social mixer.'

The call ended with repeated assurances from Liz and Claudia that they were taking good care of themselves and the children, and a reminder from Luke that it was Gatsby's night for a chewy treat. Thorneycroft found the packet of dried horn and allowed Gatsby to worry at it on the kitchen tiles. Like Bakstein, he thought, I'm dependent on the company of my dog.

XIV

AS THEY WAITED at the airport for the helicopter that was to take them to Clunbury, Dysart briefed Thorneycroft and Clay on the rules that would govern their interviews with Julian Bakstein's workmates.

'Bakstein lived within the security net provided for nuclear scientists,' he said. 'According to the super, the powers that be would prefer the investigation into his death to be led by the people who control that net; but they've been persuaded that as Trevor Cornwall was most likely murdered by the same person, and he had no connection with nuclear physics, the investigation must remain in our hands.

'That still raises difficulties. We can't ask questions about their nuclear research programmes. We can present written questions in that regard and if they're considered to be pertinent to our case, we will get answers. We'll have to do an egg dance around the work Bakstein completed before he retired.

'What we can do, and what I think is important, is establish what were Bakstein's relations with his co-workers.

'A lot of people work at Clunbury, ranging from senior scientists through juniors, to administrators, technicians, secretaries, maintenance staff and cleaners. We'll need the local police to assist in questioning them.'

Clay said moodily, 'We'll have security spooks breathing down our necks all the time.'

Dysart half smiled. 'The super thinks that at the moment they're holding their breath. We can do some heavy breathing ourselves if we have to. Right now, we gang warily.'

Once the chopper was in the air, Dysart and Clay fell to making a list of points to be cleared in the interviews. Left to himself, Thorneycroft became mired in personal worries. Were Claudia and Luke safer at Penwold than at Wimbledon? It was possible that living close to Liz put them in danger. Was he likely to be of use, in an inquiry beset by blockages caused by higher authorities? Most urgent problem of all, would the killer strike again, and if so, where, when, how and at whom?

Finding no answers, he pushed these concerns aside, and set himself to enjoy the flight through a cloudless sky. The chopper was low enough for him to distinguish pasture, crop and fallow land. He found a map in the pocket of his seat, and identified the fringes of towns and cities, the shining threads of the Cherwell, Avon and Severn rivers. Soon he saw the mountains of the Welsh border, and to the north, the rocky ridges of The Long Mynd and Wenlock Edge. The chopper veered west at the fork of two rivers, and followed a railway line to a flat plain, in which was cradled the Clunbury Research Centre.

It covered a lot of ground. The landing field was large, served by excellent roads and a railway siding. As the chopper circled down, Thorneycroft saw that the rail tracks continued past playing fields, cottages and a three-winged hostel, ending at a bank of sheds.

Thorneycroft guessed that the real heart of the research centre lay beyond a ridge of land, away from prying eyes. Fools who rushed in to the premises would get no further than the bland front facade.

The helicopter pad was next to a building that the pilot said was the visitors' reception. As they stepped onto the tarmac, three men advanced from the door of the block to meet them. The man leading them Thorneycroft recognized as Professor Langton Howard, the most senior of the Centre's scientists. He was a short, balding man with the spare build of a marathon runner, and an air of rigidly-controlled impatience. He introduced the tall young man at his side as Dr Mark Bellows.

'Our publicity and communications officer,' Howard said. 'He was the first to hear the tragic news of Dr Bakstein's death. He will be able to give you useful information about Bakstein, his CV and so on.'

Bellows nodded, unsmiling. The set of his rather fleshy features, and the rapid movements of his dark eyes, suggested that he was not in the best of tempers. He seemed to be consciously avoiding Howard's eye. Not happy, Thorneycroft decided, and wondered why.

The third man in the welcoming party, a uniformed guard armed with a rifle, was not introduced and did not follow the group into the building.

Professor Howard conducted them to a pleasant sitting room, and offered coffee and sandwiches, which Dysart refused. 'Your time is valuable, sir,' he said. 'We won't waste it.'

Howard nodded his thanks, and launched at once into what was clearly a prepared speech. He expressed Clunbury's shock and concern at Bakstein's death, and assured Dysart of his desire to do all he could to secure the arrest and punishment of the killer. He then went on to explain which questions he could and could not answer.

His tone was brusque and not a little patronizing. Thorneycroft found himself wondering if there was a bugging device in the bowl of silk flowers at his elbow, and if the large mirror in the left-hand wall was perhaps one-way glass. He saw that Dysart shared his unease.

When Howard reached the end of his address, Dysart said,

'I understand, sir, that a prime concern for you must be the security of this centre, its personnel and its programmes. I share that concern, but I have an investigation to conduct. I have to identify the person who killed Dr Bakstein. My first question to you is, do you think that Dr Bakstein's work as a nuclear scientist motivated his murder?'

'No.' Howard was vehement. 'No, I do not.'

'Can you be sure, sir? His role as a world leader in nuclear physics may have attracted the animosity of political fanatics, who'd want him out of the way.'

Howard waved a dismissive hand. 'Clunbury is not tasked with producing nuclear arms. We work to create nuclear stations that provide energy; we work to make such stations safe for the people who work in them and for the neighbourhoods they occupy. We aim to build cities, factories, ships with nuclear power, and we have a sector that helps to deal with nuclear accidents like Chernobyl. We work for peaceful ends. Bakstein was in the forefront of that peaceable research. After his retirement from Clunbury, he continued to advise our own and other governments on how to build, maintain, staff and administer nuclear facilities.

'I understand that he was also vehemently opposed to people who *do* manufacture nuclear arms. Didn't that make him political enemies?'

Howard frowned. 'No doubt there were people who hated him on that account, but I must point out that those same people resent just as fiercely all of us who strive for an end to arms proliferation. Mark here, and I, and all our colleagues at Clunbury are as much at risk from the arms pirates as was Julian Bakstein. In fact the politicians who campaign actively to limit the nuclear capabilities of places like North Korea and Iran, are far more likely to become targets of assassins than the likes of us, who are simply involved in developing nuclear power for peaceful purposes.'

'Can you think of any person, or organization that might have wanted Dr Bakstein dead?'

Howard hesitated, eyes closed, as if he were scanning some inner record. At last he said, 'No. In all conscience I cannot point to any person or organization that could be guilty of his murder. He was of such value to the world. I simply cannot get my mind to accept that he's been murdered. We're very well protected, you know. We have all the electronic devices, we have armed guards, we're informed at once if threats are made against Clunbury, or anyone who works here.'

'Dr Bakstein had retired from Clunbury. He was not employed here. Was he given the same degree of protection in retirement as he was given during employment?'

'He remained a very important member of the profession, and of society. He was entitled to claim full protection.'

'That doesn't answer my question, sir. Was he afforded full protection in his retirement?'

Howard was silent, and Dysart persisted. 'When we arrived at Dr Bakstein's property, yesterday morning, there was no sign of the protection you've described. There was no guard on the property. The front gate was not secured in anyway. The burglar alarm in the house had not been switched on and the front and back doors were unlocked. The killer was able to stroll in and conceal himself in the shrubbery. When Dr Bakstein brought his dog out into the garden at 6 a.m., both dog and master were shot dead.'

Howard raised a weary hand. 'Julian refused to have guards stationed at his house. He disliked any constraints on his freedom. He prided himself on being a man of peace. He didn't accept that there are people in the world who regard peacemakers as an obstacle to their plans. He was obstinate. It cost him his life.'

Howard's voice shook, and there were tears in his eyes. Dysart looked down at his notes, and Thorneycroft said gently, 'He was a man of peace in his work life, but how about in his private life?'

Howard stared at him. 'I'm not sure what you mean, Doctor.'

'Well, in the short time since his death, we've received a great deal of information about him. Most people describe him as a genius, but there are also some who describe him as a recluse, a man who never socialized, an atheist. He's been called bigoted, stubborn and combative. Such men tend to fall into arguments and quarrels. Did Dr Bakstein have that tendency?'

Howard sighed unhappily. 'Yes, I'm afraid he did. He saw everything in absolute terms, as right or wrong, black or white. He defended his opinions fiercely. He despised charlatans and plagiarists. His phenomenal memory allowed him to recall who had written a work. He said all writers leave unintentional foot-prints, and he could distinguish the originators from the people who plagiarized their work. He exposed several eminent people as plagiarists.'

'Which must have earned him enemies,' Dysart said.

'Enemies is too strong a word,' Howard answered. 'Julian was a genius. People allow a genius to get away with a great deal. Those spats – they were no more than spats – were disregarded because everyone recognized his great services to science, and to the sum of human health and happiness.'

Mark Bellows, who had maintained a tight-lipped silence to this point, leaned forward as if to interrupt. Howard directed a quelling glance at him, and he sat back, red-faced.

Dysart said levelly, 'Whatever Dr Baksteins's services may have been to humanity, someone killed him in cold blood. We are trying to discover what motivated that act. Can you provide me with the names of the people who had these ... spats ... with Dr Bakstein?'

Howard's patient veneer suddenly cracked. He slammed a fist on the arm of his chair and shouted, 'No, I cannot. For God's sake man, I don't have time to worry about such trifles.'

'Then can you provide me with a list of all those people who worked with Dr Bakstein, here at Clunbury?'

Howard struggled for calm. 'That would be a long list, Chief Inspector, and I would have to obtain clearance from the authorities before giving it to you. Confidentiality is important in our line of work. For the safety of our workers and our work, we refrain from bandying names about in the public arena.'

Dysart studied Howard for some moments without speaking. At last he said, 'Professor, you have your disciplines, and I have mine. Like you, I'm bound to obey certain authorities. I also have authority of my own. I can go through official channels to get the information I need, but that will take time, and like you I don't have time to waste. There's a killer out there, and it's my job to see that he doesn't kill again. I must ask you to obtain the clearance you spoke of, without delay. I assure you that subject to my duty to identify and arrest a murderer, any information you give me will be viewed as confidential, and treated with discretion.'

Still Howard sat narrow-eyed. Mark Bellows bent towards him. 'Sir, there's a great deal of public concern about these murders. If we're seen to be hampering the police investigation in any way, we'll get the sort of publicity we don't want.'

For a moment the two seemed to engage in a silent battle of wills, then Howard shrugged.

'Very well. I'll make the request, but you know the position.'

'The position,' said Bellows tartly, 'has altered since Julian's death. The old rules can't apply any more.'

'Very well. I'll make the request for clearance for the list.' He turned back to Dysart. 'I'd like you to accompany me to my office, Chief Inspector. Your input may swing the balance in favour of bending the rules.'

He got to his feet. 'Dr Thorneycroft, if you and Sergeant Clay will go with Dr Bellows to our records department, he will provide you with printouts of any documents you require for your investigation ... as long as they are not classified material. I will have lunch sent to you. It's better that the gossips in the canteen don't make you the topic of their conversation.'

Again he directed a warning look at Bellows, and this time the young man made no effort to hide his displeasure.

Bellows, thought Thorneycroft, is close to boiling point. He resents being muzzled, he doesn't like being excluded from a key discussion and he doesn't consider silence is the correct policy.

Handled right he may decide to tell us what we want to know.

The records room at Clunbury was highly computerized. Mark Bellows set to work to produce a mass of information about Julian Bakstein. Thorneycroft ate his share of a buffet lunch as he studied a twenty-page CV.

It had been carefully prepared for circulation to visiting VIPs, journalists and foreign government officials. It shed little light on Bakstein's private character. Thorneycroft suspected that somewhere else there would be a report that revealed the man's weaknesses as well as his strengths. He must have undergone stringent security tests before he started work at Clunbury.

That was another significant difference between him and Trevor Cornwall. Bakstein's life had been lived in shadow, Trevor's in full sunlight. The reason for Bakstein's murder might very well lie in this secretive way of life. Thorneycroft set himself to probe the shadows.

Tapping the CV, he said, 'This describes Dr Bakstein as a world authority on the creation of nuclear stations. What exactly did that involve?'

'He consulted with the countries that wanted to build a nuclear power station. If he was satisfied that they conformed with international standards, he examined the proposed site, checked the local demography, advised on building plans and equipment and monitored the construction work. When that was complete, he gave guidance on the way to staff, run and maintain the station.'

'That's a mammoth task.'

'It is. Julian had the ability to bring it to being. He had phenomenal gifts. He had the sort of mind that can translate plans into buildings. He often had to handle more than one project at a time, and he could switch from one to another without confusing them. That was his true genius. He could turn his knowledge of physical science and nuclear action into something concrete, and show people how to use it.'

'He must have spent a lot of time out of Britain.'

'He travelled a lot, but he didn't live abroad.' Bellows touched the screen of a computer. 'These days, this can show you what's being done on the other side of the world. I can look at a plan on my screen, make alterations and send it back to Australia electronically.'

'You do that sort of work? I thought communications was your line.'

'I did a stint in Planning.'

'Did you work with Dr Bakstein?'

'For a year, yes. Then I switched to my present job. I prefer people to things.'

'Was working with him easy?'

'It was ... immensely educative.'

'Did you have any of the spats Professor Howard spoke of?'

'Oh yes. Everyone who worked with Julian had spats. It was often impossible to agree with him. One had to submit to his wishes, or disagree and risk a quarrel.'

'How did you feel about that?'

'It annoyed me, but as Professor Howard said, one accepted his personality because one admired his genius.'

Thorneycroft continued to work through the pages of the CV, asking Bellows to explain various facets of Bakstein's aims and achievements. Bellows answered flat-voiced. There formed in Thorneycroft's mind the picture of Bakstein as a towering intelligence who had inspired respect, even veneration, among his peers, but who had made no friends.

It seemed that the tears that had shone briefly in Howard's eyes had sprung not from personal grief, but from regret at the loss of an irreplaceable skill. According to Bellows, Howard had had his share of quarrels with Bakstein, who might well have been barred from Clunbury, were it not for his genius.

The last page of the CV listed Bakstein's donations to charity, and it proved interesting. He had made huge gifts to the British armed forces, British athletes and British artists; but he had ignored the needs of children, the sick and conservation.

'He gave significant sums,' Thorneycroft remarked, and he was interested to see the flash of anger in Bellows's eyes.

'He gave away a lot of money,' Bellows said. 'He could afford to.'

'Many people who can afford to give, don't.'

Bellows made no answer, and Thorneycroft pressed the point. 'Professor Howard described Dr Bakstein as a man who saw everything as black or white. Looking at this list, it strikes me that he gave only to those people or institutions that fitted his narrow view of life. Would you agree?'

Bellows made a sound that was more a growl than a laugh. 'Yes, I would.'

'Was that the cause of your ... difference with him?'

'Yes, it was. I found it incredible that he could give so much to what pleased him, and nothing at all to what didn't.'

'Can you give me an example of his choices?'

'No.' Bellows seemed to feel he was on dangerous ground. 'My private opinions are not relevant here. Julian's dead. I don't wish to gossip about him.'

'What you consider to be gossip, the killer may have seen as motive for murder.'

Bellows shifted uneasily, and Thorneycroft held his gaze. 'The person who shot Trevor Cornwall and Julian Bakstein,' he said, 'is mentally unbalanced. He is a deliberate killer who planned his crimes and executed them without regard for the rights of his victims, or his victims' families and friends. Clearly you have strong feelings about some of the decisions Dr Bakstein made. Being a sane man, you've set those feelings aside. But I want to know why you had them. What happened that was so unacceptable that you quarrelled with Bakstein?'

Bellows shook his head and it seemed that he would refuse to answer; but suddenly he shrugged, and said, 'It was only one event that I really couldn't stomach. We had an Indian technician here. He was an excellent man, he'd lived in England for twenty years, married a local girl, they had four kids.

'Bakstein couldn't abide him. He was everything Bakstein disliked: not British, extrovert, politically to the far left, and very much pro Iraq. When the Americans started to drum up the war on Iraq, Desai was vocal against Bush and co. He said there was no evidence Saddam Hussein had weapons of mass destruction, and we shouldn't be dragged into any war.

'That was a red rag to a bull for Bakstein. He refused to work with Desai, and picked quarrels with him at every opportunity.

'About four months into the war, Desai got his brother and family out of Iraq and brought them to live in Shropshire. They had nothing but the clothes on their backs, and Desai had to provide for them. Then Desai developed cancer. A melanoma. He was dead in six weeks. That left his wife and kids, and his brother's family, without bridging finance for a while, so we got up a fund for them. Bakstein refused to contribute to it.

'I was in charge of making the collection, and I asked him for a donation, and when he refused, I called him a mean bastard and a few other things. Not that that worried him much. In time things settled down. As Professor Howard said, everyone made allowances for his quirks.'

'The killer left a note pinned to Bakstein's shirt,' Thorneycroft said. 'A poem by Shelley, *Ozymandias*. You know it?'

'I do.'

'Do you think Bakstein deserved that title?'

'No I don't. He was a mean man, but not a tyrant. He didn't leave an empty desert, he left work that will benefit millions of people.'

'A point I'd like to clear,' Thorneycroft said. 'Did Dr Bakstein keep a diary and a mobile phone?'

Bellows seemed to be relieved by the change of topic. 'He kept a diary to make a note of appointments,' he said, 'and a mobile phone for most of his calls, and to send an occasional SMS.'

The intercom next to Bellows buzzed, and he answered it. Professor Howard's voice sounded.

'We've finished our discussions,' he said. 'We'll meet all of you in the entrance lobby.'

Bellows stuffed the Bakstein CV and a number of other print-outs into a canvas carrier stamped with the Clunbury logo. Handing it to Thorneycroft, he said, 'What I told you about the Desai incident ... that's confidential.'

Thorneycroft forebore to remind him that confidentiality was not always possible in a murder investigation.

The three men joined Howard and Dysart in the lobby. Howard looked harassed, Dysart complacent. Thanks and farewells were exchanged, and the two scientists stood at the entrance door to watch the police contingent make its way to the helicopter waiting on the airpad.

XV

ONCE IN THE AIR, Dysart produced a sealed envelope from an inner pocket.

'The full list of Clunbury employees,' he said. 'I spoke to a toffee-nosed idiot in Whitehall. We'll be able to conduct our interrogations, provided we don't infringe the Secrecy Act. I'll have to come down here again to set up liaison with the local head of division. How did it go with Doc Bellows?'

'He said Bakstein was a mean bastard,' Thorneycroft answered, 'but that didn't make him Ozymandias, or justify his being murdered.'

'The killer apparently thought different,' Dysart said. He listened to the story of Bakstein's vendetta against Desai, and said. 'We'll have to talk to his relatives about it ... if they're still around.'

Thorneycroft looked at Clay. In their short acquaintance he'd learned that Clay spoke little, but observed much. 'What did you make of Dr Bellows?' he asked.

Clay sniffed. 'Ducks and dives, doesn't he. Maybe he told you that story because he'd like you to think Bakstein was topped because he was close with his cash. But I think both him and the professor believe Bakstein was killed on account of his work. Nuclear physics. They could be right.'

'What makes you think so?'

'Well, Bakstein phoned Mr Cousins, who he talks to when he has worries in the nuclear field. Cousins couldn't take the call because he's away in Seattle. There's a big conference there this week, to discuss limiting world nuclear arms operations.

Meanwhile, Iran's building up its nuclear capacity, and North Korea's firing off nuclear missiles, and planting troops on South Korea's border. Maybe Bakstein found out something he thought Cousins should know. Maybe someone shot him before he could talk to Cousins.'

'Killed because he was a mean bastard, or a defender of the peace,' Dysart mused. 'Either way he's dead, and we have a lot of work to do.' He handed Howard's envelope to Clay. 'You can start by checking if any of this lot has priors. Also see if any of Desai's relatives still live in or near Clunbury. If they don't, put the tracers on to finding their present address. They may have harboured a grievance against Bakstein.'

He glanced at Thorneycroft. 'How about you, John? Do we include you in the Clunbury interrogation schedule, or do you have a better idea?'

Thorneycroft said slowly, 'The routine work is going ahead well. I'd like to focus on aspects that fall outside of routine.'

'Such as?'

'We know certain things about the killer. He's a crack shot, a pro who uses either a sniper's rifle and special ammunition, or a pistol fitted with a silencer. He seems to know London well, and he's familiar with the areas where Cornwall and Bakstein lived. The messages he left after the murders suggest he's British, or has a very good knowledge of the English language. I'd like a computer scan done of all the known crack shots on file, to see if any of them matches this killer's profile.'

'It's a sketchy profile, John, at the moment.'

'It's all we have. We must use it.'

Dysart shook his head. 'There are a lot of people in this country who own and use guns. You could end up with a list of hundreds.'

Thorneycroft persisted. 'I know, and I'd like to make it longer by applying to the US Federal Computer Bank, and to Wiesbaden. This killer uses a hit man's techniques and ammunition. He learned those skills somewhere. The big computers may produce people with the same MO. There's also a chance that someone may turn him in. We'll build a fuller profile as time goes on, but we need to do everything we can before there's another murder.'

'All right,' Dysart said. 'I'll ask the super to set it all up. Don't be disappointed if the Americans and Germans won't play. Two murders may be top priority to us, but to the big guys, we're a long way back in the queue.'

'I don't agree,' Thorneycroft said. 'The fact that some of our top brass are back-pedalling on this case, indicates that these two murders are judged to be important, perhaps politically sensitive. We won't break this case unless we first break the barrier of silence.'

'And if foreign authorities decline their help, what then?'

'At least we will have tried.'

Dysart smiled wryly. 'We who are about to die, salute you. Very well. Talk to Ivans, tell him to be ready to run the scan in this country, and we're hoping for international cooperation. Anything else?'

'Yes. I want to make my own inquiries, talk to some marksmen on the right side of the law ... the ones who compete in shooting contests, the army snipers and amateur hunters. One of them might give us a lead to this perp. Also, I'd like another talk to Kaminsky.'

Dysart's gaze sharpened. 'Kaminsky's already shown that he won't discuss official policy.'

'I won't ask him to. All I want from him is the name of a top marksman.'

Dysart looked unconvinced. 'All right. Take Simcox with you.'

'I need to go alone,' Thorneycroft said. 'Kaminsky won't give me the time of day, otherwise.'

'John, you know the bloody rules. It's important that we have a witness to information revealed during an interrogation.'

'I shan't interrogate Kaminsky. I'll ask him for a name. He can answer or not, as his conscience dictates.'

Dysart rubbed his jaw. 'Right,' he said. 'You see Kaminsky and you ask him that one question only. No discussion, no reference to this investigation, nothing that can render any evidence inadmissible in a court of law. You are not making the inquiry on my instructions, it's your own initiative. Clear?'

'Crystal clear.'

'One more thing,' Dysart said, 'I intend to talk to Mr Cousins when he returns to England. I intend to establish what precisely is his connection with Julian Bakstein. I'll set up a meeting.'

Thorneycroft settled back in his seat, smiling. Dysart had shown that he meant to conduct this investigation in his own way, and was not to be deterred by the antagonism of people in high places.

On arriving at the Greenwich police station, late that afternoon, Thorneycroft sought out DS Ivans, who ran the computer systems.

Thorneycroft had few computer skills. A six month course had taught him how to cope with routine programmes, e-mail and Google, but the word megabyte still conjured up visions of giant fleas, or maybe a great white shark. He was impressed and humbled by the feats achieved by the likes of Ted Ivans.

Luckily for him, Ivans felt a similar reverence for men like Thorneycroft, who could use computer data to trace a missing child, nail a dope pedlar, analyze a new drug or estimate the costs and profits of a Columbian cocaine cabal. Such men could turn mere data into great stuff. They were totally cool. Ivans longed to be a forensic expert like Thorneycroft.

'I've two requests,' Thorneycroft told him. 'The first is from the chief. He wants you to run a check on this list of the Clunbury employees, to see if any of them face prior charges.'

Ivans took the list with a nod. 'Routine, no problem. What's the second?'

'You know I'm building a profile of the killer. I'd like you to do a search for a possible match.'

'That's more tricky,' Ivans said. 'There's not much of a physical description, is there? Just that he's medium height and slight build, wears a black beard that could be real or false.'

'We don't often get an eye-witness description of a murderer,' Thorneycroft said drily. 'But there are other things we know about this man, that can help to identify him.'

'Like that he's a crack shot who uses pro weapons and ammo?'

'Like that, and Ballistics and Forensics are working on that material evidence. I want you to work on something less obvious. Examine the man's actions, the things that distinguish him from other criminals, or link him to past crimes. I want your impression of him.'

As Ivans looked blank, Thorneycroft said, 'You've read all the reports, Ted, including my profile. What's your feeling about this killer? How do you see him?'

'He's a real bastard,' said Ivans promptly. 'Cruel, and with a big head. Thinks he can get away with anything. Thinks he can take us on, and win.'

'I agree,' said Thorneycroft.

Ivans warmed to his theme. 'Stupid, too,' he said. 'The way he takes risks, killing two men in broad daylight, with a good chance he'll be caught in the act. And those messages he left on the bodies. He's well educated and he likes to show it off, doesn't he? He's a weirdo. You'd think someone would have spotted him for a nutter, long ago.'

'Nutters like him can be very good at concealing their weirdness from others, even the people close to them. But you've drawn a good picture of this perpetrator. I want you to look for a match in past records.'

Ivans's dark eyes sparkled. 'I'll do that. I'll talk to Concorde, spread the net wide.'

XVI

RETURNING TO THE incidents room, Thorneycroft found
Dysart in discussion with DS Frank. By the high colour on the Sri
Lankan's normally creamy skin, there had been some difference of
opinion. Dysart beckoned him over.

'DS Frank and I have been talking about Rosa Hopewell,'
Dysart said. 'Tell him, Pramda.'

Pramda Frank fiddled with her spectacles and said nothing.
Thorneycroft smiled at her.

'Mrs Hopewell hasn't turned up, yet?'

'No, sir.' Pramda glanced at Dysart, whose gaze remained fixed
on his desk top. She took a step towards Thorneycroft. 'My father
is a silk merchant,' she said. 'He supplies many couteriers with
material.'

'Including Mrs Hopewell?'

'Yes. Chief Inspector Dysart wants me to urge my father to tell
us where she is … if he knows.'

'And do you think he does know?'

'He might, but if he does he won't tell us.'

Dysart opened his mouth then closed it again.

'*I* know it is the law to help the police,' Pramda said, 'but for
my father there are … other considerations.'

'Bad for business,' Dysart muttered, and Pramda said fiercely
'No, that is not it. He would regard it as a betrayal. She was born
in the same village as my father. If she is hiding because there is a
threat to her life, it would be a betrayal to tell anyone where she
is. So it would be a waste of time to ask him to inform on her.' She
hesitated. 'But there is something else I can ask him to do.'

Dysart looked up sharply. 'You never said that, Pramda.'

Surprisingly, she chuckled, and after a moment Dysart spread his hands. 'All right, I never gave you the chance. Tell us now.'

'It may be that my father can get a message to Mrs Hopewell. He may be able to persuade her to come to you for protection. That would be better than hiding in some place where there's no protection, and where people may see her, and talk.'

'Much better,' Dysart agreed. Pramda eyed him with suspicion.

'And it would be a waste of time, also, to put my father under surveillance. One sniff of that, and he won't lift a finger to help us. He is very firm in his principles.'

Dysart nodded. 'Talk to your father. Get his reactions. Let me know what he will and won't do. And remind him that I'm relying on you to get results in a very important case.'

'Yes, sir.' Pramda's smile was luminous. When she had hurried from the room, Dysart grinned. 'My father was very like hers, firm in his principles. The law took second place to his view of right and wrong. Did you talk to Ivans?'

'Yes, he's started looking for a match for my profile perp.' Thorneycroft settled in a chair. 'It's worrying that there's no trace of Rosa Hopewell; she seems to have vanished into thin air.'

'Or a shallow grave.'

'That's what scares me. She's linked in some way to Bakstein and Cousins. That's dangerous for her.'

'Linked how and why?'

'Let's start with the facts. Bakstein was active in trying to halt the proliferation of nuclear arms. There are rogue powers that are pushing to manufacture, trade and launch nuclear missiles and bombs. Bakstein was challenging some very nasty customers.'

'Agreed.'

'To be effective, he had to be well informed about the goings-on in the field of nuclear armaments.'

'Right.'

'So he had to have help from a high level in this country. Someone was appointed to feed him information, and to receive his reports.'

'Cousins.'

'Probably.'

'Where does Rosa come in?'

'She's British by marriage only. Pramda's just told us she was born in Sri Lanka, and her secretary says she worked as a carpet merchant in the Middle East. She speaks languages other than English. What if she's employed by Cousins to translate documents? What if she's an agent whose shop is a drop-off place used by both Bakstein and Cousins? It's also possible she received information from abroad, translated it, and handed it to Cousins for appropriate action.'

'That's speculation, not fact,' Dysart said, 'but go on.'

'When Bakstein was shot,' Thorneycroft continued, 'Rosa was sure it was because of his anti-nuke activities. She may even have had a suspicion of who set up the hit. That would be enough to make her bolt for cover.'

Dysart looked sombre. 'You're building a scenario that has Bakstein working with intelligence agents in the form of Cousins and Rosa.'

'It's a possible scenario.'

'Maybe. Why was Bakstein shot at this particular time?'

'Let's say he learned something of importance. He tried to communicate with Cousins, who was out of the country. He spoke to Rosa.'

'He asked her for the name of a good dry-cleaner, hardly a mind-blowing request.'

'That could have been an agreed code ... or Rosa could have lied to Maisie Banning about what Bakstein said to her.'

Dysart's face puckered. 'I can tell you this much, if your scenario's correct, if Bakstein was tangling with Intelligence spooks, we won't get near Cousins or Rosa. They'll be incommunicado and there's a good chance this case will be taken out of our hands.'

'I know, and I know that speculation isn't good enough, we have to have hard facts.'

'Another point,' Dysart said, 'Bakstein may have been topped because he was anti-nuke, but Trevor Cornwall had nothing to do with nuclear arms skulduggery. You've always said that Bakstein and Trevor were murdered for the same reason, but on your scenario that can't be so.'

'I still believe it's so. There's a link between the two murders. We just haven't found it yet.'

Dysart sighed. 'I'm beginning to see why this case doesn't get off the bloody ground.'

'You can try to speak to Cousins. You said you knew a couple of people.'

'I can try. I doubt I'll be given the time of day.'

As Thorneycroft started to speak, Dysart said impatiently,

'John, if your scenario's right, the question arises, how did Bakstein's killers know he was in possession of damaging information? Did someone indulge in careless talk, did someone sell out to a foreign power, do we have a double agent in our intelligence structures? You're taking these murders into the arena of intelligence and counter-intelligence. Those people play by their own rules, and they don't consort with plods in police uniform. I'll do my best to get in touch with Cousins, but don't count on my getting past Cerberus at the gate of that underworld.'

Dysart gathered up the files at his elbow. 'Clay and I will be going back to Clunbury tomorrow, to set up the interrogation of the staff. Did you fix an interview with Kaminsky?'

'Yes. Seven o'clock this evening, at a bowling alley in Chiswick.'

'Well, mind you put the right bias on the ball. Ask just the one question, don't discuss the case, make it clear you're acting on your own initiative. Phone me when you leave Kaminsky. I'll be here until about nine, after that I'll be at home.'

Driving to Chiswick, Thorneycroft wondered if the coming meeting would take place to the accompaniment of bowls smashing into pins; but on giving his name to a muscular doorman, he was told to go to the room next to the cold-drinks stand. There he found Kaminsky listening to a CD of Judith Baskin singing alleluias.

Kaminsky waved a hand towards an array of bottles on a table. Thorneycroft poured himself a pint of Heineken and sat down in a chair facing his host. The alleluias soared to a triumphant conclusion and Kaminsky turned off the player.

'What d'you want this time?' he demanded.

It wasn't a propitious start. Kaminsky looked tired and very much on his guard.

Thorneycroft was not to be rushed. He took a long swig of his beer and studied his surroundings. The room was an odd mix of snuggery and workplace. At one end were the TV, easy chairs and booze; at the other were all the machines of modern communication.

'Who owns this place?' he asked.

'My brother-in-law,' Kaminsky answered. 'It's nice and private. I can talk to people without being interrupted. Who sent you?'

'No one. I'm here on my own authority.'

'There's no such thing. So, Lone Ranger, what's on your mind?'

Thorneycroft set aside his tankard. 'Plenty, but I won't burden you with it. I have just one question. Will you give me the name of a top-ranking British marksman or woman.'

'Why do you want that?'

Kaminsky's face set in a squinting scowl. It was plain he was debating whether to grant the request. The silence lengthened and Thorneycroft was tempted to break it, but he remembered Dysart's instructions, and held his tongue. At last Kaminsky spoke.

'There are dozens of good marksmen and women.'

'Then give me the best.'

Kaminsky rubbed a hand over his face. He met Thorneycroft's eyes. 'Have you heard of Jack Langley?'

'Vaguely. Wasn't he an international champion, a few years ago?'

'Yes. Talk to him. He's on the national selectors' team, he knows a lot of people. His address is Hapgood Manor, Loop Road, near Worth Priory, Sussex.' Kaminsky scribbled the address and telephone number on a scrap of paper and handed it over. 'I don't know if he's in England right now. He travels a lot.'

'You know him?'

'I know of him. We never met.'

'If he's away, is there a wife I can talk to?'

'There's a wife. I'm told she's flakey, away with the fairies. That's four questions. Don't push your luck.'

Kaminsky stood up, and Thorneycroft abandoned his unfinished beer and walked with him to the door of the room. He started to offer his thanks, but Kaminsky cut him short.

'Goodbye, Dr Thorneycroft. Bear in mind that we never had this conversation.'

'You have my word,' Thorneycroft said, but he spoke to Kaminsky's retreating back.

He made his way past the cool-drink kiosk and the alleys filling now with bowlers. The doorman was sitting in a cane chair, reading a folded newspaper. He flicked a glance at Thorneycroft but offered no goodnight.

The exchange with Kaminsky, Thorneycroft decided, had been short and not sweet, yet he left the building with a tingling of the nerves, a sense that some important barrier had been breached.

His telephone was ringing as he stepped into his house. It was Claudia, sounding anxious.

'Is everything all right, John? I've been calling you all evening.'

'I'm sorry, love. I had a meeting.'

'Luke and I miss you so much. When can we come home?'

'When it's safe. I know it's hard, not being together, but if you and Luke were in London, I'd be worried. I wouldn't be able to concentrate on the job.'

'Yes, I do see.' Claudia turned to more comfortable topics. Presently she said, 'Liz wants to speak to you, I'm putting her on.'

Liz's voice was brittle. 'Have you any news?'

'We went to Clunbury, where Bakstein worked. It was productive. We're gathering small pieces of information. Put together they can be important, but it's a slow process.'

'I know, I know I have to be patient.' She sighed. 'It helps, having Luke and Clo with us.'

'It helps me, too. Liz, tell me, did Trevor know Julian Bakstein?'

'No, I'm sure he didn't. I've thought about it, and I can't remember his ever mentioning Bakstein's name. Why?'

'I'm just trying to get the facts straight in my mind,' Thorneycroft said. 'I'll try to get down to Penwold soon, but we have a lot of work to do. Just hang in there, Liz.'

He spoke to Claudia again and when the conversation ended he tried Jack Langley's number. There was only a recorded answer.

Dysart phoned.

'The super's setting up the regional investigation unit,' he said. 'He's had pressure from the politicos, but he's handled it. We'll have police on board, not politicians. We're renting extra space in the Waverley building next door. Kevin's seeing that computers and phones go in. Departments in the investigation will be allotted to drafted officers. I'll be in overall command, responsible to the super, and you, as a consultant, will report directly to me. I'd like you to give a talk to the whole unit as soon as its assembled, give them your take on the perp. I suggest you use my original team members whenever possible – they're familiar with both cases. We'll talk more tomorrow evening when I'm back from Clunbury. Did you speak to Kaminsky?'

'Yes. He's tetchy, but he gave me a name … Jack Langley, a top-level marksman. I tried to call him, but there was no one at home. I'll try again tomorrow, set up an appointment.'

'Where's he live?'

Thorneycroft gave him the name, address and telephone number.

'If you arrange a meeting,' Dysart cautioned, 'take Simcox with you. Let the super have the results at once and put Ivans and Frank in the picture. And John, remember that the spooks have their beady eyes on us. Do everything by the book.'

Thorneycroft fed Gatsby a late snack and took him into the garden. The night was warm and humid. Insects circled the street lights, and down the road merrymakers sang in the pub. Trapped in a web of murder and suspicion, Thorneycroft felt a longing for the humdrum things of life.

He lay awake for some time that night, going over the events at Clunbury, wondering how the enlarged investigation unit would accept a profiler's views, puzzling over Bakstein's link with Cousins and Rosa Hopewell, and who or what was powerful enough to muzzle the ebullient Mr Kaminsky.

XVII

THORNEYCROFT WOKE TO a hot dawn, the heat haze shimmering over ground mist. He spoke to Jack Langley at eight o'clock, introduced himself and apologized for the earliness of the call.

Langley answered briskly, 'No matter, I'm an early riser. What can I do for you, Doctor?'

'My doctorate's in forensic psychiatry,' Thorneycroft said, 'and I've been retained as a consultant by the police investigating the murders of Trevor Cornwall and Julian Bakstein. No doubt you've seen the news reports.'

'Read the papers, seen the television. Dreadful crimes, but I don't see how I can help you. I've no skills in that field.'

'You've been described to me as the best shot in England. The killer of those two men is an expert shot. We have to identify him, and it will help if we can determine whether he's British or a foreigner. We need the names of acknowledged marksmen who may be familiar with the man, or who can give us further names to consider.'

Langley said slowly, 'I know a number of fine marksmen and women, but I'm sure none of them includes a cold-blooded murderer in his circle. However if you want to discuss it, by all means come and see me. When would suit you?'

'Today, if possible. We must prevent this man from claiming another victim.'

'Yes, quite. Let's see, I can give you an hour or so this morning. I have a meeting at 12.30. I'm one of the selectors choosing a team to tour the US. Can you be here by ten?'

'Yes, certainly. I'll be bringing Detective Sergeant Simcox with me. If you will give me the directions to your home....'

Langley gave them, and within minutes Thorneycroft was driving to Morden to collect DS Simcox. Simcox had spent half the night garnering information about Jack Langley, and he regaled Thorneycroft with it as they sped south past Croydon and Redhill.

'He's a farmer's son,' he said, 'that's where he learned to shoot. By the time he was twenty-one he was a crack shot, but he didn't go in for the competitive stuff right away. He went to Hollywood.'

'Hollywood?' Thorneycroft was incredulous, and Simcox laughed.

'Not to act. He worked with the lads who toted the six-guns in the Westerns, and the sawn-off shotguns in the gangster movies. He made a bit of money, developed an eye for moving targets, came home and joined a team of professional marksmen. He went to the top pretty damn quick, and stayed there longer than most, though he's been retired for some years.'

'How old is he now?'

'Sixty-eight.'

'Kaminsky mentioned he's married.'

'Yeah.' Simcox shuffled a bundle of notes. 'I got it somewhere. Here. He married when he was thirty-five. A Mrs Sybilla Moorland.'

'Mrs? A divorcee?'

'No, a widow with one son, and plenty rich. Her dad was a jeweller. He made things for the royals and the American pop stars.'

'Kaminsky says the woman's flakey.'

'I wouldn't know about that. I didn't have time to cross-reference. There'll be lots more stuff waiting for us when we get back.' Simcox laid his notes aside. 'You were in the SAS, weren't you, sir? You must know a bit about firearms, yourself.'

'That was a while ago,' Thorneycroft said. 'Today, a lot of the guns are in private hands.'

Simcox nodded vigorously. 'It's a trigger-happy world. It's not that hard to get hold of a revolver or an automatic, and then ... bang, you're cock of the walk. Crazy world. This perp we're after now, he's crazy isn't he?'

'He may not be legally insane. I'd say he knows what he's doing, and knows that it's wrong.'

'That didn't stop him killing Cornwall and Bakstein. That's first degree murder, in my book.'

'It is,' Thorneycroft said, 'and I want him put away for a very long time.'

Reaching Crawley they branched southeast on minor roads. Once past Worth, they reached forested land and a hamlet circling a small brick chapel.

'Straight on for four miles, if Langley's directions are precise,' Thorneycroft said.

They were, and at five minutes to ten he drove through a carved gate and up a short drive to a square modern house.

Looking about him, Thorneycroft decided that Jack Langley liked precision. The neatly clipped hedges and lawns, the weed-free borders, the exact placing of a sundial, all spoke of an orderly mind.

To the east of the house was a block of buildings that could be garages or storerooms. To the west, beyond a wide lawn was a tarmac landing strip and a hangar. A small plane was standing in front of the hangar. Beyond that was a long stretch of open ground peppered with shooting targets.

There was no swimming pool in sight, no tennis court. The east end of the building appeared to be a conservatory. Thorneycroft left the car close to its glass panes, and saw that it sheltered a profuse display of exotic tropical plants.

As he and Simcox walked back to the front door, a woman in the conservatory raised a hand and smiled at them. They glimpsed a dead white face and a shock of yellow hair.

Simcox murmured, 'that must be the flakey lady,' and Thorneycroft nodded.

'I don't think we mention her unless we have to.' They reached the door and he raised his hand to press the doorbell, but before he could do so, the door swung back and Jack Langley waved them through. He greeted them by name and led them along a passage to their right.

'We'll talk in the morning-room,' he said. 'The air con's on. We don't often need it in this climate but today's going to be a stinker. Would you like tea, coffee, a cool drink?'

The offer declined, they settled into chairs facing a window that overlooked the garden. Before Langley could take his place, the mobile in his pocket jangled, and he answered it, raising an apologetic hand to his guests. Thorneycroft studied him as he moved about the room with the phone.

He was not a big man, but his movements had the strength and ease of an athlete. His face was round, his skin evenly tanned and surprisingly smooth for a man of his age. His nose was small and hooked, his eyes bright and intensely blue. He put Thorneycroft in mind of a Pathan sniper he'd encountered in his army days. The man had had this same blue, ingenuous stare. One did not turn one's back on him for a single moment.

Langley ended his conversation and returned to his chair. He smiled at Thorneycroft. 'I've looked out some names for you, Doctor, but I must emphasize that the marksmen I know compete for cups, and the hunters go after big game. None of them shoot humans. You'd do better to apply to the police gunmen, wouldn't you?'

'We're working on our own and foreign computer records,' Thorneycroft said, 'but frankly, we need short cuts. The faster we run this killer to ground, the better.'

Langley scratched his jaw. 'I might be able to narrow the field if I knew what sort of gun he used.'

'In the murder of Cornwall he used a sniper's combat rifle with an accelerator bullet. He used a handgun with a silencer to shoot Bakstein.'

Langley's face creased in distaste. 'That sounds like a hired butcher, to me, not a sportsman.'

'It does, but there are certain factors which are not typical of a paid assassin.'

'Such as?'

'The messages he left on the bodies.' Thorneycroft described the obituary and the Ozymandias poem, and Langley shook his head.

'That sort of thing's out of my ken,' he said, 'but this may help you.' He fished a booklet from the pocket of his shirt and handed it to Thorneycroft.

'It contains the register of most of the above-average shots in Britain,' he said. 'Names in isolation don't tell one much. If you like I can run through them with you, shed a little more light on them.'

'Please, if you will.'

Langley went through the booklet page by page, describing various men and women, their abilities, their preferred weapons, and in some cases their personal idiosyncrasies. Simcox took notes and Thorneycroft asked questions. Finally Langley laid the booklet aside.

'I've one more contribution to make,' he said. This time he produced a handwritten list. 'I'm giving you these names in confidence. They are people who are proficient with a rifle or handgun, but who in my opinion shouldn't be allowed to handle either.'

Thorneycroft was startled. 'You mean they have criminal tendencies?'

'Oh no, no, I've no knowledge of that. They are just too careless, too undisciplined. To handle a potentially lethal weapon, you need good eyesight, steady nerves, and complete self-control. People who let their emotions get the better of them, don't shoot well, and they're a danger to others. That list covers the reckless cowboys and cowgirls in our ranks.'

'Are any of them reckless enough to be homicidal?'

'I don't believe so.' Langley hesitated. 'There are huntsmen who enjoy the hunt, and possibly the kill, but as I've said they don't go after human prey.' Langley glanced at his watch. 'I still have time in hand. Would you like to see my own little armoury?'

He ushered them across the passage to a locked room. The little armoury he'd spoken of proved to be extensive. Strapped to the walls were racks of antique guns; flintlocks, an arquebus, a blunderbuss, and a range of early sporting guns. Langley opened safes to display more modern weapons, rifles, duelling pistols, police revolvers and automatics. He pointed to a long-nosed six-shooter.

'Gary Cooper gave me that,' he said. 'It throws a trifle to the right.'

Gazing about him, Thorneycroft said, 'a collection like this is a big responsibility.'

'Yes, it is. I had to get a lot of permits, and jazz up the security on the property, laser beams and so on. He smiled. 'Most of the stuff is too old to be safely fired. It's of historic interest only.'

'Are they loaded?' Thorneycroft asked, and Langley gave him a sardonic smile.

'No, Doctor, nothing here is loaded. The ammo's in the safe over there, and its combination is safely locked in my head. I may add that my collection does not include any combat rifles. And now, I'm afraid I have to leave to keep my appointment with a group of peaceable marksmen. If you need to ask me any more questions, do just give me a call.'

He walked with them to the entrance hall, and Thorneycroft expressed his gratitude for Langley's co-operation. 'You've given us plenty to work on. DCI Dysart will let you know if he has further questions.'

'I meant what I said,' Langley said. 'I want to see this man exposed and punished. Killers with guns cast a shadow over my profession.'

He started for the door, but before he reached it, a woman came hurrying up the passage, calling Langley's name. She was tall and gaunt, her body so thin as to be almost skeletal. The skin of her jaw and neck hung loosely, and the round patches of rouge on her cheekbones gave her a feverish look. Only her eyes, large, amber and lustrous, suggested that she might once have been beautiful. A second woman appeared behind her and tried to restrain her, but she was knocked away by a petulant swing of the arm.

It seemed to Thorneycroft that for a moment Langley froze. Then he stretched out a hand. 'What is it, Sybilla?'

Sybilla Langley marched across the hall to his side. The second woman followed, and Thorneycroft saw her direct the faintest of shrugs at Langley.

'Lunch is ready,' Sybilla said. 'It's set for five. I ordered poached salmon and creme brûlée, your favourites.'

Her voice was high and tremulous, like a child on the brink of tears.

Langley put an arm round her shoulders. 'You know I can't dodge this meeting, darling.' He turned her to face Thorneycroft. This is Dr John Thorneycroft, and his colleague Detective Sergeant Simcox. My wife Sybilla, and her dear friend and companion, Mrs Jane Blarney.'

For 'companion' read 'minder', Thorneycroft thought. He shook Sybilla's hand. It was thin and cold as a bunch of twigs, but her smile was brilliant.

'Oh, delightful,' she said. 'You both must stay and enjoy Jack's luncheon.' She leaned to plant a light kiss on her husband's cheek, and hooked an arm through Thorneycroft's. 'We shall sample delicious wines, and have coffee out on the patio.'

Thorneycroft knew he should claim pressure of work, and remove himself and Simcox from a situation that Jack Langley clearly disliked. There was a tension in the hallway that he recognized as the unease of people anxious to cover up the truth, and he wanted to learn what that truth was.

He smiled at Sybilla. 'I can't resist poached salmon,' he said. 'We'll be delighted to join you for lunch.'

Sybilla beamed at her husband. 'There, you see. We four will be as happy as sandboys. You run along and attend your meeting.'

She turned away to say something to Jane Blarney, and Langley spoke quietly to Thorneycroft.

'Sybilla tires easily. She must have her rest after lunch. I rely on you to see she gets it.'

He walked quickly to the front door and out to a Lexus saloon with chauffeur that was waiting on the driveway. Sybilla tugged at Thorneycroft's arm. 'Everything's ready,' she said. 'We'll feast ourselves, and you and Sergeant Simcox shall tell me about the wonderful work you do.'

This proved to be an empty promise. Sybilla, once settled at the head of the dining-room table, showed no interest at all in police work, nor was she curious about their presence in her home. She embarked on a steady flow of small talk, while keeping an eye on the maid who served the food and wine, and directing an occasional triumphant glance at Jane Blarney.

Her loquacity gave Thorneycroft the chance to study her. It was a little like watching an old movie, for she used outdated slang and gestures; but it was plain that whatever flakiness assailed her, it was not Alzheimer's disease. Her memory was good. She recalled past events, and items from the current newspapers; she spoke knowledgably about the plants in her greenhouse and when Simcox admired a picture on the wall, she gave a detailed account of its provenance.

'It was a present from my son Eric,' she said. 'He met the artist, Raoul La Roda, in Spain and recognized his talent. He bought that picture for me, and would have bought more, but sadly La Roda was killed in a road accident soon after he painted that scene. Eric has never found any other examples of his work, although he visits Spain from time to time.'

Jane Blarney said flatly, 'I don't imagine that after all these years, any more of his pictures will turn up.' She looked irritated, as if she and Sybilla had had this argument before. Sybilla laughed, and waved her fingers airily.

'All it means, dear Jane, is that some clever dealer is keeping Raoul's works on ice until the price is really high.' She smiled at Simcox. 'Eric has a very good eye for art. If you come across a painting by La Roda, buy it. You won't waste your money.'

The meal over, she rose to her feet. 'Coffee on the patio,' she said brightly, but Thorneycroft shook his head. 'We really must be going, or we'll be in trouble with DCI Dysart.'

Sybilla's face crumpled. 'You can't leave without seeing Eric's room,' she said. 'It's the finest room in the house. It looks across the downs, it's full of air and light.'

Jane Blarney came to stand beside her. 'Sybilla, you know what Jack always tells you, you must have your rest.'

'I don't need rest.' Sybilla's voice soared high and tears shone in her eyes. Her grip tightened on Thorneycroft's wrist. 'Please, it will make me so happy.'

Again Thorneycroft's conscience told him to leave, but this time it was compassion that intervened. He saw that Sybilla Langley was suffering, and that she was seeking in some bizarre way to ease the pain. Eric's room might be Aladdin's cave, or Bluebeard's chamber; the fact was that she placed some deluded faith in its powers, and it would be cruel to deny her that solace.

He said gently, 'We can stay a little longer, and then we must get back to work, and you must have your rest.'

She nodded eagerly. 'Yes, very well. Come then.'

She hurried them up a broad flight of stairs, dragging on Thorneycroft's arm, with Jane Blamey and Simcox hastening to keep up. She was trembling, and once she gave an excited chuckle. They followed a corridor to the eastern end of the building to reach a panelled door. Sybilla leaned confidingly towards Thorneycroft.

'Eric travels a great deal,' she said, 'but whenever he comes home he finds everything ready for him. I keep everything exactly the way he likes it.'

She opened the door, and beckoned them through it with a theatrical sweep of the arm.

There was nothing abnormal about the room. It was, as Sybilla had said, a fine room, light and airy, and the picture window at the far end looked across a belt of forest to fields, pastures and the rising slopes of the North Downs.

It was beautifully furnished in the best modern style, the thick carpet deep cream, the fabrics and hangings umber, sage green and deep soft gold. It was clear that the easy chairs and sofas, the Swedish desk and the many decorative fittings, were impeccably maintained. Through an archway was a marble and gilt bathroom. There were fresh flowers in a bowl beside the bed. It was opulent and comfortable in every aspect, but what Thorneycroft was drawn to, were the books.

Bookcases lined the inner walls of the room, and they were well filled. Thorneycroft walked along their ranks. The titles covered many subjects. One section was devoted to fiction, old and new. A couple of the novels had only been published in recent weeks.

Sybilla was close to him as he moved, and he said, 'I see you keep the library up to date.'

'Oh yes. Eric tells me what he likes, and I add to the shelves regularly. The books he no longer wants go to charities, or the hospitals.'

She spoke with confidence now, a woman satisfied that she was doing a good job.

'Judging by his books, I'd say your son's a scientist. Am I right?'

'Oh yes, he's a doctor of physics, but he's not tied down to research. He's a lecturer. He has engagements to speak all over the world. Some people try to belittle him, they say he's prostituting his knowledge, but that's just petty jealousy. He doesn't let it bother him. He makes a very good living, and he's doing what he enjoys. I'm proud of him. Very proud.'

Thorneycroft replaced the book he had lifted from its shelf and turned to face her.

'He hasn't followed in your husband's footsteps, then?' For a moment she looked blank, as if bringing her thoughts back from a great distance. Then she smiled.

'No. Eric takes after me. When he was in his teens he tried target shooting, but his heart wasn't in it. I persuaded him to go to university and study for his degrees, and it's paid off. He's in demand everywhere.'

She drew Thorneycroft away from the bookshelves and showed him the contents of the walk-in wardrobe. It held suits in plastic bags, freshly laundered shirts and underwear, jerseys, rows of shoes, riding boots and ski boots.

'He prefers Zermatt to Grindelwald,' Sybilla said.

The circuit completed, they arrived back at the door, where Simcox and Jane Blarney were waiting. Thorneycroft took Sybilla's thin hand.

'Thank you for showing us the room. You've done a great job here. It's a place any man would appreciate.'

She nodded without speaking. The energy that had suffused her was dwindling visibly, like sand running out of a broken bag. Jane Blarney stopped between her and Thorneycroft.

'Will you show yourselves out? I must stay here. She's exhausted.' She spoke in a low voice and there was anger in her eyes.

'Yes, of course. And thank you for your patience.'

'I care for her. That's my job. Just go straight down the stairs, past the dining room door to the front. I shall ring for the maid to let you out.' Jane turned from him and went to sit beside Sybilla, who was crouched on the edge of the bed.

Thorneycroft and Simcox made their way back through the silent house. The maid was waiting to let them out. The front door closed behind them and they climbed into their car and drove away, with Simcox at the wheel.

As they passed through the entrance gates, Simcox said, 'Sir, while we were going up the stairs, I spoke to Mrs Blamey; I asked her how Mr and Mrs Langley came to meet. She said they met during an international shooting competition. She said Mrs Langley was a very good shot before her mind went. I don't suppose she could be a suspect, could she?'

'I doubt it,' Thorneycroft answered. 'She hasn't the power to plan and to concentrate, and I don't see her riding a Cougar bike.'

'No, much too flakey.' Simcox hunched his shoulders. 'I shouldn't wonder if that's why her son travels a lot. Like living in a morgue, it'd be, and I bet she spends her time telling him what to do. I'm glad my mum was never that possessive.'

'I don't think he's travelling anywhere,' Thorneycroft said. 'I think he's probably dead. She's built a shrine, to help her pretend that one day he'll be coming home.'

XVIII

THORNEYCROFT WAS SILENT on the journey back to London, thinking about the Langley household. He scanned the lists that Jack Langley had given him. Could one of the so-called cowboys be the killer? It seemed unlikely. Langley had described them as lacking discipline, without self-control, and that certainly didn't typify this killer's actions.

There'd been immense tension in that house, something stronger than a wish to conceal Sybilla Langley's fixation on her son's room.

There's something I've missed, Thorneycroft thought, something I should remember. Try as he might he could summon up nothing that seemed to have any bearing on the case. He stopped brooding about it, and concentrated on coping with the flood of afternoon traffic.

On reaching Greenwich, he found Dysart and Clay were back from Clunbury. Dysart was looking depressed.

'A wasted journey,' he said. 'All the workers at the research centre have cast-iron alibis, couldn't possibly have shot Cornwall or Bakstein. And the Desai family have gone back to India, no way any of them could have committed the murders.'

'The killer could have hired someone,' Thorneycroft said, but he didn't believe that to be true. The man who shot those two men had put his indelible stamp on the crimes.

Dysart wanted to know the outcome of Thorneycroft's meeting with Jack Langley. Thorneycroft made his report and handed over the booklet and the list of names Langley had provided.

'He went through the lot with us,' he said. 'He has personal knowledge of a lot of the marksmen in this country, but he doesn't think any of them are capable of murder.'

'We'll check them,' Dysart said. He was turning over the pages of the booklet. 'Langley's own name is here.'

Thorneycroft smiled. 'He's certainly an expert shot, but I don't see him as a double murderer.'

'Did you question his wife?'

'We had lunch with her, but there was no point in asking her about the murders. She's delusional. Langley is very protective of her.'

Dysart wagged an impatient hand. 'That's sad, but it's not our problem.' He passed the booklet and list back to Thorneycroft. 'Talk to Ivans, tell him to circulate them to the relevant divisions, let's see if any of them bear a resemblance to your profile of the perp.'

Ivans accepted the fresh material with stoicism. 'We're plugging away at lists of marksmen,' he said. 'There are hundreds of them in Britain, not to mention the rest of the world.' He brightened. 'I did dig up some info on Rosa Hopewell. She's a British citizen by marriage. Hopewell, the man she married, was a dealer in Persian carpets. He met Rosa in Isfahan. She owned a shop there. That's Iran, isn't it?'

'Yes. That could be important.' Thorneycroft was *distrait*, glimpsing a truth that dodged out of sight before he could grasp it. He came back to earth. 'Is Thomas Hopewell still alive?'

'No, he died fifteen years ago. Rosa left the carpet business and went in for fashion designing. She's done very well at it. Clay says Bakstein bought her clothes.'

'Yes, he did. We badly need to find her, to establish just how well she knew Bakstein.'

'No sign of her yet,' Ivans said. 'I suggested we offer reward on the web, but the super vetoed it. He said it might increase the risk to her. Why would he think that?'

Thorneycroft didn't answer. His mind had jumped a gear. He got to his feet.

'I need you to check something,' he said. 'Jack Langley has a wife named Sybilla. She was married before and has a son by the marriage. I need to have copies of the certificates of the marriage and the birth.'

'Piece of cake,' Ivans said. 'One of the lads can go to Somerset House and get what you want.'

'Thanks.' Thorneycroft was on his way to the door when a thought occurred to him. 'Is Nosey Turner in the building?'

Ivans shook his head. 'He's in Scotland. His sister died and he went up for the funeral. He's taken some leave, to help her family sort things out.'

'When will he be back?'

'In a few days. You need something urgently?'

'Not really. It'll keep.'

Thorneycroft headed for Dysart's desk in the incidents room. 'How did you fare on the Cousins issue?' he asked.

'Stalemate,' Dysart said gloomily. 'Bakstein worked with Cousins and Rosa Hopewell and we can't reach either of them. Cousins is locked in the nuclear proliferation talks in Seattle, and won't be back here for a couple of days. The super is putting pressure on the Foreign Office to expedite his return, but they're playing hard to get. As for Rosa Hopewell, we've not found a trace of her, despite our all-station alert.'

'Ivans told me she owned a carpet shop in Isfahan, before her marriage. She lived in Iran, possibly learned the language. It could be her job is to translate documents from Iran. Iran opened a new nuclear development facility last year, and still hasn't signed the Non-proliferation Treaty.'

'So?'

'Let's surmise that Rosa received information about Iran's nuclear intentions. She handed the information to Bakstein, who tried to communicate it to Cousins, but was shot dead before he could do so. It explains why Bakstein was shot, and why Rosa's in fear of her life. She knows what Bakstein knew ... and what we need to know.'

'Which is why we're making every effort to find her.'

'We haven't offered a reward. Ivans said he suggested it, but the super turned it down.'

'Rightly so. For one thing, a reward has to be approved in principle by the proper authorities before an offer can be made. For another, a reward offer could increase the danger to Mrs Hopewell. We publish the offer, some clot tells the press he's seen her at such-and-such a place and the killer gets to her before we do.'

'I'm not suggesting a big public appeal. The reward should be funded by someone outside of the police. I imagine Liz Cupar would be prepared to put up the money, and her lawyers could make the offer. They'd make it to just one person, Rosa's assistant, Maisie Banning. She's a tough cookie with an eye to the main chance. She won't gab about the reward, for fear of competition. It's worth a try. I could speak to Liz, sound her out.'

Dysart stared at Thorneycroft. 'You're proposing that we bribe Maisie Banning to turn in her boss.'

'Not "we". Liz's lawyers offer an inducement to Maisie to help us find a woman who's in danger of assassination. If that's not legally kosher, the lawyers won't do it.'

'You're a chancer.'

'Loose cannon,' Thorneycroft agreed.

'Get out of here before you corrupt the whole team,' Dysart said, but he was smiling.

On reaching home, Thorneycroft put through a call to Liz Cupar and explained his idea to her. She agreed at once to funding a reward. 'Tell me the amount and I'll send you the money.'

'First,' cautioned Thorneycroft, 'I need your lawyer's consent to the deal. They can make the offer on behalf of Cornwall Electronics, your name needn't feature in it at all.'

'I'll talk to them at once, and let you know what they say. Thank you, John, for giving me this opportunity. It's good to feel I can make some contribution.'

The senior partner in the legal firm retained by Cornwall Electronics called Thorneycroft two hours later.

'I've spoken to Ms Banning,' he said. 'She wouldn't admit to knowing where Mrs Hopewell is hiding, but she undertook to try to get a message to her, urging her to put herself under police protection.'

'How much will that cost you?'

'Oh, we didn't talk in terms of cash. I suggested we sponsor Roxanne's next fashion parade in a minor way. My wife will go to Friday's show and buy a caftan or two. Provided, of course, that we are able to find Mrs Hopewell.'

'A win-win situation.'

'Exactly. Goodnight, Dr Thorneycroft.'

Thorneycroft reflected that Rosa Hopewell would now be under pressure from two sources: DS Frank's father, and Liz Cupar's lawyers. That might well persuade her to come to the police ... unless, of course, she was already dead.

XIX

THORNEYCROFT'S BEDSIDE PHONE rang at seven o'clock the next morning. The caller was Ivans, talking fast.

'I have something very interesting to report. I can't discuss it on the phone. The super and Dysart are on their way here and I have some things to do before they arrive. Can you come in asap?'

Thorneycroft dressed, asked the Bladen guard to see to his own and Gatsby's breakfast, and drove to Greenwich. Superintendent Buxton and Dysart were already in Ivans's office, and as Thorneycroft joined them, Ivans handed him a clip of certificates.

'Your hunch about Sybilla Langley paid off, sir,' he said. 'Before she married Jack Langley, she was Mrs Thomas Moorland. They had one son, Eric. You'll see that his birth certificate lists him as Eric Romney Moorland. His grandfather was Rubin Romney, the jeweller, and Thomas Moorland was in the same trade. Moorland died young of a heart attack, and a year later Sybilla married Jack Langley. Eric Moorland was Langley's adopted son.'

As Thorneycroft looked mystified, Dysart intervened.

'Eric Moorland was the nuclear physicist who was kidnapped and murdered by bandits in the Middle East, eight years ago. You must remember the case? The bandits kidnapped Moorland and two other scientists. They were on a lecture tour of Middle Eastern countries. They were captured on their way to Baghdad.'

Thorneycroft nodded slowly. 'I do remember. I was in Denver when it happened, doing a course on forensic pathology. There was a report in one of the newspapers, but I was closeted in my study group at the time, and I didn't pay the story much attention. Soon after it broke, the Americans launched their attack on Iraq, and that wiped everything else off the news pages. I must say, I didn't connect Langley to Moorland when I spoke to him yesterday. How does this affect our investigation?'

'Straws in the wind,' Superintendent Buxton said. 'Moorland was a nuclear scientist. He worked at nuclear power development for thirteen years. Then he broke from research work, and took to the lecture route. He made a name for himself as a speaker and wrote articles for the scientific and popular journals. He was already a rich man through his inheritance from his Romney granddad, and his father. The lectures merely swelled the coffers.'

'The money made him a target for kidnappers?'

'Exactly. The other two scientists were also well-heeled. Jefferson Wheeler was an American agronomist, and Michael Coolidge was an Australian expert on water conservation and desalination. They were warned it was crazy to make the trip at that time; the Iraqi war was imminent, and the Arab states were in turmoil. They didn't listen, they made the trip and were kidnapped on their way to Baghdad.

'The kidnappers demanded a ransom of £15 million. £5 million for each of the three victims. Jack Langley undertook to co-ordinate the collection of the money, and he achieved the full amount very fast; but before it could be paid, the Iraqi war erupted, and two days later, all three captives were shot execution-style by the kidnappers.'

'Why?' Thorneycroft was startled. 'Why did they kill the captives before they'd made sure of the ransom money?'

'Probably they saw that the war was going to make it very difficult to lay their hands on the money. My own view is that the murders were an act of revenge against the nations that were attacking Iraq. The murders were a result of the politics of the time.'

'The kidnapping happened eight years ago. Why do you connect it with the present investigation?'

'Moorland and his companions were murdered because they were citizens of countries that supported the attack on Iraq, and vocally opposed the proliferation of weapons of mass destruction.

Bakstein also vigorously opposed the proliferation of nuclear arms. Moorland and Bakstein were both nuclear physicists.'

'That may be so, but Trevor Cornwall had nothing to do with nuclear physics, or weapons of mass destruction.'

'Cornwall did support Britain's participation in the Iraqi War.'

'As did thousands … millions … of other people in Britain.'

'They weren't mega-rich, internationally influential citizens. Cornwall may have been killed as a warning to other magnates not to interfere in Middle Eastern controversies.'

Thorneycroft shrugged. 'It seems a weak argument to me, but it's true that a mad killer acts on mad premises. You say Langley collected the £15 million ransom money. That's a lot of cash. What happened to it after the captives were shot?'

The superintendent said, 'It was placed in trust, I believe. Ivans will chase up all those details.'

Dysart, who had been examining the certificates supplied by Ivans, looked up. 'We'll have to talk to Jack Langley again. It's strange he never mentioned his son's death to you. He must have been aware that both Moorland and Bakstein were nuclear physicists – they may well have known each other. They both opposed nuclear arms proliferation. That could have made them targets for a revenge killer. We must check it out.' He turned to Ivans. 'Get all the available information on the three kidnap victims. There may be no connection between their murders and the two present cases, but it's an area we have to examine.'

'I'll lay odds that Kaminsky believes that there's a connection,' Thorneycroft said. 'Why else would he point me to Jack Langley? Out of thousands of British marksmen, why did he choose that one to advise us on this case?'

'Perhaps Kaminsky will explain why he made that choice.'

'He won't. He made it crystal clear that he won't give us any more information. Kaminsky's been muzzled. He's already broken ranks by giving us Langley.'

'And it paid off.' Dysart laid aside the clip of certificates and reached for a telephone. 'I must meet Mr Langley, see what else he hasn't thought to tell us.'

*

Dysart and Thorneycroft drove to the Langleys' home that after-noon. Langley was undismayed by this second visit. As he led the way to his study, he said, 'I can give you more time today than I did yesterday. I've no appointments, and Sybilla and Jane are away, shopping in Epsom.'

There was resignation in his voice, as if he had made up his mind to confront a tiresome problem.

As the three men entered the study, Thorneycroft noticed a colour photograph on Langley's desk. The subject was unmistak-ably Sybilla's son. The same amber-gold eyes, ringed with tawny lashes, glowed at the observer.

Dysart lost no time in broaching the purpose of the visit.

'I'm sorry to raise a subject that must be very painful to you, sir,' he said. 'I'm informed that your son Eric was murdered by kidnappers, eight years ago. He and his two companions were captured, and later shot. They were on their way to give lectures in Turkey. I am trying to discover if there is any connection between that crime and the recent shootings of Mr Trevor Cornwall and Dr Julian Bakstein.'

Langley seemed hardly to hear the last part of what Dysart said. His gaze was fixed on the photograph on the desk. Dysart prompted him.

'It's been suggested that all these killings were inspired by a desire for revenge ... in the case of your son, revenge on the people who waged war on Iraq. Does that seem plausible to you?'

Langley turned slowly to face Dysart. 'Plausible? The men who killed my son and his friends were driven by hatred and blind malice. It happened, but nothing will ever make it seem plausible to me.'

Dysart reddened. 'I'm sorry. It was a foolish word to use. If you can give us the facts of your son's journey to the Middle East, it may help us to prevent more killings.'

'Yes.' Langley drew a deep breath. 'As you probably know, they were warned by the authorities not to attempt the tour. The

Middle East was a tinderbox. Eric and his friends not only chose to ignore the warnings, they opted to drive across Iraq to Turkey. They'd been offered big money for their lectures and they believed they could complete the tour and be home again before the war broke out.

'They delivered their lectures in Israel and Dubai without trouble. They set out for Istanbul, but never arrived there. Their car was found abandoned near Kirkuk. Two days later, the ransom demand arrived.'

'For £15 million?'

'Yes. Five million for each man.'

'How was the demand sent?'

'By devious routes. There was involvement of the British authorities, and authorities in the Middle East, but the lines of communication were very shaky.' Langley ran a hand over his neck. 'The government did its best to get information, and passed it on to me and the families of the other two men, but there wasn't much.'

'Did the kidnappers claim affiliation to any specific group?'

'No, never. The man who was my chief informant said they probably weren't terrorists, just bandits on the make.'

'Who was your chief informant?'

'A Mr Jeremy Cousins, he's with the Foreign Office.'

Dysart paused a moment, making a note. Then he said evenly, 'Are you still in touch with Mr Cousins?'

'Oh no, not for many years. The case was closed. We never knew who was responsible for the murders. We never recovered the bodies.'

'Were there other demands from the kidnappers, after the first one?'

'They sent messages. Threats of what they would do if the ransom wasn't paid. Eric and the other two were moved about from place to place. There was never a chance to locate the kidnappers, or even to determine which country they were in. The video didn't provide any clues.'

'Video?' said Dysart sharply. 'There was a video?'

'Yes.' Langley's face twitched and he pressed his fists against his cheeks. 'After the three men were executed, a video arrived at the Foreign Office. It showed the murders. The men trussed like chickens. Shot in the back of the head. I had the money ready but they never let me pay it. They slaughtered my son and sent those vile pictures.'

Langley fell silent and Dysart waited for him to recover. At last he said quietly, 'Do you have a copy of the video?'

Langley straightened up, eyes blazing. 'No! I would never harbour such filth in my home.' He turned to Thorneycroft. 'I have to think of Sybilla now. You've seen how it is with her. She refuses to believe that Eric is dead. Her mind's broken. I find her talking to space. She thinks she's talking to him.'

'Yes, I've seen,' Thorneycroft said. 'I'm sorry we have to ask questions about things that must be deeply painful for you.'

'I should have told you all this yesterday. I just couldn't bring myself to speak of it. Last night I thought about it and I realized I must tell you about Eric and his friends. If you hadn't phoned, I would have called you. I have to help in any way I can.'

Dysart said, 'You have helped us a great deal, sir. Tell me, what was the official position, after the video was received?'

'Position?'

'Was it accepted as genuine? There was no possibility that it was a fake?'

'None at all. It showed their faces ... Eric, Jefferson Wheeler and Michael Coolidge. It showed them all being shot. There could be no doubt.'

'So their deaths were officially confirmed.'

'Yes.' Langley closed his eyes. He said tiredly, 'People tried to investigate, to get information, but there was none.'

'I'm sorry to ask you this, but what arrangements were made for the ransom money?'

'It was placed in a trust. All the donors were approached and asked to put in a claim for the return of their share of the money. Most of them gave instructions that it be given to the families or dependants of the three men. Sybilla and I had contributed the five million for Eric. We left it in the trust. For Eric, Sybilla said, and I couldn't argue with her. Some day it will be used to create a memorial for him ... a bursary or something useful.'

Dysart was making notes. He will get in touch with the victims' relatives, Thorneycroft thought, to confirm that they agreed to this settlement of the ransom funds. Like Langley, they would have to endure the probing of old wounds.

Dysart laid his pen aside. 'Mr Langley, will you give me a list of the names of those who donated to the fund?'

Langley stiffened. 'No, Chief Inspector, I can't do that. The people who made donations were given an assurance – my personal word – that their names would not be divulged to anyone. There was a natural fear that donors might become targets of the kidnappers.'

'I can assure you that the names would remain confidential.'

'I said no! I gave those people my word, and I won't break it.'

Dysart was not deterred. 'Let me put it another way,' he said. 'Did Dr Bakstein or Mr Cornwall contribute to the ransom fund?'

'I have told you, I will not discuss that matter. I will not risk putting other lives in danger. Is that clear?'

'It is.' Dysart closed his notebook and Thorneycroft saw that he was on the point of ending the interview. He said quickly, 'Your son and Julian Bakstein were both nuclear physicists. Did they know each other?'

Langley made a visible effort to recover his calm. He said, 'They had met, of course. Each of them was prominent in his particular area of nuclear science, but they never worked together. Eric thought Bakstein an old fusspot.'

'Fusspot?'

'A hot-air balloon, always rabbiting on about some minor point of procedure, full of old-fashioned notions. They met at conferences but they seldom saw eye to eye. Bakstein was a difficult man; quarrelsome, a loner.'

'Unlike your son?'

'They were chalk and cheese. Eric was creative. When he first qualified, he concentrated on designing nuclear facilities, research stations, power stations and the like. Later he turned to lecturing on nuclear physics. He believed science should be made understandable to ordinary folk. He was good at doing that; people flocked to his lectures. There were always plenty of organizations eager to provide him with a platform.'

'I understand you married your wife Sybilla when Eric was five. Did you formally adopt him?'

'Yes, I did.'

'Yet he retained the Moorland surname?'

'That was to please Sybilla. Eric was left a great deal of money by his grandfather, Rubin Romney, and also by his father Thomas Moorland. Eric was christened Eric Romney Moorland. Sybilla held that their names should endure.'

Langley glanced at the faces confronting him, and smiled. 'I didn't mind that Eric didn't bear my surname. He was my son. That was what I wanted. I wanted him to be my son, but himself. His own man.'

'He didn't pursue your career.'

No. He said guns were for people who couldn't earn a living any other way. That was a good description of his murderers, wasn't it? Unreasoning, brutish people, contemptuous of the rights of others. I retired from competition after Eric died. I couldn't get it out of my mind that a bullet ended his life.'

The sadness in Langley's voice had sharpened to anger. He looked from Dysart to Thorneycroft. 'You believe that Eric was the victim of a revenge killing, because we invaded Iraq. So be it. Let his death be avenged. Let his killers be brought to justice. You are the instruments of justice, do your work. I will help you in any way I can.'

There was no more to be said. Langley accompanied them to the parked police car.

'You'll keep me informed?' he said.

'We will,' Dysart replied.

Driving away from the house, Thorneycroft thought of the rooms kept ready for a man who was never going to return, of Sybilla talking to a ghost, of Jack Langley whose life had been so brutally disfigured.

'He's had eight years of hell,' he said.

'He has.' Dysart's eyes were cold. 'He's lost his son, and his wife, too, in a sense. He's never had closure. That's enough to turn a man into a killer.'

Thorneycroft was disconcerted. 'Surely you don't suspect Langley of the murders? What possible motive could he have for shooting Bakstein and Cornwall?'

'None that I know of, yet, but what I do know is that Langley is full of killing rage. You're a psychiatrist, you must recognize the signs.'

'Yes, but I also recognize the pain that causes the rage.'

'And rage may trigger violence. Langley has all the skills shown by the perpetrator of these crimes; he's a crack shot, he lays plans and carries them out;. he has access to weapons and ammunition, he's rich enough to buy a Cougar III, or to hire a hit man if need be.'

'That's circumstantial, Iain. There could be hundreds of people with the same skills and attributes.'

Dysart's jaw set. 'I also know that Langley is withholding information. He didn't tell us all *he* knows.'

'He was cooperative except in his refusal to name the donors to the ransom fund, and in that he was simply keeping a promise.'

'Withholding information can cost an innocent victim his life. Langley's suffered, that doesn't mean we have to defend him blindly, does it?'

'No, of course not.' Thorneycroft was silent for a space, then he said, 'I think we should have asked him if there were people who refused to give to the ransom fund. If Bakstein or Cornwall refused, that could have engendered deep resentment in Langley. He might have believed that if the money had been collected more quickly, it could have been paid to the kidnappers before the Iraq war broke. We know Bakstein was mean about money. He refused to help a sick colleague at Clunbury, because he disliked the man.'

'Right, then, that could be Langley's motive for murder. He killed a man who he felt contributed to his son's death.'

'That might apply to Bakstein, but I can't imagine that if Trevor was asked for a donation, he'd have refused. He was the most generous of men.'

'He was also a stickler for the rules. Those three scientists had been warned not to make the tour. They made it at their own risk. A lot of people believe that paying a ransom will encourage other kidnappers to try their hand. Cornwall could have felt it was wrong to give to the fund.'

'I'll try to discover if Bakstein and Trevor were approached for donations, and what their response was.'

'How will you do that? No use asking the trust. Langley heads it.'

'I'll speak to the people who were close to Bakstein and Trevor, see if they can recall anything about the ransom appeal. But to be honest, the only link I can see between the kidnapping of Eric Moorland, and our present investigations, is the fact that Jeremy Cousins of the Foreign Office figures in both. Eight years ago Cousins was the government's link with Jack Langley. Recently, he's been in cahoots with Julian Bakstein.'

'Cousins has a lot of explaining to do,' said Dysart grimly. 'I'll be talking to him as soon as he sets foot in England.'

Thorneycroft called Liz right away, and asked her if her father had donated money to the ransom fund for Moorland and his two companions.

'I've no idea,' she said. 'He didn't like talking about his donations; he believed charity must be private, no self-advertisement. I'll ask Larry Taylor, he handled all Dad's personal donations. It may take a while, to go back eight years, I'll let you know as soon as I can.'

Thorneycroft's next calls were to the Clunbury research centre, They were not fruitful.

Mark Bellows, when asked if Bakstein had contributed to the ransom fund for the three kidnapped men, answered snappishly that he had no information on the matter. Pressed further, he announced that he was extremely busy, and cut the connection.

Professor Howard was more polite. 'I'm afraid I don't know what Julian did or didn't do in that regard. Staff members gave from their personal funds, without disclosure to anyone.'

Thorneycroft concluded that Howard was evasive as a matter of policy.

Given the responses of the Clunbury men, Dysart grunted.

'They don't want to be involved,' he said. 'The bell tolls for other people, not for them.' He leaned back in his chair. 'I've been thinking, money's the motive for most violent crimes. Once Moorland's death was officially confirmed, the ransom money was released from trust and returned to the donors. The Langleys left their five million where it was. Langley told us it hasn't been touched, but five million is enough to make a man change his mind, don't you agree?'

As Thorneycroft made no answer, Dysart continued. 'I'll be having that trust fund checked. We'll see if all the donors got their money back. And we'll ask Mr Cousins what he knows about Jack Langley. Cousins is due back tomorrow evening so we don't have long to wait.'

That remark apparently tempted Fate too far, for at that moment the telephone at Dysart's elbow set up a clamour. He took up the receiver and listened in silence, his face darkening. Finally he uttered a brief thanks and hung up.

'That,' he said, 'was my FO pal. He tells me that flight control at New York received an anonymous tip-off that there was a bomb on the plane due to bring a bunch of nuclear scientists back to Europe. The informant said the bomb was due to explode when the plane was over the Atlantic. A lot of flights have been cancelled, and the US authorities are holding the passengers and crew of the bomb-threat plane for questioning.'

'Cousins among them?' asked Thorneycroft.

'Cousins among them,' Dysart replied.

XX

THE STORY OF the bomb threat to the Seattle flight hit the headlines next morning. Thorneycroft bought a selection of newspapers on his way to work, and laid them on Dysart's desk.

The more sedate publications were guarded in their reports, but the sensation seekers published pictures of scientists scrambling from the aircraft, and hinted at terrorist attacks on countries opposing the proliferation of nuclear arms.

'Now we'll have a diplomatic meltdown,' Dysart growled. 'The Yanks will hyperventilate about another 9/11, and their security buffs will be suspicious of anyone who was within a hundred miles of that airport. It'll be days before we get to talk to Cousins.' He pushed the papers aside. 'Clunbury,' he said. 'They must know if Bakstein subscribed to the ransom fund, or not.'

'Bellows and Howard professed ignorance.' Thorneycroft considered the picture on the front page of the *New York Times*. 'But you're right. A bomb threat must have given them thought.'

He reached for his mobile and called Mark Bellows's office number. Bellows answered at once, and his voice was tremulous.

'Dr Thorneycroft, I'm very glad you called. When we spoke yesterday, I wasn't very forthcoming, I'm afraid.'

You lied through your teeth, Thorneycroft thought, but he made placatory noises and Bellows continued:

'I saw on *Sky News* this morning that Jeremy Cousins was on a plane that had a bomb on board. Is that true?'

'Cousins was on a flight back from Seattle. There's been no official confirmation that there was a bomb on the plane. It could have been a hoax call.'

'But the flight was grounded. That means the officials are taking the threat seriously. I must talk to you. Not here, not on the phone. Can we meet somewhere else? London, say?'

Thorneycroft fanned the flame of Bellows's panic. 'I have a heavy work programme. Does your concern relate to my call regarding Dr Bakstein?'

'Yes. Yes, I have information. I should have given it to you. I can come up to London today. I'll say that I need to order equipment.'

'Well, if it's urgent, I could give you an hour at lunch time. Where do you obtain your equipment?'

'Raeburn's, in Earl's Court.'

'Then let's meet there. That way, your sudden visit to town will seem routine ... should anyone be watching your movements.'

'Watching me?' Bellows's voice rose an octave. 'God, I never thought of that. We're all at risk....'

'Can you make lunch time at Raeburn's?'

'Yes. I'll leave here at once.'

'Will they admit me to the premises?'

'Oh yes. It's not classified equipment, just ordinary laboratory stuff. I'll tell them to expect us. We can talk in one of their rooms. Thank you, Thorneycroft, I'm much obliged....'

'One o'clock at Raeburn's,' Thorneycroft said, and rang off. Dysart looked at him inquiringly, and he said,

'Mark Bellows has caught the bomb scare stories, and he's scared silly. Yesterday he told me he didn't know anything about Bakstein's response to the ransom demand. Now he wants to tell all.'

'He should have come straight to us,' Dysart said.

'He should, but I think he finds me less intimidating than HM's finest. I'll tape the interview.'

'If he agrees to that.'

'He will. He's been uneasy from the start, about the way Clunbury's handling Bakstein's murder. Remember how he tried to speak out the first time we interviewed them, but Howard shut him up? The bomb scare has convinced him he's on the killer's short list. He'll babble like a brook.'

'I don't like off-the-record chats,' Dysart said, 'but do it your way. If anything goes wrong, I'll feed you to the super.'

Raeburn's Laboratory Equipment was an unimposing building on the fringe of Earl's Court. Thorneycroft arrived early for his appointment, and was shown to a small room furnished with a table, hard chairs and piles of order forms.

Mark Bellows arrived on time, out of breath and apologetic. His normally florid face was pale, and the hand he offered to Thorneycroft was cold and clammy.

Dumping a briefcase on the table, he said, 'Thank you for coming, Doctor. I made a mistake yesterday. I shouldn't have listened to Professor Howard. He has this idea that one must not discuss Clunbury affairs with anyone, ever. He said that if ever you called me I must say nothing about Bakstein. I see now that that's wrong. Bakstein's death involves us all. I'm sorry.'

Thorneycroft nodded. 'You're here now, that's a positive move. Why did the bomb scare make you change your mind?'

'I realized that Bakstein's death, and the bomb on Cousins's plane are linked. Bakstein and Cousins were both targets for a killer because of their job, and that means that all of us at Clunbury are in danger, doesn't it?'

'It's a possibility,' Thorneycroft lifted his tape recorder from its carry-bag and placed it on the table.

'I need to record this interview, Dr Bellows. Do you have any objection to that?'

'None at all. I want to assist you, any way I can.'

Thorneycroft switched on the recorder and made the formal introduction, stating his own and Bellows's names, and the time and place of the interview. That done, he said,

'Let's take this one step at a time. You've said that Bakstein and Cousins were both targeted by a killer because of their job. Cousins isn't a nuclear scientist. What do they have in common, workwise?'

'I meant, they are both ... Bakstein was bitterly opposed to the proliferation of nuclear farms, and that's the main purpose of Cousin's job.'

'You're talking of illicit arms proliferation?'

'Yes, by terrorists, or some rogue producer.'

'What makes you say Cousins was the target on that plane? There were dozens of nuclear physicists aboard it.'

'Jeremy Cousins is the government watchdog for Clunbury,' Bellows said. 'Because we're involved in nuclear research, we need to be kept informed of nuclear development around the world – any activity that could contribute to the success of our work, or endanger it. We have to be warned about unprincipled competitors, theft of ideas or equipment, breaches of international law and outright terrorist threats.

'Cousins is our link man, and when Bakstein was at Clunbury he was our link with Cousins. They worked closely together. After Bakstein retired from Clunbury, he kept in touch with Cousins and with us. He was a sort of unofficial go-between.' Bellows broke off, biting his lip. 'I don't want to breach Clunbury's confidence, by idle talk.'

Thorneycroft spread his hands. 'The police are investigating a double murder. I'm part of the investigating team. Our discussion here is not idle talk. My questions should be answered quickly and truthfully.'

'Yes, you're right. It's just ... hard to break the customary rules.'

'Dr Bellows, are you personally against the creation, stockpiling and use of illicit nuclear arms?'

'Of course I am, as are all of us at Clunbury.'

'Has the illicit activity increased?'

'It has.' Bellows seemed to relax a little. Leaning back in his chair, he said, 'The building of nuclear arms has accelerated over the past decade. We know that several nations have developed nuclear powers. We can't be sure if their intentions are for peace or war. Iran continues to enrich uranium, North Korea has launched nuclear missiles. There's cause for grave concern.'

'What was Dr Bakstein's view of the situation?'

'He was ... ambivalent. On the one hand he castigated the renegade scientists who are helping countries that won't conform to the NPT aims. On the other hand he insisted that every effort must be made to win over the countries in the Non-aligned Movement by diplomatic means, and not by punitive sanctions.'

'But in general he was opposed to the proliferation of nuclear arms?'

'Oh yes, vehemently. He said it would lead to World War III.'

'What about Cousins? What was his stance on the matter?'

Bellows tucked in his chin and his expression became cagey. 'You must ask him that question, not me.'

'Aren't all our government authorities against nuclear arms?'

'God, no! There are some who swear that the only way to prevent nuclear war is to possess nuclear arms. They're convinced that owning an atom or hydrogen bomb will discourage others from launching a nuclear attack.'

'Better armed to the teeth than a toothless tiger?'

'So some think. Owning nuclear arms makes them feel safe, but other countries, like Iran for instance, feel threatened because they don't have nuclear arms. There are also those fanatics who may take it into their heads to launch a nuclear attack. The victim responds in kind, and planet Earth becomes a desert.'

'You've said that after retiring from Clunbury, Bakstein kept in touch with the people there. Did he, in the days preceding his murder, express anxiety about anything?'

'No, I'm sure not. We've discussed that point thoroughly. I assure you that neither Bakstein nor Cousins has given us any hint of trouble, or danger. Bakstein always played his cards close to his chest. He liked to claim the kudos for success. He was a control freak.'

'Like Ozymandias?' Thorneycroft suggested. 'Dr Bellows, at our first meeting you told me that you didn't get on with Bakstein. You mentioned that he refused to subscribe to a fund for the Desai family, and that you took him to task.'

'I did.' Bellows's jaw protruded. 'I called him a mean bastard, which he was.'

'Was he too mean to contribute to the ransom fund for Eric Moorland and his companions?'

The question caught Bellows off guard. He shifted uneasily in his chair. 'Yes,' he said at last. 'He refused to contribute a penny to the fund. He said Moorland and the others had been told not to go on that tour, they'd brought their capture on themselves. He said that paying the ransom would set a precedent for other kidnappings. Finally he said that Moorland wasn't worth such a huge amount of money, that his boastful ways had caused a bunch of criminals to think he was at the top of his profession, which he wasn't.'

'Did Bakstein make these views public?'

'He did indeed, and in the most disgraceful way. Moorland's father, Jack Langley, came to Clunbury to make an appeal for donations to the fund. Most of us gave what we could, but Bakstein stood up at the meeting and gave his reasons for not donating. He virtually told Langley that his son wasn't worth saving. Langley was deeply distressed and angered. He left the centre without allowing anyone to apologize for Bakstein's remarks.'

'Did Bakstein and Moorland know each other?'

'They did, and they hated each other. Bakstein held that Moorland prostituted his scientific knowledge by giving popular lectures. He said a patriot didn't throw hard-won knowledge to people who were no better than scavenging dogs. In a way he was right, there. Moorland struck lecture deals with anyone who would pay his fee. He claimed that ordinary folk have the right to be informed about scientific matters.'

'Do you believe that's true?'

'Well, yes, I do; but the fact is, Bakstein and Moorland were temperamentally poles apart. Moorland was an opportunist. He put himself first. Bakstein was an idealist. He didn't care a damn for popularity or wealth, I'll say that for him.'

'You say they hated each other. Hate's a strong word.... Reasonable people can generally come to terms with people they dislike.'

Bellows waved a dismissive hand. 'It wasn't just a matter of dislike. They differed fundamentally, they clashed on every subject. The only thing they had in common was that they were both nuclear physicists.'

'Did you like Moorland?'

'I didn't know him well. He didn't work at Clunbury. The times we met, I found him stimulating, amusing company. Easy to get on with.'

'Which Bakstein wasn't.'

'No. It was impossible to get on with him. No one liked him. But he was not an Ozymandias, just an unlikeable curmudgeon.'

'You say Bakstein and Moorland clashed. How was that, if they didn't work together?'

'They fought publicly, at conventions, at scientific meetings, in the media.'

'That's not uncommon. Experts clash with other experts.'

Bellows shrugged, tight-lipped, and Thorneycroft knew that they'd reached the end of that topic.

'You've suggested that Bakstein was murdered, and Cousins was exposed to a bomb threat, because of their stance in halting the proliferation of nuclear arms. What I'm trying to do now is establish whether there are other possible motives for Bakstein's murder. His refusal to give to the ransom fund must have roused strong feelings in a great many people. There may be other of his actions that caused people to dislike, or even hate him.'

'There were.'

'Such as?'

'Bakstein made no secret of the fact that he outshone all of us. He treated us like retarded schoolchildren. He also tried to impose his theories and codes on everyone. He had the most inflated ego of anyone I ever met.'

'Yet he was respected, even revered.'

'Yes.' Bellows stared into space. 'He ... he had a feel for the universe. Its laws, mysteries, possibilities. He was capable of carrying vast development plans in his head, all the ramifications and pitfalls. It's hard to explain. He could do things that seemed impossible. He was a giant. Unfortunately he made the rest of us look like pygmies.'

Bellows warmed to his theme. 'Another thing, he had an incredible memory. He could remember formulae and figures as if he had a computer in his brain. He could recognize who was responsible for a statement made years back, even if it was published under a pseudonym. He had a trick of accusing scientists of plagiarism if they used material originated by another man or woman.'

'An uncomfortable trick. Did he ever accuse anyone at Clunbury of plagiarism?'

Bellows's face darkened. 'Oh yes. He accused me, once, of stealing another man's work. I was able to prove that I'd asked the man's permission to use his research results to illustrate a paper I was working on.'

'Did Bakstein ever accuse Eric Moorland of plagiarism?'

'Yes. Moorland wrote an article in which he quoted material established by Ilse Watsek, without giving her credit. Bakstein wrote to the scientific journal that published Moorland's article, citing the sections that he said plagiarized Watzek's work.'

'What was the outcome?'

'Moorland explained that he had had a relationship with Ilse years before. He was able to show that before she died of kidney disease, she gave him the rights to her published and unpublished work. There was an enormous row and some scandal; it was that episode that decided Moorland to abandon research and construction work, and go over to public lecturing.'

'Which eventually took him to the Middle East and his death.'

Bellows frowned. 'I suppose one might say so, but he was warned not to make that tour. He got what he asked for.'

Thorneycroft thought of Jack and Sybilla Langley. They might well have hated Bakstein, for his criticism of their son, and his total lack of compassion for him and the other two men executed by terrorists.

'Stupidity doesn't justify murder,' he said. 'How did Bakstein react to the news that the captives had been shot execution style?'

'I don't know. He was away in Australia when it happened.'

'One last question,' Thorneycroft said. 'I've heard that Bakstein was patriotic to the point of jingoism. That could have been a cover. Do you think he would have been prepared to sell his phenomenal knowledge to illicit buyers?'

Bellows looked shocked. 'No. Never. I've said a lot of unpleasant things about him, but he was devoted to this country. He worked on difficult projects, under very arduous conditions, and never expected extra reward or praise.'

Bellows was becoming defensive, and Thorneycroft decided it was time to wind down the interview. He said, 'Dr Bellows, what you have told me is important, and helpful. Thank you for your cooperation.'

Bellows gave a brief nod. 'Will we be provided with protection against this killer?' he asked. 'Everyone at Clunbury must be at risk.'

'DCI Dysart has already arranged for your local police and your own security guards to keep watch over Clunbury.'

'But this man is a crack shot, he could operate from beyond our security fences. He could—'

Thorneycroft said quietly, 'I don't think you are any more at risk than thousands of scientists around the world. The best protection is to identify the killer and lock him away in a maximum security prison. Your information will help us do that.'

Bellows smiled weakly. 'I must sound very cowardly. I wonder if Raeburn's supply bullet-proof vests.'

'Nobody who works with radioactive materials can be called a coward,' Thorneycroft said. He spoke the formal sentences that concluded the interview and switched off the tape recorder.

They walked together to the street and parted there, Bellows to return to Clunbury, Thorneycroft to drive to Greenwich. On the journey he received a phone call from Dysart.

'Good news,' the DCI said. 'Cousins is back in England. The FO claims he's suffering from shock and can't be interviewed, but the super's called that bluff. Cousins will make his report to his superiors tonight, and tomorrow he's all ours. How did you go with Bellows?'

'I think you'll be pleased,' Thorneycroft said. 'He told me Bakstein hated Eric Moorland and refused to give a penny to the ransom fund. He refused publicly, and belittled Moorland's abilities to his father's face.'

'So Jack Langley had a motive for murder,' Dysart said.

'Langley, and the relatives of the two other men who were murdered and probably dozens of other friends and colleagues. And why would any of them wait eight years to take revenge?'

'Time will tell,' said Dysart complacently. 'Time will tell.'

XXI

JEREMY COUSINS PUT Thorneycroft in mind of processed cheese. His face was wedge-shaped, creamy-pale and moist, and the hair combed neatly from a centre parting was yellow-white. He was dressed in holiday mode, baggy shorts, a Hawaiian shirt and straw sandals. His pale blue eyes regarded Thorneycroft and Dysart with dislike. The FO cream was decidedly sour.

'Officially I am still on leave,' he announced as he waved them into his office. 'I can't spare you much time. I'm off to Clunbury in two hours, to make my report on the Seattle conference.'

He gave Thorneycroft a tight-lipped smile. 'One is thankful to see you on the investigating team, Doctor. I've followed your career with interest. Crime work is so much more sophisticated, these days. Technology has replaced Constable Plod ... no offence to you, Chief Inspector. One just feels that solving the murder of Julian Bakstein demands all available forensic skills.'

Thorneycroft wondered if the prat was attempting to drive a wedge between him and Dysart, but he was reassured when Dysart said affably,

'I know you're anxious to get to Clunbury, Mr Cousins, so let's not waste time. Can you begin by explaining why the authorities at Seattle failed to give you Superintendent Buxton's urgent messages relating to the murder of Dr Bakstein?'

Cousins's mouth contracted to a peevish button. 'It was the fault of the American convenors,' he said. 'They decreed that the delegates should not be interrupted in their deliberations. The conference halls were under siege from day one ... a mass of media representatives, not to mention several hundred demonstrators who made repeated attempts to break through the security cordons. US security is inclined to overreact. When they heard that Bakstein had been shot, they went ballistic. They were sure it was the forerunner of another 9/11. To do them justice, there are constant attacks on American citizens, and it's hard to distinguish between a bunch of lunatic demonstrators, and organized hardline terrorists.'

Dysart nodded. 'With regard to the bomb scare on your plane, I'm informed it was found to be a hoax.'

Cousins examined his fingernails. 'Yes. Apparently it was the work of a group calling themselves the Earthsavers. They staged their little joke very neatly. The media was told of the supposed bomb in the hold of our plane, just minutes before it was due to take off. We were all hustled off the airfield to what was termed a place of safety. We were kept in virtual detention for hours. They took their time about announcing that it was a hoax.'

'A section of the media trumpeted the tale that there was a bomb on board, due to explode over the Atlantic. Stirring stuff.'

'Mere thumbsucking. There was no bomb.' Cousins looked pointedly at his watch, and Dysart said briskly,

'That point cleared, we can move to my real concern, which is the murder of Dr Bakstein. I take it you know that he spent the last two days of his life desperately trying to get hold of you?'

'I know it. You must understand that Seattle was a top-level conference. We had a lot of vital discussions in process. We were not allowed to take mobile phones into the conference areas. The convenors wished to prevent our being harassed by outsiders, and they also needed to prevent any leakage of information from the conference to the outside world.'

'Understandable.' Dysart leaned forward in his chair. 'I believe you are the government's link man with the Clunbury Research Centre?'

'I am.'

'What does that entail?'

'I keep the Clunbury people in the loop. Inform them of nuclear developments around the globe, advise them of new techniques and improvements in methodology. I also keep our government up to date with whatever Clunbury is doing.'

'Does that include warning them of illegal nuclear activity by countries outside of the Non-proliferation Treaty?'

Thorneycroft noted that, at this question, Cousins folded his arms across his chest, classic body-language of unwillingness to answer. Cousins took his time about answering.

'Naturally I inform Clunbury of any such activity. We don't withhold information from our experts, Chief Inspector. It's vital to keep them advised of everything that occurs in their field, good or bad.'

'Vitally important,' Dysart agreed. 'So I assume you instructed the organizers at the Seattle conference that a message from Bakstein, or any other of our nuclear experts, must be conveyed to you at once?'

Anger sparked in Cousins's eyes, and he fiddled with a paper-weight on his desk. 'I did so instruct them. Unfortunately my orders were not complied with. I have explained the circumstances obtaining at the conference.'

'So you have.' Dysart made a note on the pad before him. 'Have you received information from any source that reveals why Bakstein wished to talk to you?'

'No I have not.'

'So you have no idea what he considered important enough to warrant his breaking the conference barrier of silence?'

'I have no idea what he wanted. None at all.'

'And he was shot dead before he could communicate with you?'

'Yes.' A faint colour suffused Cousins's pale cheeks. 'I don't know why he was shot, and I cannot think why he failed to speak to someone else in this office. If he had important information, one of my colleagues could perfectly well have dealt with the problem.'

'Perhaps he trusted you, and was not sure he could trust your colleagues.'

Cousins made no reply, and Dysart's smooth smile became tigerish. 'Dr Bakstein worked closely with you, even after his retirement from Clunbury, did he not?'

'He kept in touch, yes.'

'Two days before he was murdered, he phoned this office, asking for you. He was told you were on leave, attending the Seattle conference. He refused to speak to anyone else. After he was murdered, Superintendent Buxton tried to reach you in Seattle, but you didn't receive his messages. Is that correct?'

'I have told you, it was due to—'

'Official stupidity, yes, which may have resulted in Bakstein's death. He had something important to convey to you, something he would not consider discussing with any of your colleagues. He tried to reach you, but failed. The delays gave the killer time to silence him before he could speak to you.'

Cousins's hands trembled and he clasped them together. 'There is no proof that his information, if there was any, was important. Bakstein was a fusspot, always trying to intervene in matters that didn't concern him.'

Dysart's eyes glinted. 'Like, for instance our government's policy towards the nuclear ambitions of the non-aligned nations? I understand he vigorously opposed illicit efforts to achieve nuclear power.'

'He opposed such efforts, but there isn't a jot of evidence that that is what Bakstein wished to discuss with me.'

'I agree. We don't yet know if his problem was of national importance, or just the niggling of a fusspot. It's my job to try to establish which it was.'

'And how will you do that? Bakstein's dead.' Cousins was waxy pale, and sweat shone on his forehead. Dysart watched him coldly.

'You worked closely with Dr Bakstein. Was Mrs Rosa Hopewell also part of your team? Did you use her as a translator of material relating to nuclear physics?'

Cousins hesitated, then waved a negligent hand. 'I employed her as a translator from time to time. I myself am fluent in German, French and Italian, but for other languages I need efficient translators. They aren't easy to find. They have to be politically trustworthy as well as skilled linguists.'

'Does Mrs Hopewell fit that bill?'

'She does. She's a Sri Lankan by birth, but she's acquired a number of Middle Eastern languages. She's one of those people to whom languages come easily.'

'What exactly does she translate?'

'Scientific reports, articles from foreign newspapers, the sort of humdrum stuff that keeps us in touch with nuclear activities elsewhere in the world.'

Dysart was silent for a space, apparently referring to his notes. Raising his head he said, 'Do you employ Mrs Hopewell as an intelligence agent, Mr Cousins?'

'No, certainly not! I am not a spy. I am an information officer. As for Mrs Hopewell, she has no training for such work, and no wish to undertake it. She simply translates a stack of dull material relating to nuclear physics.'

'Dr Bakstein was acquainted with Mrs Hopewell, wasn't he? He was a good customer of her shop, Roxanne's, in Sloane Street. He liked to dress like an Eastern potentate. Did he also read Mrs Hopewell's translations?'

Cousins glared. 'Yes. What of it? He was incredibly thorough in keeping up with what was happening in his field. He read everything from official reports to the gossip columns of foreign publications.'

'Are you aware that Mrs Hopewell has ... disappeared?'

'Yes I am, and it's imperative that we find her. I'm told she took flight when Bakstein was shot. My office has been making every effort to reach her at her known addresses, without success.'

'Why are you so anxious to find her?'

'Well, naturally, she's our employee, we are all concerned about her.'

'Concerned for her safety? Do you think she's in danger?'

'No, I don't. We're concerned because she's evidently terrified. It's our job to reassure her, and if necessary to provide her with protection until the assassin has been apprehended and locked up ... and that is your job, Chief Inspector, not mine.'

'Quite,' said Dysart smoothly. 'We're as anxious as you are to find and protect Mrs Hopewell. We believe she may be able to shed light on what was causing Bakstein such concern. She could be a key witness in this murder case.'

Cousins stabbed a finger at Dysart. 'May I remind you that Mrs Hopewell has a citizen's rights. If she decides to return to her normal way of life, my office will be at hand to look after her.'

'If she comes to you.'

'She will, and we will see that she is not subjected to harassment by police interrogators.'

Dysart smiled. 'We have work to do, sir, and we will do it without infringing any citizen's rights, or ignoring the rule of law. I must caution you not to obstruct us in our duty, in any way.'

Cousins got to his feet. 'Very well. We understand each other, I see. I'm afraid I have no more time to give you. A car is waiting to take me to Clunbury.'

Once clear of the building, Dysart chuckled. 'Naughty temper, hasn't he? He'll be a gift in the witness box.'

'You rattled him.'

'How much of what he said is true?'

'I think he indulges in half-truths. He doesn't want us to dig into the reasons for Bakstein's murder. He's toeing some official line, probably connected to his job as a go-between for the nuclear buffs. I think he spoke the truth when he said he didn't know why Bakstein was so anxious to reach him; but he lied when he denied that Rosa Hopewell is part of his private information network. I'd say he used her and Bakstein as unofficial agents. I think he suspects that Rosa Hopewell knows why Bakstein was murdered.'

'I can't see Bakstein as a paid agent,' Dysart said. 'He'd have considered it beneath him.'

'Perhaps, but I'd say he was a willing unpaid helper. Saw himself as a patriot protecting the free world against nuclear pirates. As for Rosa, aside from being on Cousins's payroll as a translator, she may well have developed a sideline of her own, receiving reports from pals in the Middle East, and getting Cousins or Bakstein to pay her for translating them.'

Dysart pulled a face. 'That'd be a dangerous occupation. She'd be antagonizing the countries of origin, as well as getting up the noses of Cousins and his backers.'

'My guess is, Rosa's a tough little grafter. If she's acted as some kind of double agent, she's done so knowing the risks; which explains why she's gone to ground. She knows she could be victim number three.'

Dysart made no reply. He was silent until they reached the carpark where he'd left his Volvo. Then he said, 'Cousins is the link between the two murders. He was Bakstein's confidant; he involved Bakstein in operations that exposed him to danger and he was Jack Langley's contact man at the Foreign Office when Eric Moorland was kidnapped.

'You've said all along you wanted to know what linked two such different victims, and the answer is, Cousins. I want to know more about his dealings with Jack Langley. He'll know the details of the kidnapping, and of the execution of the three victims.'

Dysart glanced sideways at Thorneycroft. 'I know you don't agree that Langley's the perpetrator, but he had the means and the opportunity and the motive to kill Bakstein. Cousins can help us to sew up the case against Langley. My worry is that he might try to slide out from under.'

'He won't leave London,' Thorneycroft said. 'He has to stay in London. He wants to talk to Rosa Hopewell, he wants to question her about Bakstein's last two days, he wants to know the cause of Bakstein's anxiety.'

Dysart grimaced. 'I hope to God Rosa doesn't go to Cousins. He'll whisk her away to some place we can't reach her.'

'She won't go to him,' Thorneycroft said. 'She'll come to us.'

'Why? Why should she choose us over people she's known and worked with for years?'

'Because one of those people has been murdered. Because DS Frank's father will tell her to trust the police to protect her; because she'd like to collect the reward Liz's lawyers are offering and most of all because she wants to tell us what she did that earned Bakstein a bullet in the brain. It's also possible she wants to attend her fashion show on Friday. She'll come to us.'

XXII

THE NEXT DAY produced no encouraging events. Dysart set the unit to routine work, checking statements, verifying facts, fielding calls from people who claimed to have information to give.

Thorneycroft studied the lists of expert marksmen spilled out by the computers of Britain, America and Germany. A number of the names were of known killers, but none of them displayed the idiosyncrasy of the man who'd murdered Cornwall and Bakstein. None of them had left arcane messages on their victims' bodies.

Thorneycroft was becoming convinced that the killer did not have a previous record. His crimes seemed to have resulted from an extraordinary set of circumstances, generated by Bakstein and Cornwall. The circumstances were real, not the fantasies of a hallucinating mind. It might or might not be possible to discover what they were. The truth might already have been lost in the rubbish bins of daily life.

It seemed to Thorneycroft, as he ploughed through the stacks of computer printouts, that this case might never be solved. He left Greenwich that evening feeling tired and depressed, and the phone call he received from Liz did nothing to lift his spirits.

'I've had a message from Dad's accountants,' she said. 'You asked if he donated money to the ransom fund. The answer is, he did. He gave half a million pounds to the fund, but he did it anonymously. His name won't be on the list of donors.'

'You're sure of this?' Thorneycroft asked.

'Positive. The chief accountant remembers the donation very clearly, because he and Dad discussed whether it was right to meet kidnappers' demands. They decided that there were three valuable lives at stake, and they should be saved.'

Thorneycroft called Dysart and gave him the news. 'Bakstein refused to give to the fund, Trevor gave handsomely. Bakstein may have been killed for his parsimony, but the killer had no reason to want revenge on Trevor.'

'So there were two killers, not one,' Dysart said. 'Langley killed Bakstein in revenge for his son's death. He staged a copy-cat killing, hoping that Bakstein's murder would be attributed to Cornwall's killer.'

Thorneycroft didn't argue the point. He still believed they were looking for a single killer, but he had to agree that Jack Langley had had the motive, means and opportunity to shoot Bakstein. It was also true that Jeremy Cousins was linked to both Bakstein and Langley. He had worked with Bakstein, and liaised with Langley at the time of the Moorland kidnapping. The link had to be investigated.

He fell asleep quickly, but was woken by the jangle of his bedside telephone. He fumbled the receiver to his ear.

'Thorneycroft.'

'Yes, Doctor.' The voice was at once harsh and tremulous, the accent not English. 'I am Rosa Hopewell. I must meet with you. It is urgent.'

Thorneycroft squinted at his watch: 3 a.m. He said, 'Yes, Mrs Hopewell, I'm glad you called. Tomorrow—'

'No. Tonight. At once.' The voice rose a tone. 'This cannot wait, I am in danger, I need a safe place. I also claim the reward.'

Driven by fear and greed, he thought. Two powerful forces. 'Who told you there was a reward?' he demanded.

'Maisie. My assistant.'

'So she knew all along how to reach you.'

'No. She did not. I called her to talk about our show on Friday. She told me that there was a reward for the person who told the police where to find me. So I'm telling you.'

'Where are you, Mrs Hopewell?'

'At the Stella Maris Home. You know it?'

Thorneycroft did know it. It was a shelter for abused women. Claudia's church supported it.

'Are you injured?' he asked. Sister Claire, who ran the shelter, had no time for any but battered women.

'No, I am not hurt. Sister Claire is my friend. My late husband was patron of this place for many years. I am allowed to stay here tonight, but not longer. The police must find me a safe place. I will make it worth their while.'

'And how will you do that?'

'I have information to give them.' Her voice was impatient, now. 'You know where is this house?'

'Yes. In Winder Street, Chiswick.'

'You come, and bring that policeman, the one in charge. I will only negotiate with authorities.'

'I'll speak to DCI Dysart,' Thorneycroft affected uncertainty. 'He'll need a good reason to turn out at this time of night.'

There was a pause. He could hear her breathing, rapid and uneven. She was scared, but she was also scheming how to lay her hands on the reward.

'Mrs Hopewell?' he prompted, and she answered abruptly.

'I have good reason. You tell him I know why Julian Bakstein was shot.'

Thorneycroft left his car opposite the Stella Maris Home. The building was in an area that had once been prosperous Victorian, but the big old houses had been converted into bedsits or offices, and parks and gardens had been replaced by pubs and betting shops.

As he locked his car, a group of people erupted from an alley, shouting and gesticulating. At the centre of the group two men were fighting, both of them holding knives. A police car rounded the corner of the block, and the group scattered in all directions.

The police car drew up behind Thorneycroft's, and Dysart stepped out of the passenger seat. He waved a hand at the dispersing gang.

'Punks,' he said. 'All wind and water. They haven't the brains or guts to pull anything big.'

'You know them?' Thorneycroft asked, and Dysart grinned.

'Aye, that's Rab Bartle's gang. I broke Rab's nose for him, a way back.'

'You served here?'

'A few months, yes.' Dysart turned towards the shelter. 'Sister Claire does good work, hereabouts.'

They walked together through a steel-barred gate topped with razor wire. 'More like Fort Knox than a charity refuge,' Dysart said. 'Some abusers come round looking for a favourite punch bag.' He pressed the button on the front door of the building.

A voice box established their identities and the name of the inmate they wished to see. They were admitted by a man in a white suit who ushered them up a flight of stairs and along a passage to a closed door. Their guide tapped three times and called,

'Mrs Hopewell? Dr Thorneycroft and Inspector Dysart to see you.'

Footsteps sounded beyond the door, a key scraped in the lock and the door opened slowly. The woman facing them was small and plump. Grey-white hair framed a round face like a pastry cut-out; bright black eyes, small flat nose, wide thick-lipped mouth. She wore a red silk caftan and red leather sandals. She extended a pudgy hand, snapping the thumb and finger.

'Identification,' she said.

Thorneycroft and Dysart produced identity cards which she examined and handed back to them. She signed them into the room, closed and locked the door and turned to face them.

'Sister Claire knows you both,' she said. She pointed at Dysart. 'You worked here,' and at Thorneycroft, 'your wife brought you to a cake sale. She said you are to be trusted, and I must speak to you.'

Dysart smiled. 'Good. I'm in charge of the investigation into the murder of Dr Bakstein. You say you have information for me. If you do, don't withhold it, Mrs Hopewell. If we can arrest the killer, that will give you more security than any safe house, I assure you.'

She made a chewing movement of her jaws. A piranha, thought Thorneycroft, a man should mind his fingers in her vicinity, but at the moment she was a fish out of water.

'Sit down,' she commanded, and watched them settle on a well-worn sofa. She chose a wooden chair, facing them. Reaching into a pocket of her caftan, she produced a wedge of paper, folded several times. She leaned forward to hand it to Dysart.

'I have friends in Iran,' she announced. 'They send me articles about nuclear science. This arrived three days before Julian died.'

Dysart did not at once examine the paper. 'What sort of articles do they send?' he asked.

Mrs Hopewell shrugged plump shoulders. 'Nothing secret. Just articles about nuclear power in civil life. That one is about a facility that was completed last year in Iran. It is not news. It has been in the papers here, everywhere.'

Dysart unfolded the several sheets of paper and scanned them one by one, handing each one in order to Thorneycroft.

Thorneycroft nodded as he read. 'You're right. I read about the facility in *The Independent*, months ago.'

Dysart kept his gaze on Mrs Hopewell.

'Did you make this copy, ma'am?'

'Yes, as always, I make a copy to keep.'

'And the original?'

'I gave to Dr Bakstein.'

'Who sent you this document, Mrs Hopewell?'

She fixed her boot-button eyes on him. 'I do not give names. I do not embarrass my friends.'

Dysart seemed tempted to warn her against withholding information from the police, but he changed his mind.

'When did you give this document to Dr Bakstein?'

'Two days before he was killed.' Suddenly her fear was apparent in the sweat on her temples and the quivering of her mouth. She pressed fingers to her lips, shaking her head. Dysart retrieved the papers from Thorneycroft. 'As you say, it's stale news. I can't see that it helps my investigation, or entitles you to protective custody.'

Her eyes widened. 'It does. It was a death warrant for Julian, for me also. You must listen what I'm telling you.'

'I'm listening. You gave Dr Bakstein the document. What happened then?'

'He took it home with him. A few hours later, he phoned me, very agitated. He said he must at once get hold of Jeremy Cousins. I told him, Cousins is in Seattle, speak to someone else at the Foreign Office. He said no, that was not advisable.'

'Why wasn't it advisable?'

She shrugged.

'I don't know. Julian didn't say.'

Dysart watched her closely. 'When he phoned you, what exactly did he say?'

'I told you, he said he must speak to Cousins, urgently.'

'What else did he say?'

'Nothing. Just goodbye.'

Dysart's voice became silky. 'Mrs Hopewell, according to Maisie your assistant, she asked you what Bakstein had spoken about, and you said he asked you for the name of a good dry-cleaner.'

'Oh, that. Yes, it was not important.'

'He was agitated, you say, he urgently wished to speak to Mr Cousins, yet he asked about a dry-cleaner? Was he trying to convey a message to you? A warning of danger, perhaps?'

She blinked and turned her head away from him, and he persisted. 'Why did Dr Bakstein, at a time of great concern and agitation, ask you for the name of a dry-cleaner? The truth, please.'

'It was not a warning,' she muttered. 'All Julian meant was that I must not mention the document to anyone at all.'

'Asking about a dry-cleaner was an agreed signal between you?'

'Yes. When handling material from abroad, we must be very discreet, always.'

'Did that message, that stressed the need for secrecy, cause you anxiety?'

'No. There was no reason. Julian was not afraid. He was just agitated. He was an old woman, always excited, about nothing. There is nothing in those papers to cause such a brou-ha-ha. You can see for yourselves, there is nothing to cause alarm.'

'Yet here you are, Mrs Hopewell, calling at dead of night, demanding police protection, claiming your life is in danger.'

'It was the next day,' she cried, 'when I saw on the television Julian was dead, shot dead … then I became afraid. I left my shop, left town, I hid myself away.'

'Did you go straight to the Stella Maris Home?'

'No. I went to a hotel in Southend. I stayed there. I never left my room. I sent out for newspapers. One of them said that Cousins was back in England. I knew he would start a search for me, maybe advertise. I was afraid the hotel people might turn me in. I came here to Sister Claire. I called Maisie. They both said I must talk to the police.'

'From the moment you learned about Dr Bakstein's murder you've been afraid for your life, yet you didn't consider getting in touch with me until now.'

'I was afraid that there would be publicity, that the man would know where I was. I would be like a sitting bird for him.'

'Or did you change your mind when you learned there was a reward waiting for your finder?'

'No! I want protection, I'm afraid!' And patently, she was. Fear showed in her shaking hands, the tears in her eyes. Yet she still could not resist asking the question:

'Can I claim the reward?'

Dysart shook his head. 'I can't discuss the reward. It's not a police offer.' He leaned towards her. 'Have you been in touch with Mr Cousins since his return to England?'

'No.' She drew a long breath, searching for self-control. 'I don't wish it.'

'He's anxious to talk to you.'

'Of course.' Malice sparked in her eyes. 'He wants me under his thumb.' She pressed the ball of her thumb into her palm with a grinding movement. 'I will not allow him. I am finished with him and his friends. You must find me a safe place until you have caught the shooter. Then I will go back to my shop, to my own work. Not to his.'

'I'll see what can be done to find you accommodation,' Dysart said.

'How soon?'

'I'll be in touch with you first thing tomorrow. I'll arrange transport.'

She sighed and nodded. 'Thank you. I have told you the truth. One thing I know, in here.' She laid thick fingers on her chest. 'The papers I have given you ... that dull thing that is not news ... it is the reason Julian was killed.'

Back in the street, Dysart and Thorneycroft discussed the document Rosa Hopewell had given them.

'It could be a signal in itself,' Thorneycroft suggested. 'A coded instruction that Bakstein recognized, but she didn't. The thing seems innocuous, and as she said, it's stale news, but Bakstein found it important. He warned her not to discuss it with anyone. And what did he do with the original papers? They weren't found on his premises. Did he destroy them?'

Dysart frowned. 'Perhaps the killer took them, along with Bakstein's diary and mobile. He may have had the papers on him when he was shot.'

'At six in the morning? He was wearing shorts and a zip jacket,' Thorneycroft's mind reverted to the scene of the crime; Bakstein dead on the grass, the unlocked house, the dead dog. 'He thought the document was important, he felt the need for secrecy, but he wasn't scared. He felt no danger to himself. If he had, he'd surely have asked for protection, he'd not have stayed in that house alone, or gone out into the garden as he did.'

'The last, worst mistake of his life,' Dysart agreed. He folded the papers into his pocket. 'I'll get the boffins to look at this, see if they can detect any coded message. That'll be more time lost. We're not moving fast enough.'

'It gives us bargaining power,' Thorneycroft said.

'The document? How?'

'With Cousins. If he gets to hear of it, he'll want to see it. He'll want to put his own boffins to work on it. He's entitled to do that – Mrs Hopewell was employed by him. We can tell him about the document, promise him a copy … on terms.'

'Such as?'

'The video showing the execution of Moorland and his mates. Jack Langley said it's in the authorities' possession. Cousins was the government's link with Langley when the kidnapping took place. I'll lay odds Cousins has a copy of the video. We offer a trade.'

Dysart smiled. 'That'd be quicker than applying through the proper channels. I must get back to the nick at once, I've a lot to do. By morning we'll have Mrs Hopewell in a place of safety. Once that's fixed, I'll make a date with Cousins.' His eyes gleamed. 'I'll enjoy putting that twister over a barrel.'

XXIII

THORNEYCROFT PHONED GREENWICH early next morning and found Dysart at his desk.

'You been there all night?' he asked.

'Yup. Mrs Hopewell's in a safe place, close enough so we can keep tabs on her. She still has some questions to answer. I've given a copy of her document to Harry Quin, to check for coded messages.'

'Have you spoken to Cousins?'

'Not yet. He's due back at work today. I'll call him at nine sharp. I'm going to take a shower and send out for breakfast. Come in and join me. We need to talk.'

By 8.30 Thorneycroft had consumed an egg and chips from the take-out next door, and agreed with Dysart on the best way to handle Cousins.

'It's time for him to learn that possession's nine tenths of the law,' Dysart said. He swallowed the last of his coffee and rolled an eye at Thorneycroft.

'You ever wanted to play good-cop bad-cop?'

Thorneycroft grinned. 'Since nobbut a lad.'

'Right then, I'm the black hat, you're the white hat. I get the mannikin unsettled, then you come in and suggest he gives us the video, we give him a copy of the document.'

'What if he refuses?'

'He won't. I've been in touch with the people who managed the Seattle conference. They told me that far from instructing them to put all calls through to him, Cousin said he would only take calls authorized by our Foreign Office.'

'And Bakstein chose not to obtain that authorization.'

'Exactly. It seems he did make one personal call to the conference centre, which Cousins declined to take.'

'He didn't make that call from his home. His landline and mobile phone records show only the two calls, one to the Foreign Office, and one to Mrs Hopewell. He must have made the third call from an outside phone.'

'The point is, he never reached Cousins, and the super's calls from here after Bakstein was shot were only referred to Cousins when the conference closed, and Bakstein was dead.'

'You think Cousins's refusal to communicate contributed to Bakstein's death?'

'It was certainly a dereliction of his duty, and a black mark against him if his superiors get to hear of it. I think Cousins will see the benefit of cooperating with us.'

'If we give him a copy of the document, he may try to suppress it.'

'He won't chance that. I shall make it plain to him that Harry Quin already has a copy. If Harry decides the thing falls in the Intelligence court, Cousins won't have any say in how it's handled. No, we have him where we want him, cornered and very nervous.' Dysart stretched his arms, smiling. 'This is one of the times I really enjoy my job.'

Cousins received them alone. He ignored Thorneycroft's polite 'good morning' and eyed Dysart coldly.

'Well, Chief Inspector, what prompts this visit?'

Dysart appeared not to have heard. He chose a chair and settled his large frame in it, gazing about him at the office furniture.

'I take it this is a private interview, Mr Cousins? No two-way mirrors, no bugs in the light fittings?'

Cousins scowled. 'You've watched two many police procedurals,' he said. 'Kindly answer my question.'

'Which was?'

'Why are you here?'

Dysart's eyebrows soared. 'For the same reason I was here last time, sir. To further the police investigation into the murder of Julian Bakstein.'

'I have told you all I know about that dreadful event.' Cousins's fingers drummed rapidly on his desk. Dysart was searching the pages of his notebook.

'Yerss ...' he murmured. 'We know that during the two days prior to his death, Dr Bakstein made three phone calls. One to you at this office, one to Mrs Rosa Hopewell at Roxanne's and the third to you at the Seattle conference. Unfortunately you had instructed the organizers there that you would only take calls authorized by your superiors in London. You never took Bakstein's calls. You never learned why he was so anxious to talk to you. Why did you block Bakstein's calls?'

'I did not block them. I merely placed my duty to the vitally important nuclear discussions in process, above my need to field calls from unauthorized persons.'

'Unauthorized? Is that how you rated Dr Bakstein? Your expert on nuclear research? A genius you had worked with for years?'

Cousins's tallowy features darkened. 'A genius perhaps, but one who habitually niggled about minor breaches of protocol. I have told you, he could have spoken to anyone here.'

'Apparently he didn't see it that way. He believed it was essential to speak to you. He made that clear to the conference officials and they repeated that message to you, but you flatly refused to take the call. You failed to talk to a desperately worried man. The next day he was shot dead. Britain lost one of her most valuable citizens. I imagine that must raise questions about where precisely your duty lay.'

Cousins stiffened. 'You exceed your authority, you are not entitled to judge me or to moralize about my actions. If you have legitimate questions to ask, then ask them. For the record, I must point out that neither in his call to this office, nor in those to Mrs Hopewell or Seattle, did Bakstein give the smallest hint that the situation presented any danger to himself or anyone else.'

'Agreed, but how do you know what he said to Mrs Hopewell?'

'I asked her assistant, who told me what was said.'

'Ah. Then you know that he asked Mrs Hopewell for the name of a good dry-cleaner. I'm informed that that was an instruction to Mrs Hopewell that she must not discuss his call or its subject with anyone else. Dr Bakstein intended to converse with you alone. No one else.'

'He gave no hint of danger,' Cousins insisted. 'I simply thought he was indulging in his usual nosey-parker capers.'

'But he wasn't, was he? The document Mrs Hopewell gave him apparently caused him great concern, even though Mrs Hopewell herself describes it as nothing to cause alarm, stale news.'

Cousins's eyes were bulging. 'Document? What document? You've seen her, haven't you? You know where she is, you're deliberately withholding information from me. I demand to know her whereabouts, now, at once.'

Dysart tilted his head. 'I'm afraid I'm not at liberty to tell you that, Mr Cousins.'

'As her employer I have the right to know. If you've found her—'

'No no, she found us. She invited Thorneycroft and me to meet with her. She gave me a document.'

'She had no right to do so. It is the property of my department.'

'Mrs Hopewell doesn't seem to think so. She said it was sent to her by a friend in Iran. A private gift.'

'There is no such thing for anyone handling government business. Where is Mrs Hopewell, Chief Inspector? I must talk to her, set her head straight....'

'I'm afraid she made it clear that she won't communicate with you in any way.'

'I demand to have her present address.'

'I'm sorry, sir. As you pointed out to me at our last meeting, Mrs Hopewell has rights, which I'm bound to respect.'

'She does not have the right to withhold information from me. She is in my employ. She knows the terms that apply to her position. The national interest demands that I know where she is, and just what she's been up to during my absence from this country.'

Dysart folded his hands. 'You told me that Mrs Hopewell

worked for you as a translator, nothing more. That she did a mundane translating job for your department. She has decided to quit that job and to end all contact with you and your colleagues. There's nothing in that to infringe normal labour practices. Nothing that allows you to harass her.'

Cousins pointed a shaking finger at Dysart. 'That woman is a lying, scheming opportunist. She's been warned time and again not to set herself up as an unofficial post office for all the dissidents and refugee riff-raff of the Middle East; but she's greedy. She can't resist taking the money such people offer her. She has broken the terms of her agreement with me, and I insist that you tell me where she's hiding, and that you hand over the document she gave you.'

'That's not possible, she gave it to Bakstein.'

'I'm damn sure she took copies of it. She gave you one, didn't she?'

'She did. She believes it brought about Bakstein's murder, that it's germane to the police investigation. It was her duty to inform me of it.'

Cousins surged to his feet. 'This is preposterous. If you don't hand over those papers immediately, I shall speak to your superiors. I shall inform them of your arrogant, obstructive behaviour.'

'Do, by all means. You'll find they have strong views about people who obstruct the police in the performance of their duty.' Dysart too was on his feet. 'You have failed to assist me in my investigation of the murders of Trevor Cornwall and Julian Bakstein. You have lied to me about the nature of your employment of Bakstein and Mrs Hopewell. You have used both of them to gather information relating to nuclear arms proliferation. In doing that, you must have known that you were exceeding your powers, and putting them at risk. Now Bakstein is dead and Mrs Hopewell is in fear of her life. Those are the facts, Mr Cousins. Those are the results of your setting untrained persons to act as amateur intelligence agents.'

Cousins gasped like a stranded fish. 'My aim,' he said in a quavering voice, 'is to halt the proliferation of nuclear arms by negotiation, not by threats and sanctions and sabre-rattling. You and your sort ignore the merits of diplomacy, you press for verbal and physical attacks to force non-aligned countries into line. You will drag the world into a nuclear war!'

Dysart laughed, and Cousins's control snapped. 'You may laugh,' he screeched, 'but you know nothing of nuclear power and the pirates who will do anything to possess it. You are nothing but a flatfoot ignoramus and I shall make sure that authority puts a stop to your antics. Get out of my office, do you hear me?'

'It's impossible not to hear you.' Dysart stooped to pick up his briefcase, but before he could do so, Thorneycroft stepped to his side.

'Wait, Iain, let's not be hasty. Mr Cousins has a point, you know.'

'What point?' Dysart's jaw jutted, and Thorneycroft put a hand on his shoulder.

'Like most of us, he wants to end the threat of nuclear war. I'm sure that he also wants to see the arrest and punishment of the criminal who shot two of our most valued citizens. Moreover he's correct when he says that Mrs Hopewell is responsible to him, and should abide by the terms of her contract.'

Dysart favoured Thorneycroft with a stubborn stare. 'There's no way I'll break my undertaking to Mrs Hopewell.'

'No one can ask that of you. Mr Cousins must appreciate that Rosa Hopewell has made up her mind on certain matters. She will not agree to see him, and if an attempt is made to invade her privacy, she may well go to law to foil it.' Thorneycroft turned to face Cousins. 'She could make things very uncomfortable for this office, sir.'

Cousins switched his glare to Thorneycroft. 'Rosa Hopewell may avoid me, but you can't withhold the document she gave to Bakstein. That falls in my domain, I have a right to it. It must be examined by my staff to see if it contains anything prejudicial to national or international security.'

'I agree, and so does DCI Dysart. He has already sent a copy of the document to Harry Quin for expert examination.'

'He refuses to give me a copy.'

'No. He has refused to give you Mrs Hopewell's address, which he's entitled to do, as she's under police protection. Now, can't we all sit down and discuss things quietly? I assure you that both the Chief Inspector and I regard you as of key importance in our investigation.'

Cousins gave him a suspicious glance. 'I know nothing about the murders,' he said. 'I was out of the country when they were committed. I never met Trevor Cornwall. I have nothing to contribute to your inquiries.'

'I think you do. Shall we sit down? Iain, please?'

Dysart resumed his seat, and Cousins slowly followed suit. Thorneycroft perched on the edge of his seat, facing Cousins.

'You knew Bakstein very well, Mr Cousins,' he said. 'You worked closely with him for many years.'

'I knew him, his genius, his great services to this country, I deeply regret his death, but I have no idea why he was killed. I can only think it was the work of a lunatic.'

'Let me suggest a possible reason for his murder. Eight years ago you were our government's representative in the negotiations to secure the release from kidnappers of Eric Moorland and two other scientists. All three men were executed by their captors.'

Cousins looked mystified. 'What possible connection can that have with the current murders?'

'I'll explain. Julian Bakstein was linked to the Moorland case. Mr Jack Langley, Moorland's father, was charged with the task of collecting the ransom money for all three captives. You, at that time, were not only on the negotiating team, but you were operating as counsellor to the Clunbury Nuclear Research Centre. Bakstein was their link man with you. Is that correct?'

'Yes.'

'Were you present when Jack Langley visited Clunbury to ask for donations to the fund?'

'I was. I accompanied Mr Langley to Clunbury. I knew the employees. They donated a lot of money to the fund.'

'Did Dr Bakstein make a donation?'

Cousins was silent for a moment, then he said flatly, 'No. He refused to support it. He said to do so would encourage other kidnappers to snatch victims and extort huge amounts.'

'In what manner did he make his refusal?'

'Brutally. He stood up in a packed hall and harangued Langley. The audience booed him, but he refused to retract. Bakstein never cared what people thought of him. He did what he felt to be right. That was his strength, and at times his fatal weakness.'

'What was Langley's reaction?'

'He was very distressed, and very angry.' Cousins turned to look at Dysart. 'What has this to do with the present murders?'

As Dysart made no reply, Cousins's gaze became incredulous.

'You can't believe that Jack Langley nursed that anger for eight years! That he killed Bakstein? Langley's a national hero, a man of integrity, he's incapable of such a crime.'

Dysart shrugged, hands spread, and Thorneycroft said smoothly, 'It's a line of investigation that has to be followed. We need to understand why Bakstein was killed. His failure to give to the ransom fund could have provided a motive, not just to Langley but to relatives and friends of the other two victims.'

Cousins shook his head. 'I still fail to see how this line of thinking concerns me.'

'You may be able to give us information about the kidnapping. No one is better informed on the subject than you. We've come to the fountain-head.'

Cousins's eyes narrowed. 'Don't soft-soap me, Doctor. I can see through such stratagems. What do you want of me?'

Thorneycroft sighed. 'I want a win-win situation. You are anxious to see Mrs Hopewell. We can't grant that wish. You also want the document she received and passed to Bakstein. We concede your right there. DCI Dysart is aware of it, and has no wish to dispute it.'

Thorneycroft glanced at Dysart who nodded.

'For our part,' Thorneycroft continued, 'we are anxious to study an article you have in your possession.'

'What article?' Cousins looked uneasy, but interested. Thorneycroft's voice became confiding.

'The video your department received eight years ago from the kidnappers. The one showing the execution of Moorland and his companions.'

Cousins raised both hands. 'Impossible. Cabinet at the time ruled that the video must not be shown to any unauthorized person. It is still embargoed.'

'That ruling was made eight years ago when the war in Iraq was about to break. That war is ended, the video can't influence its course or alter the situation in Iraq. The document we hold, on the other hand, is relevant to the present. As you say, you need to examine it to see if it affects national security.'

Cousins was silent, chewing his lip, and Thorneycroft smiled.

'Mr Cousins, you can pursue your right to obtain Mrs Hopewell's document by legal action. We can follow official channels to gain access to the video. I confess that I find the proper channels tedious and time-consuming, and frankly we don't have time to waste. The killer is out there. He could kill again while we fill in forms and answer silly questions.'

Cousins spread his hands on his desk. 'Are you suggesting an exchange?'

'You can show us the video here, in private, and we can give you a copy of Rosa's document. It's simply a quick way of seeing your rights and ours are realized.'

Cousins turned to Dysart. 'Is that your offer? You see the video, I get a copy of the document?'

Dysart considered. 'We see the video and get a copy of it, you get a copy of the document.'

'Very well, but you will have to give certain assurances before you see the video, and you will only receive a copy under the conditions of safekeeping and confidentiality that the Cabinet imposed eight years ago. Are you ready to abide by those conditions?'

'Yes, within reason. I can't make promises that could inhibit me in my duty as a police officer. I can promise discretion, and a strict regard for state security.'

'The discretion must apply also to our discussions today.'

'That I can't promise, but this I know: there's more chance of discretion if we see the video now, in the privacy of this room, than if we make a formal application to view it. That always gets to the ears of the media. Gives them a chance to enjoy a feeding frenzy.'

Still Cousins hesitated, and Thorneycroft said quickly, 'I know very little about the kidnapping. I was on a course in Denver when it happened. There wasn't much coverage in the American papers.'

'Or any other papers,' said Cousins heavily. 'Publicity was kept to a minimum. The Iraq war was about to break. Public opinion was very inflamed. To screen atrocities and terrorism would have made things worse. The video was shown only to certain high-ranking officials ... politicians, heads of the armed forces, and of course security heads.'

'Was the opinion that the kidnappings and executions were politically inspired?'

'No. No political or terrorist organization ever claimed responsibility. It was considered to be a simple act of banditry, staged to make money. The victims were all rich men.'

'If it was a money-making exercise, why was the ransom never claimed? The men were executed only days before it was to be paid.'

As Cousins hesitated, Dysart intervened.

'Jack Langley believes his son and his companions were murdered as an act of revenge for the invasion of Iraq.'

'That may be true. Only a very powerful motive could have prevented the thugs from getting their hands on the ransom. Langley had the full amount in readiness, but the executions took place before he could deliver it.'

'Which left Langley holding £15 million. Could that have meant more to him than his stepson's life?'

Cousins was outraged. 'Jack Langley formally adopted Eric Moorland. He raised him as his son, he loved the boy. He was shattered by the executions. He didn't *hold* the ransom money, it was placed in trust. Any donor who wanted his donation back, got it, but most of them directed that the money should go to the victims' families.'

'You showed Langley the video, didn't you?'

'Yes, for the purpose of identifying his son.'

'Moorland was a nuclear physicist, like Bakstein.'

'They were alike only in respect of their profession. There was little resemblance between them in character or achievement.'

'Was the video shown to the relatives of the other victims:'

'Yes, and with the same response as Langley gave. Shock, deep pain, anger.'

'Were the mens' bodies recovered?'

'No. Nor were the killers. It's believed they are dead. Lots of thugs were eliminated during the course of the war.

'How was the ransom demand made?'

'By telephone, to this building. After that, messages were sent to other parts of London: to a prominent bank; to the French Embassy; to the lawyers in charge of the ransom trust.'

'What form did these messages take?'

'They were threats of what would be done to the captives if the ransom wasn't paid. They were all very brief. We had no chance of tracking the position of the captives. They were moved constantly.'

'Does the video give any indication of where the executions took place?'

'Only that it was in a rock cave. There are plenty of those in the mountains of Iran, Afghanistan, Kashmir, India ... and in Turkey and Iraq.'

'How did the video reach you?'

'It was delivered to a post office in the City,' Cousins ran a hand over his face. 'It was a terrible shock to us. We were expecting to deliver the ransom money and to negotiate the release of the men. Instead, there was this vile evidence of their murder.'

Dysart said abruptly, 'The history of what went on between the kidnappers and this office will be on record. I will apply for permission to access your files. The video is to hand now. Will you show it to us, Mr Cousins?'

Cousins straightened in his chair. 'I will show it to you, on the conditions I stipulated. Discretion and confidentiality, and a proper attention on your part to the needs and laws of this country.'

Dysart smiled, his truculence vanished. 'Thank you, sir. I will abide by your conditions, to the best of my ability.'

'Very well.' Cousins rose and crossed the room to a locked cabinet. He took from it a slim cassette which he slotted into the video section of a television set.

'I must warn you,' he said, 'it's not pleasant viewing.' He pressed the starter button and returned to sit at his desk as the screen flickered into life.

XXIV

THE VIDEO WAS in colour. Though not the work of a professional photographer, it had the terrible stamp of professional crime.

It opened with a display of the identity documents of the three kidnap victims. These were replaced by the image of a masked man, standing against a rock wall. He delivered a tirade, first in Arabic and then in English, accusing America and Britain of the rape of Iraq.

The three captives were labelled spies of the West and enemies of Islam. They must pay with their lives, the speaker said, for the lives of murdered Iraqi civilians.

They were dragged before the camera. They had been trussed with wire so that they could do no more than shuffle. Their clothes were filthy and bloodstained, and three weeks' growth of beard could not conceal the livid bruises on their faces and bodies. Plastic tape was strapped across their mouths.

Thorneycroft leaned close to the screen to study their faces. Wheeler and Coolidge looked drugged, the pupils of their eyes contracted to pinpoints. Morphine, he thought, administered not for mercy's sake, but to prevent any show of resistance.

Eric Moorland seemed less affected by the drug. He struggled against his bonds, and the man guarding him struck him across the face so that blood ran from his nose.

A narrow bench was brought forward and the three men were forced to sit on it. Behind each victim stood a masked guard armed with a long-barrelled combat pistol which he held pressed to the back of the victim's skull.

Wheeler and Coolidge sat quietly, but Moorland tried to get to his feet. Again the guard struck him and Moorland slumped to the bench, swaying. The guard reached for a sack and pulled it over Moorland's head, drawing it tight across his face.

The camera shifted back to the speaker. This time he spoke only in English. Iraq, he said, had been violated by pigs, and it was time for justice to be done. The camera moved back so that it was possible to see the whole of the cave, the victims slumped on the bench and the guards behind them.

The speaker moved to the side of the area. He raised his arm, pointing at Wheeler. The guard behind him pulled the trigger of his pistol. Wheeler's head exploded and his body toppled to the ground.

The camera shifted to Coolidge, the speaker raised his arm and Coolidge was shot.

Moorland was struggling again, and the first two guards moved to pinion his arms. The guard behind him fired two shots, and he fell, the shreds of the sack and the wreckage of his head mingling in a bloody pool.

The speaker crossed to examine the three bodies, then turned to face the camera.

'This is what we will do to all spies and murderers of our children,' he said.

Abruptly, the screen went blank. There was no further picture or sound.

Cousins went to switch off the machine. He extracted the cassette, brought it back and laid it on his desk.

Dysart was the first to speak. 'I'm sure this has been studied exhaustively by Intelligence.'

'Many times,' Cousins said. 'It was never possible to identify the kidnappers.'

'Did you hear from them again?'

'No. That video was their swansong. I believe and hope that they are dead.'

Thorneycroft said, 'The men were drugged before they were killed.'

'Yes, with some sort of opiate.'

'Moorland tried to put up a fight.'

'It didn't help him, poor sod.'

'It must have been a hell of a thing for Langley to watch.'

'He insisted on seeing it. He said he had to be sure the men were dead. He saw to it that the ransom money was returned to the donors, or to the people they nominated.'

'So the families of Coolidge and Wheeler got around five million each, and Jack and Sybilla Langley got their stake back?'

'It was Sybilla Langley who put up their share. Jack Langley administers her affairs. She's in no shape to manage them.' Cousins held out a hand. 'And now, please, the document.' He pushed the cassette forward, towards Dysart.

Dysart laid the papers on the desk. Cousins snatched them up and scanned them, at first eagerly, then with obvious disappointment and annoyance.

'This is rubbish,' he said. 'It's rough notes for a news article referring to the nuclear facility Iran opened last year. The article appeared in papers worldwide. It contained nothing of value from the point of view of nuclear research. Rosa Hopewell was right. It's valueless.'

'Julian Bakstein was concerned by it. Agitated, Mrs Hopewell said. And someone shot him dead before he could tell you why.'

'As I've explained, he was given to getting worked up over trivial matters.'

'If the document was trivial, why was he shot?'

'Because he constantly frustrated the ambitions of countries who refused to sign the Nuclear Non-proliferation Treaty. He earned himself a lot of dangerous enemies. We warned him time and again not to tease the tigers, but he wasn't a man who listened to advice. I believe he infuriated the fanatics to the point of murder. But Bakstein didn't feel personally threatened by the document. He was just irritated by it.'

Dysart turned to Thorneycroft. 'Do you have any questions, John?'

Thorneycroft stared intently at Cousins. 'You don't believe that the Rosa Hopewell document brought about the murder of Bakstein?'

'I think it extremely unlikely.'

'Tell me this. If that document does contain information that could be damaging to a pirate country or individual, how did the killer know it was in Bakstein's possession?'

Cousins said tiredly, 'The modern world's a small place. Technology has greatly increased the spy's arsenal. Bakstein was watched by hostile countries and individuals. If radical foreign elements learned that a document they considered damaging had been sent to Rosa Hopewell, they would know she would pass it to Bakstein. That might have decided them to get rid of Bakstein. But I repeat, I believe he was killed because of his opposition to their nuclear aims. The killing just happened to coincide with the arrival in Britain of an outdated and harmless report from Rosa's pal.'

'Do you really believe that Bakstein was kept under observation by people outside of this country?'

'I do. He was watched by hostile and friendly nations, including ourselves. He was one of the most valuable scientists in the world. Everyone kept an eye on him.'

Thorneycroft moved closer to Cousins's desk. 'Bakstein may have been killed because of his actions as a nuclear scientist, but why was Trevor Cornwall shot? He knew nothing whatsoever about nuclear physics.'

Cousins got to his feet. 'That is your problem, Doctor, not mine, for which I am truly grateful.' He handed the video cassette to Dysart.

'I shall expect to hear from you, Chief Inspector, when you receive Harry Quin's report. I will do my best to regain contact with Mrs Hopewell, and to restore some sort of order and decorum to her relations with my office. Now, if you will forgive me, I have a great deal of work to do. I wish you success in your investigations. Good day.'

*

Dysart was elated by the morning's work.

'The video provides what we've lacked all along,' he said, 'the motive for Bakstein's murder. Langley must have hated him for his refusal to support the ransom fund. Langley was shown that disgusting video. It could well have turned hatred into a passion for revenge.'

'On those terms, it could provide a motive for any member of the families or close friends of all three captives.'

'We'll be checking them, too, I promise you, and a hard time we'll have of it, tracing them after eight years. My point is, Langley is a crack shot who had the motive, means and opportunity to kill Bakstein.'

Thorneycroft made no answer, and Dysart said sharply, 'Why the long teeth, John? You've said all along it was vital to find the motive for the murders. Now we have.'

'For Bakstein's murder, not for Trevor's. He gave handsomely to the ransom fund.'

'It's probable that the two murders were committed by different people. Cornwall was killed by an expert shot. Langley, also an expert shot, saw it as a chance to kill Bakstein in a copycat murder that would be attributed to Cornwall's killer. We still have to find the motive for Cornwall's murder ... a separate investigation, not linked to Bakstein's death.'

Thorneycroft stopped in his tracks. 'The two murders were committed by the same person,' he said.

'Why do you keep saying that?' Dysart demanded. 'You can't cling to an argument that doesn't fit the case.'

'My job,' retorted Thorneycroft, 'is to draw a profile of the killer, to assist you to track him down and lock him away. The profile I've drawn is of a single killer who is an expert shot, probably English, well-educated, well-funded—'

'All of which applies to Jack Langley....'

'And who left messages on the bodies of his victims. Those messages describe the characters of the victims. Reliable people have confirmed that the descriptions are close to the truth. Trevor was described as a prominent citizen, good family man, popular sportsman. Bakstein figured as a power-hungry, egotistical colossus, an Ozymandias. The killer either knew both men, or had made a close study of them. But it wasn't a lust for revenge that drove him. There was another reason why he decided to kill them … a more urgent necessity.'

'You're drawing on your imagination, not on the known facts.'

Thorneycroft bit off an angry reply. He said levelly, 'We have plenty of facts, but so far we haven't been able to link them together in a coherent form.'

'I think we have.' Dysart paused and looked away from Thorneycroft as if to avoid a quarrel. 'I agree we need to strengthen our cases. I must pursue the possibility that Langley's the killer, but I grant there may be other solutions to the murders. I think you should pursue your own line, see if you can build the available facts into what you feel is a more coherent form.' He turned to face Thorneycroft. 'You have great skills, John. I respect them. I will always welcome your thoughts, but I have to follow up on a man I see as a likely suspect.'

Thorneycroft: 'Of course. I understand. I'll do as you suggest.'

Travelling back to Greenwich, they spoke little. Dysart was busy mapping out the work to be done following the acquisition of the video. Thorneycroft, oddly, was thinking of his grandmother.

Granny Bess Thorneycroft had been a sturdy countrywoman whose decisions were based on common sense and life experience; but she was credited with second sight. From time to time she would be assailed by an unshakable conviction that seemed to defy reason. Sometimes what she 'saw' would involve taking a course of action. More often it conveyed a warning of danger. Her family had learned that it was wise to heed her apparently unreasonable visions.

Thorneycroft had, from time to time, experienced this same inexplicable certainty. Twice, during his career in the SAS, he had obeyed an unreasonable compulsion that proved to be lifesaving. He attributed these warnings not to an occult influence, but to the as yet untapped capabilities of the human brain, which he believed were capable of putting the world's computers in the shade.

Now, driving to Greenwich on a sunny day, he found himself in the grip of a dark foreboding. He sensed the menacing presence of a killer, knew without doubt that he was planning further mayhem.

'We're on the wrong track,' he muttered. Dysart turned towards him.

'What did you say?'

Thorneycroft did not answer. Now wasn't the time to quarrel with Dysart. When they arrived at the police station, he commandeered an empty interview room, a computer and a secure phone line, and asked for his own file of reports, and other sections of the accumulated data of the case to be delivered to him.

That done, he put through a call to Bunny Rourke, at Penwold.

XXV

BUNNY ROURKE WAS reassuring about the situation at Penwold. 'The security here's A1,' he said. 'They're right on the job, and the local coppers send regular patrols. DCI Dysart phones me every day, and I've told him we haven't seen any suspicious strangers hereabouts. I keep my eye on the staff and stables. We're doing fine.'

'Just make sure that everyone on the property keeps to the rules,' Thorneycroft said.

'I will that. What makes you think that that bastard would come to Penwold? Have you had a tip-off?'

'No. It's because I don't know where he might attack that I want everyone to be on guard. The man's psychotic, Bunny, and he knows he's being hunted. That puts him under huge stress, which may lead him to kill again. I rely on you to let me know if there's any incident, however trivial, that strikes you as out of the ordinary.'

'Will do, and I'll keep a special eye on the ladies and the kids, see they stay in the safe area.'

With that, Thorneycroft had to be satisfied. He spoke for some time to Claudia, whose concern was for Liz.

'She's feeling the strain, terribly,' she said. 'She has nightmares about finding Trevor dead at their gate. I've made her move into the old nursery at night, with me and the kids. It helps us all to be together after dark.'

'Liz should have professional counselling, but that would mean bringing her to London, and she's safer at Penwold.'

'Yes, and she'd miss working with French Toast. That's good

for her. Iain Dysart has been very kind. He phones her every day to keep her informed. I think he's very fond of her.'

'They're old friends.' On impulse, Thorneycroft said, 'I miss you and Luke.'

Claudia picked up some tension in his voice. 'What's wrong?' she said. 'Is it something in the case?'

'It's moving,' he answered.

'Be careful, John. Look after yourself. Promise?'

'I promise,' he said.

The call ended, he turned to the mass of material piled on his desk. He smiled wryly, remembering that Dysart had accused him of relying on imagination rather than on fact.

The truth was that a profiler had to study the known facts of a crime, apply his forensic and psychiatric knowledge to the facts and then add the catalyst of imagination to the mix. From that he drew a profile of the sort of criminal who might be responsible for the crime. That definition formed the basis of all his later work and research. It determined the advice he gave to the investigating team.

Thorneycroft thought about the profile he'd drawn.

He remained convinced that a single marksman had shot both Trevor Cornwall and Julian Bakstein. The man was not a typical serial killer; he had left messages on his victims' bodies, but they didn't follow the repetitive pattern favoured by a serial murderer.

Nor was this man driven by a perverted sexual compulsion. His motive was cold necessity. Cornwall and Bakstein were in some way a threat to him, so he had removed them from his path.

He was pathologically unbalanced. He felt no remorse for his crimes. He was egocentric, a careful planner, intelligent, well-educated, capable of quick and decisive action. He was probably English, wealthy enough to afford a Cougar III. He knew who could provide him with arms and ammunition not available to law-abiding citizens.

It had to be admitted that this description fitted Jack Langley in some respects. It was possible that Langley hated Bakstein enough to kill him. But try as he might, Thorneycroft couldn't see Langley as the killer.

Somehow, he thought, we've gone off track. We've placed the wrong interpretation on the facts we've gathered. We have to go back to the beginning.

Sighing, he set himself to separate from the papers on the desk, all the material relating to Bakstein's death. He began his revision by considering the scientist's character. The character of the victim played a part in every murder investigation. What Bakstein was, what he knew, what he did, had made him the target of a killer.

Those who knew him described him as a genius, a patriot, a man who served his country with unswerving loyalty. They also called him pugnacious, reclusive, a sybarite who affected exotic dress, an irritating fusspot who waged battles both against nuclear pirates and colleagues who cashed in on other people's work.

He was rash and stubborn. On retiring, he had refused to accept security guards on his property. He had done work for Jeremy Cousins, without appreciating the dangers such work exposed him to.

He was ambivalent in his handling of money. He'd refused to donate to a man dying of cancer, or to three kidnap victims, yet he'd given generously to his pet charities.

His only real friend had been the dog that died with him. Bakstein took the dog into the garden at 6 a.m. The dog sensed the presence of another person. It started towards the shrubbery but it didn't bark. Had it picked up the scent of someone it knew?

If Bakstein recognized the man who shot him, he wasn't given time to react. He was shot dead at once. The weapon was most likely a silenced pistol, the tool of a professional killer.

Bakstein's diary, his mobile phone and the document given to him by Rosa Hopewell, were not found on his person or in his house. They were probably removed by the murderer ... which lent strength to the view that the document was the reason Bakstein was shot.

The document was central to solving the riddle.

It was possible that the three missing items were removed to conceal the links Bakstein had with Cousins and Rosa Hopewell.

Cousins's actions before and after the murder of Bakstein were far from praiseworthy.

He had refused to take the call Bakstein made to him in Seattle. He had lied about that refusal, and about the work done for him by Bakstein and Rosa Hopewell. He had emerged badly from Dysart's questioning, insisting that Bakstein was killed by one of the nuclear pirates he so vigorously opposed.

Could Cousins be attempting to conceal some error, or crime? Was he guilty of killing Bakstein?

Dysart did not suspect him. Dysart believed that Jack Langley was the killer.

Thorneycroft sat with closed eyes, allowing the mass of facts settle in his mind.

Surprisingly, he found himself agreeing with Mrs Hopewell that Bakstein had been killed because he was in possession of a packet of stale news.

He thought about the document. It had not frightened Bakstein, it had caused him serious concern. What was his concern, if it was not fear for his own life?

What was the significance of the document?

Thorneycroft dug through the files before him and retrieved the clip of papers.

It was five pages long, the rough draft, the skeletal background of a nuclear facility. Cousins and Rosa Hopewell said it had been completed months ago, and a statement released to the media.

This draft was written in English. No need for Rosa to translate it. Why had Bakstein made such a fuss about it? There was no way of telling, but the ghost of an idea crossed Thorneycroft's mind, and he made a note of it.

He turned next to his own interview with Mark Bellows. He fed the tape into the recorder on his desk and listened to Bellows's summary of Bakstein's qualities: genius, patriot, quibbler over minor matters, a man who did great work, and made too many enemies for his own good.

Finally he considered the kidnappers' video. Was it enough to topple Jack Langley's reason, to cause his hatred of Bakstein to fester for eight years, until he took his revenge?

Dysart wanted facts, not imaginings.

Thorneycroft collected a pile of his own notes, including those he had made in the last few hours. He added the Bellows tape and Rosa's document, and carried them all to Ivans's desk.

'Can you do a bit of lateral research on these?' he asked. 'Any supporting documents, any cross reference to other similar situations, you know the kind of thing. I'm especially interested in the Hopewell document, although I'm told it's innocuous.'

'A cigarette end's innocuous until you test it for DNA,' Ivans said.

Something sparked in Thorneycroft's mind. 'You're right. Unfortunately, we don't have the original. The killer removed it. Maybe his DNA is on the papers.'

'Sweat would do it.' Ivans was already sorting Thorneycroft's notes. 'I'll get back to you asap.'

'Try Clunbury first,' Thorneycroft said. 'They probably have stuff on record. Tell them it's very urgent. I think the perp's getting ready to make another hit.'

Ivans nodded, reaching for the telephone.

Thorneycroft realized that it was past two o'clock and he was hungry. He left the station, bought a hamburger and ate it on a park bench. He could hear the distant throb of the river traffic, and the clang of a clock striking the half hour.

Time is measured from Greenwich, he thought. East meets West here. What's the meeting point of the murders of Cornwall and Bakstein?

Trevor was the first to be killed. Was he the prime target, and Bakstein a secondary victim? We have a better understanding of Bakstein's death – the nuclear physicist with many enemies, always a potential victim of a political assassin.

Arriving back at the station, he found Ivans waiting for him. He handed Thorneycroft a folder. 'Clunbury came to the party,' he said. 'I'm running a check on newspaper records, to see if I can dredge up pictures for comparison.' He hurried away, whistling happily.

Thorneycroft settled at his desk and studied the items Ivans had given him. They affected him like a blow in the solar plexus. He buzzed Dysart on the intercom, but the duty sergeant told him the DCI was at a media conference and not expected back until 3.30.

'When he comes in, tell him I must talk to him at once,' Thorneycroft directed.

He set himself to do a rapid review of material that would back up the report from Ivans. He re-ran the video, stopping it at a key point, and repeated that process with the tape of his interview with Bellows. He made notes of the conclusions he'd drawn from the tapes, and added points he recalled from his meetings with Langley, Cousins and Rosa Hopewell.

It all added up. There were shreds of evidence that pointed to who killed Bakstein, and why. The shreds must be added to, and woven into a web of fact that would provide a case that would hold up in a court of law.

Most important of all, the link between the killings of Bakstein and Trevor Cornwall must be established beyond doubt.

Thorneycroft spoke to the duty sergeant and asked if Nosey Turner was back from leave.

'He came home last night,' the sergeant answered. 'He'll be back at work tomorrow.'

'I need to speak to him at once,' Thorneycroft said. 'What's his home number?'

He made the call and Nosey took it on the second buzz. 'Dr Thorneycroft? Is it about the photographs? I collected them an hour ago from Concorde Street. I'll bring them in if you need them.'

'I do need them, Nosey, and I need you to show them on your magnifier.'

'I'll be there in twenty minutes.'

Thorneycroft thanked him, and, pulling a file from the stack on the desk, he reviewed the reports on the death of Trevor Cornwall.

XXVI

DYSART AND NOSEY Turner arrived together at Thorneycroft's door. Dysart's expression was thunderous, and he lost no time in saying why.

'That cow Hopewell,' he said, 'before she came crawling to us for protection, she sold her story to Ty Hudson of *The Daily Despatch*. She told him she was in fear of her life. Said she'd worked for Jeremy Cousins as a translator of material relating to nuclear piracy, and advised Hudson to ask Cousins why he didn't take the call Bakstein made to him at the Seattle conference, the day before he was murdered.

'Hudson drew no comment from Cousins, so he spoke to the Seattle organizers. His story's in this evening's *Despatch*. It hints that Bakstein was killed because our authorities didn't protect him against an assassin hired by "some nuclear pirate".

'Rosa Hopewell has put Bakstein's concern about nuclear piracy slap bang in the public eye. I told her that what's she's done is a serious offence. Her answer was that when she sold the story to Hudson she was "just taking out insurance".'

'That's crap,' Thorneycroft said. 'She's warned the killer that we're investigating the links Bakstein had with Cousins and herself. He knows now that we're closing in on him and that makes him immensely dangerous, not just to Rosa and Cousins but to everyone on the investigating team. All of us and our families.'

'Exactly. It's too late to kill the story. We must just hope that Langley doesn't read *The Despatch*.'

'Forget about Langley,' Thorneycroft said. 'He's not the killer.'

Dysart blinked, and pointed at the material piled on Thorneycroft's desk.

'Are you saying you have a better suspect?'

'I have a theory.' Thorneycroft indicated the package in Nosey's hands. 'Those are the enlargements of the photographs Trevor took at Dubai. I believe they can identify the killer.'

'Then what the hell are we standing here for?'

Dysart turned and headed for the stairs that led down to Nosey's basement laboratory, Nosey at his heels. Thorneycroft followed, carrying a filing tray loaded with files, his own notes, the video cassette and his tape of the Bellows interview.

In the basement Nosey set chairs to face a television set and its clutch of satellite machines. Thorneycroft shuffled through the photographs from Concorde Street.

All Trevor's Dubai photos had been developed and three of them had been enlarged to poster-board size. Thorneycroft selected two of the smaller prints and laid them aside. He held up the first of the enlargements.

'Trevor took a full roll of photos of a race at Dubai. He developed all of the negatives himself and printed three at portrait size. At my request, Concorde Street has blown those three up to poster size. They provide a record of the horse French Toast winning the mile race.' He held up the first enlargement.

'This shows the start of the race,' he said.

The photograph was technically superb, and showed in clear detail the Dubai starting gates flown up and the horses surging onto the racetrack.

'Sixteen horses in the race,' Thorneycroft said. 'The favourite's well placed in the centre of the track, and French Toast is here, close behind.'

He held up the second enlargement.

'This one was taken in the final stages; you can see the seven-furlong post to the left of the picture. There are six horses in the picture, bunched together. You can see that French Toast's jockey has moved him to the edge of the bunch to give him a clear run to the finishing post.

'And in this picture,' he held it up, 'French Toast is passing the post. There are no other horses in the picture. He is the unchallenged winner. In fact, he won by three lengths. The pictures show his tremendous finishing speed, the sort of acceleration power that owners and trainers dream of.

'After watching that race, Trevor knew he had a potential champion. He developed these three pictures to show what French Toast can do against good competition. He trimmed off the edges of the prints because he wanted pictures of his horse, he didn't need the other runners or the crowds. He'd have used his photos for publicity purposes when the right time came.

'But it's the crowds that we actually have to look at now.'

He gave Nosey one of the smaller prints he'd selected.

'Can you magnify this for us,' he asked, 'and focus on this area?' He traced a circle on the print.

Nosey fed the picture into a box linked to the side of his television set, and pressed buttons. The picture appeared on the television screen, much magnified. Nosey shifted the focus to the right until Thorneycroft said, 'stop there'.

They were looking at something out of a slapstick movie. The photo showed the crowd close-packed at the rail of the track, mouths wide, yelling in excitement. In the centre of the designated area, a young man leapt exultantly, his outflung arm striking the face of a bearded man in Arab dress.

Nosey chuckled 'Bashed off the sheik's dark goggles,' he said. 'Pricey ones, I hope the gent backed French Toast.'

Thorneycroft handed him another print. 'Show this one. Focus on that same area.'

Nosey obliged. The picture appeared on screen, shifted to hone in on the same portion of the crowd. Now the young man stood aghast, while the bearded man clawed at air as his dark glasses soared skywards. His face stood out in crystalline detail; snarling mouth, bared teeth, eyes as cold and gold as a lion's. He appeared to be staring straight at the camera.

Dysart sprang to this feet, leaned to the screen, swung to face Thorneycroft.

'It can't be,' he said. 'Moorland's dead!'

Thorneycroft shook his head. 'He's alive. He was at Dubai race-course that day. Trevor photographed him without meaning to. He was only interested in getting good pictures of his horse. But that one cost him his life.'

Dysart recovered his breath. 'They faked Moorland's death. They cooked the video.'

'Yes.' Thorneycroft touched the cassette. 'I can show you the place where they switched him for another man.'

'Don't trouble, I can guess,' Dysart said grimly. 'The video opened with a thug ranting about the rape of Iraq. Then it showed the three captives. They were trussed like turkeys but they weren't blindfolded. Then Moorland struggled, and a guard pulled a sack over his head.

'Then there was another burst of hate speech and the camera stayed on the speaker. When it reverted to the victims, Moorland was still struggling, his head was in the sack and the sack was strapped across his mouth with plastic tape. The man was masked and gagged. They substituted another man for Moorland. Some poor sod was butchered in Moorland's place.'

'Yes,' Thorneycroft agreed, 'and the sack concealed his eyes, which would have shown it wasn't Moorland who was shot.'

'Why did they shoot any of them?' Nosey said. 'They were only a couple of days away from £15 million. What made them change their plans?'

'The Iraq War,' Thorneycroft answered. 'They must have real-ized they'd little chance of collecting the ransom money; but they had Moorland, a nuclear physicist. He was pay dirt. They kept him alive and sold him to a country outside of the Non-prolifera-tion Treaty. Willing seller, willing buyer. Some country reckoned Moorland was worth the cash, and he went along with the deal. Being a traitor was preferable to taking a bullet in the brain.'

'Why did they have to fake Moorland's death?'

'Pirate buyers need secrecy, they need to hoodwink the world into thinking they've abandoned their nuclear arms programmes. If Moorland was officially declared dead, he couldn't be working with an illegal manufacturer. His two companions were killed to make that story more convincing.'

Dysart was still staring at the picture on the screen. 'Moorland must have been standing directly opposite Cornwall when that picture was taken,' he said. 'He was looking right at Trevor's camera when his glasses were knocked off. He saw Trevor take the picture. He must have realized he'd be on it. If it was published, there was a good chance he'd be recognized. Unmasked.'

'Yes. I think he decided then and there to kill Trevor. The last photo on Trevor's roll shows Moorland pushing through the crowd, heading for the winner's stall. He stood and watched Trevor lead in French Toast. The course officials would have been able to supply him with Trevor's name and address. Moorland saw Trevor as a man who could prove he was alive, mark him a traitor and a sell-out. That would be the end of his profitable career as a nuclear snitch. Not even a rogue country wants to employ a man who's charged with treason, and figures on the world's most-wanted list.'

Dysart turned back to face Thorneycroft. 'So he came to England to silence Cornwall. What about Bakstein? How does he fit in?'

In reply, Thorneycroft handed him the copy of Rosa Hopewell's document, and the printouts Ivans had received from Clunbury.

'Jack Langley told me that Eric Moorland started his career designing and building nuclear research stations in various countries. Clunbury kept his early designs on file, with the press reports on his work. Moorland always wrote his press releases himself. If you compare the Clunbury material with Rosa Hopewell's document you can see there are similarities.'

Dysart was comparing the papers. 'You can,' he said, 'not just in the designs but in the press releases. Moorland uses certain designs and certain phrases. He has his own style. You think Bakstein picked that up?'

'I think so, and he realized that Moorland might still be alive.'

'Why didn't he come straight to us with his suspicions?'

Thorneycroft hesitated, and Nosey spoke.

'Maybe he thought Rosa's document was just a copy of something Moorland wrote years ago.'

'That must have crossed his mind,' Thorneycroft agreed, 'and he evidently wanted to discuss it with Cousins, perhaps urge him to make discreet inquiries. If it turned out that Moorland was alive, they could try to get him home without a scandal that would damage Britain's reputation for clean dealing in nuclear power matters.'

Dysart laid the papers aside. 'Moorland knew for a fact that Cornwall photographed him at Dubai, and so he killed Cornwall. But how did he know that Rosa Hopewell had been sent a copy of his press release about the nuclear station that was opened six months ago?'

'There's no way of knowing. He could have been tipped off by a friend, or by his recent employers or by the people who provided him with cash and accelerator bullets and a Cougar III. That's for Intelligence to unravel. One thing I'm sure of is that Moorland's out on his own, now. His usefulness as a nuclear advisor must be over, and if Trevor's photos are made public, Moorland will be exposed as a traitor and a sell-out. He'll be seen as unemployable, and therefore expendable. He'll be looking for a new place to hide, where he can change his appearance, and make a new life for himself. To do that he needs cash ... a lot of it, and fast.'

'He'll go for what's most easily available.' Dysart looked appalled. 'Jack and Sybilla Langley. They control the five million given to the ransom fund, and there's the money left to Eric Moorland by his grandfather and father ... that would have passed to his parents when he was presumed dead.'

'He may even believe if they refuse to hand over, the money will come to him if they die.'

'Rising from the dead?'

'He could fabricate some story. He's not sane, Iain, he knows we're close. My fear is, he'll use Sybilla Langley as a hostage, and get Jack Langley to sign over some colossal amount. We must warn Langley to take his wife and everyone else in that house to some safe place.'

'Yes. You speak to him, John. I have to report to the super. We need to alert the ports and airfields to watch for Moorland, and I must arrange Special Force protection for the people he may attack. The local cops can watch the roads round Worth, but if Moorland shows, they mustn't try to take him, they'll get themselves killed. They must have trained backup. I'll tell them I'll get down there myself as fast as I can.'

'I can go now,' Thorneycroft said.

'No, you can't, you're not a policeman.'

'I'm an army reservist. I'm permitted to carry arms, and use them if the life of an innocent person is threatened. I can make a citizen's arrest.'

Dysart hesitated. Then he said, 'For now, just warn Langley to get himself and his people out. We'll deal with the rest once they're safe. You have my mobile number, keep in touch.' He turned to Nosey. 'You come with me, and bring all the material, particularly the photos. They'll convince Buxton quicker than a thousand words.'

He and Nosey hurried away. Thorneycroft moved to the telephone and punched in Jack Langley's home number.

XXVII

LANGLEY'S PHONE RANG unanswered for what seemed a long time. Thorneycroft wondered uneasily if there was anyone at home. When at last Langley spoke, his tone was unwelcoming, but it softened when Thorneycroft gave his name.

'Yes, Doctor, what can I do for you?'

'I'm calling on behalf of DCI Dysart,' Thorneycroft explained. 'We've identified a suspect in the murder of Julian Bakstein. We have reason to believe that Bakstein was killed by a person or persons involved in the illegal production of nuclear armaments. They have a hit list, and your name may be on it.'

'For God's sake, why would it be?' Langley sounded almost amused. 'I have nothing to do with that unholy trade, or with the criminals who run it.'

'You son was kidnapped and executed by thugs who do have such links. I understand you raised the ransom money demanded by the kidnappers, and that you still control the trust fund set up to contain it.'

'True, but what has that to do with Bakstein's death? I find this conversation pointless. If the police are going to indulge in thumb-sucking, I prefer—'

Thorneycroft cut him short. 'Please, Mr Langley, we don't have time to argue. Just accept that knowledgeable people believe you and the members of your household are in danger. DCI Dysart urges you to move everyone on your property to a safe place, and to stay there with them until we can provide all of you adequate protection.

Langley brushed the advice aside. 'What's this suspect's name?' he demanded.

'I'm not at liberty to reveal that,' Thorneycroft said, 'but I can tell you that the suspect will probably try to lay hands on the ransom money you raised.'

'That's impossible. It's secured by a trust. It takes three signatures to access the funds, and I for one won't give a brass farthing to that bunch of murderers.'

'You may have no choice. The killer may well take a hostage … your wife, for instance. Will you deny him money in those circumstances?'

'Dr Thorneycroft, you're offering me imaginings, not facts. Is what you say grounded on evidence gained by the police, or is it just wild theory?'

'I'm giving you advice from a seasoned police investigator. DCI Dysart does not indulge in imaginings. As for myself, I'm a forensic psychiatrist with experience of such killers, and I'm telling you that this man is psychotic, and extremely dangerous. I believe he will try to extract money from you, and use it to escape from this country to whatever haven he's marked down for himself. Until he is arrested, you and your dependants are in grave danger.'

'Then it's the duty of the police to protect us.'

'DCI Dysart is trying to arrange that, but I must point out that protection will be far more difficult if you and your people remain in that house. Please hear what I'm saying. Leave your home. Move your household to a safe place. Don't discuss the move with anyone else, and see that your people don't try to communicate with anyone at all. Just put them in your car, and go. Now. At once.'

Langley was silent for so long that Thorneycroft feared he had ended the call, but at last he spoke.

'Very well, Doctor. I will do as you ask.'

Thorneycroft heaved a sigh of relief. 'Good. Call Iain Dysart as soon as you're in a place of safety.' He gave Langley Dysart's contact numbers. 'And understand,' he concluded, 'you must stay with your people, and follow whatever instruction the chief inspector gives you. We'll let you know as soon as it's safe for you to go home.'

'I understand,' Langley said. 'Goodbye Doctor, and thank you for your concern.'

The line went dead. Thorneycroft wiped sweat off his face. He wondered if Langley would in fact keep his word. There'd been a disturbing note in his voice at the last. He'd made up his mind, but to what?

Could Dysart's suspicions be justified? Was Langley a deranged killer? Or might he have guessed that his son was alive and guilty of two murders? How would he act over the next few hours? As an ally, or an enemy?

There was no profit in speculation.

Thorneycroft made his way to the incident room where Dysart and his team were working to create the network that could prevent Moorland's escape from England. Dysart came to Thorneycroft's side.

'You spoke to Langley?'

'I did. He'll take his wife, her companion and the three staff members to a safe place. He'll inform you when that's done. I told him to stay with them, but I'm afraid he may go back to his house.'

'Why would he? He could get himself killed.'

'He may have guessed that Eric's our suspect. Eric may already have made contact with him.' As Dysart grimaced, Thorneycroft said, 'It's his son in question, Iain. Would you just sit on your hands if it was your boy?'

'I don't know what the hell I'd do. This whole thing is guess-work. I've been arguing with Special Branch, they say they can't mount an operation against a man who's officially dead and who's never been charged with any crime. They don't see their way clear to protecting a figment of my imagination.'

'It's imperative we have trained men to corner Moorland. Cops from the beat will be helpless against him.'

'I know, and the super's doing all he can to bring in an attack unit. In the meantime I've fixed for the Worth police to watch their approach road to Langley's property, and the Epsom nick will post men on all the other routes. If Moorland's spotted we'll know at once.'

'I'm going down there,' Thorneycroft said. 'I'll get onto Langley's property, keep an eye on the house and grounds. I think Moorland may try to use Langley's plane. It's got a good enough range to get him to France, Spain, maybe even North Africa.'

Dysart was shaking his head. 'No, John, this man has to be dealt with by law. You have no police status. You can't play the avenging angel.'

'I don't intend to. I know the law. I know I can't shoot anyone unless he threatens my life or the life of another innocent person. I've been trained to defend myself and others. I may be able to prevent Moorland killing again.'

'Wait until we have a unit in place.'

'There's no time.' Thorneycroft was already moving towards the door. 'Thanks to the piece in *The Despatch*, Moorland will be on the move. If you do manage to engage a unit, see they're posted in the woods on Langley's boundary, but they must not break cover without your say-so. If Moorland shows and tries to get to that plane, I'll do what I can to stop him. If I fail, destroy the plane and him.'

'John,' Dysart said.

Thorneycroft turned in the doorway, smiling.

'You keep in touch,' Dysart said. 'Understand?'

'Of course.'

'Just don't do anything I wouldn't do,' Dysart said, but he spoke to empty air.

Thorneycroft drove fast to Wimbledon.

The night guard from Bladen's had come on duty, and Thorneycroft explained that he would be away from London for twenty-four hours.

'I hope to be back tomorrow evening,' he said. 'I'll leave the protection of my property to you and Gatsby. If you have any problems at all, call the local police.'

Gatsby met him at the front door and followed him up the stairs to his dressing room. He changed quickly into long-disused gear: a dark camouflage suit with teflon under-jacket, dark socks and boots, a knitted cap and a helmet. He slipped a pot of black face paint and his mobile phone into the pockets of his jacket.

Unlocking the gun cupboard at the rear of the room, he lifted out his rifle, an ammunition belt and a backpack that held articles not designed for peaceloving citizens. He extracted a sheathed knife and balanced it on his palm. It was good for throwing, or for close combat. He attached the sheath to the clip on his belt.

His rifle was in prime condition. He slid his hand along its length and felt a cold pleasure that he'd thought was a thing of the past. This gun was made for war, not sport. It was fast and deadly accurate. It gave the possessor an advantage over any ordinary rifleman. Against Moorland, an advantage was to be welcomed.

At his side, Gatsby whined unhappily, scenting anger. Thorneycroft stooped to hug his neck. Gatsby followed him down to the door that led to the garage, and scrabbled wildly when Thorneycroft shut the door in his face.

The gun and backpack safe in the boot, Thorneycroft reversed the car to the street. The guard lifted a hand in salute, and closed the gate. The clang of its metal against the gatepost seemed to mark the end of peace, the start of a journey to a battlefield.

Driving south, Thorneycroft considered his chances.

With luck there would be backup, some of it armed and trained to handle combat, some of it unarmed and virtually a danger to themselves and others. All of them would be working in unfamiliar territory, and without proper briefing.

The heavy afforestation round Worth would provide ample cover for a marksman like Moorland. He had the advantage of knowing the area from childhood, the paths through the surrounding woods, the possible weak points in the encircling fences. He knew the layout of the house, the hangar and the airstrip. The airstrip was long and wide enough to allow an aircraft to take off from either end.

The shooting range had been built only two years ago. Moorland might or might not know of its existence and its geography. Thorneycroft visualized the permanent fixed targets, set on their pyramids of rough stone. Those could provide cover for advancing men … or for a resident sniper. But in the dark, the range could also present unguessed obstacles.

Was Moorland a qualified pilot? Did he hope to escape that way, hedgehopping around the radar patterns, making for Europe or North Africa?

He would want to enter the house, to search for money or valuables, or, if Langley was there, to persuade him to hand over money.

Did Moorland have allies at hand, who could set him on his way to some dark sanctuary? He was facing the might of international law, but there were plenty of organizations outside of the law which would shelter anyone who could pay their price.

It all came down to money. Money meant life and freedom to Moorland. He would come to his father's house for money, he was on his way; he would kill anyone who stood in his way.

He was a ruthless psychopath who planned every detail of his crimes. That could prove to be his weakness. He liked to work to a meticulous plan. He killed and made his escape according to plan.

He would have a plan tonight. He would expect it to run smoothly. The key to defeating him was to disrupt his plan, put him off balance.

Thorneycroft saw in his mind's eye the Langley property, the house standing foursquare on its manicured lawns. If Moorland gained entry to the house, he could hold out there for some time. If he knew the combinations of the safes, he would be able to draw on Langley's bankroll and his armoury. It might take an assault unit with stun grenades and tear gas to dislodge him. In the process he could kill several people.

If he entered the house and found it deserted, what would he do? Would he lie in wait there for the householders' return, or would he decide to get out quickly?

Thorneycroft considered the plane and the airstrip. Could they be put out of action? Moorland would need the airstrip lights. It was already twilight. In a couple of hours it would be dark, with only the sliver of the young moon to illumine sky and land.

The most vital question centred on Jack Langley. If he broke his word and returned to the house, if he encountered his son there, how would he react? Would he give Eric money and help him to escape, or would he try to turn him over to the police? There was no way of knowing.

At Crawley, Thorneycroft pulled off the road and called Dysart. He gave him his position, and asked if he had left London.

'Clay and I are approaching Redhill,' Dysart answered. 'The rest of the team will follow with backup. Langley phoned me to say his lot are with friends in Reigate.'

'Is Langley with them?'

'I don't know. He just gave me that message and rang off. I called him back, but his mobile's switched off.'

'Not good news. He may have headed home.'

'I've warned our men to keep a lookout for him. The super's onto an armed assault unit stationed at East Grinstead, I hope to meet them at Crawley. We'll deploy the trained men to points on Langley's garden fence, but keep them under cover until we know what we have to deal with. If you give me the word, they can move in fast.'

'I'll be going in from the Worth side. Who's in charge there?'

'A Sergeant Hopgood. When you reach Worth, stop at the foresters' depot, leave your car there. Hopgood will show you a path through the woods that will take you close to Langley's house. The woodsmen cleared the path a week ago, thinned the brushwood and undergrowth, so you shouldn't be ambushed, but watch your step. Hopgood thinks Moorland's more likely to come in from the north fence – that's where the house is closest to a tarred road, if he tries for a quick getaway.'

'A plane is quicker.'

'If he can fly it, yes.'

They discussed communication with each other and with the support groups. Thorneycroft wished Dysart well and headed for the narrow lanes that would bring him unobserved to Worth.

XXVIII

HOPGOOD LED THORNEYCROFT to a gate in the woods. The twilight was fading, but it was still possible to see the path to Langley's property.

Thorneycroft paused to apply camouflage paint to his face, neck and hands. As he traced the streaks and blotches that had become habit on his army missions, he found himself repeating his mantra of those days: breathe deeply, stay cool, focus on the job in hand, do it and get out.

He set out along the path, stepping quietly, rifle at the ready, watching for any sign of another presence. None appeared. Another gate admitted him to Langley's property. The path skirted the back of the building, threading its way through woodland to debouch in a small clearing. Langley's house was visible through the trees to Thorneycroft's left. He advanced to the shelter of thick undergrowth and studied the building.

It was silent, no light showing. Curtains were drawn across the windows. The garage at the rear was closed. Was Langley's Lexus there, or with his friends in Reigate?

Thorneycroft surveyed the territory. The east, west and north sides of the clearing were formed by thick stands of birch, pine and bracken. The south side overhung the path from the house to the hangar. He found a place there that afforded good cover, but allowed him to see the house to his left and the hangar a hundred yards to his right.

There was no light showing anywhere on the property, no sign of human occupation. He moved to his right down a slope that abutted on a ditch running from the foot of a hillock, to the back corner of the hangar. A pipe had been laid along the length of the ditch. Water from a spring? The ditch provided a channel down which he could move unseen.

He walked along the pipeline to the point where the ditch ended. The back wall of the hangar was a couple of yards away. The door in the back of the hangar was padlocked.

Away to his right lay Langley's practice range, with its stone-based targets. Its northern boundary was formed by the roofed colonnade that housed the moving targets. The colonnade curved south, to the far end of the airstrip.

The moving targets must be electrically operated. Was the switchboard inside the hangar, or out?

Thorneycroft scanned the sky. It was darkening fast, and a bank of cloud was moving in from the west, increasing the gloom. He slipped quietly across a narrow strip of turf, to the west side of the hangar.

A porch protruded from the hangar wall and he stepped into its shelter. He shone the light of a pencil torch over the interior of the porch. The switchboard was at the back. A master switch controlled the board.

Did it turn on the airstrip lights as well as those of the target areas? He examined the rows of minor switches, reading the label over each one.

There was no switch for the airstrip lights. That must be controlled from inside the hangar.

There was a single switch for the stationary targets. On or off.

The movable targets each had a switch that activated lights, movement and sound.

Thorneycroft recalled similar training systems. Set one going, and figures sprang into view, lights flared, voices yelled. The marksman had split seconds to decide whether the target was friend or foe, to shoot or hold his fire. To further confuse him there were sound effects of enemy forces, the rattle of AK47s, the ploff-ploff of mortars.

Thorneycroft turned on all the switches except the master switch. Activate that, and it would all happen.

He edged from the porch to the front corner of the hangar. Its huge doors stood open, shielding him from the open ground. Langley's plane was on the tarmac apron. It waited, ready for flight.

Langley must have left it there. Had Moorland already communicated with him? Was Langley preparing to fly him to safety? Or was Langley lying dead in one of those silent rooms?

If that was the case, Thorneycroft thought, I'd be dead too. Moorland's not here yet.

He crept back to his hide in the forest. He called Dysart and reported what he'd seem and done. Then he settled down to watch and wait.

It was a bird that gave him warning, rising in panic with a loud cawing. It was some way away, to the north.

Thorneycroft kept his eyes on the house. It remained silent and dark. Some ten minutes passed before a shape moved from the trees at the rear of the building. A man with a rifle. He stepped onto the path and edged forward, halted. A torch flared briefly and went out. The man moved forward again, seemingly unaware that he was observed.

At the corner of the house the man paused again, his head turning slowly as he scanned the reaches of the garden and woods. Satisfied, he walked swiftly along the front facade, reached the front door and pressed the doorbell. The door swung open at once, throwing a narrow band of light across the doorstep. A figure leaned out, arm outstretched in a beckoning movement. For a moment the two faces were visible.

Then Jack Langley drew his long-dead son into the house.

Thorneycroft called Dysart. 'Moorland's here,' he said. 'He's in the house, and so is Langley.'

Dysart swore. 'I knew it. They've set this up. Langley lied. We'll have to take them both. The unit's arrived, we're in place. We can rush them.'

'No.' Thorneycroft spoke softly but with force. 'We can't be sure that Langley's an accomplice. He may be trying to contest Moorland's demands. He'll do whatever's best for Sybilla. We have to give him the benefit of the doubt. We'll see how things stand when they leave the house. Have the men ready, but warn them that Moorland's the target. Not Langley and not me! Tell them, if they hear gunfire, it doesn't mean they can fire at random.'

'John, you're taking too much on yourself.'

'It's the best way. I'll tell you when they quit the house.' Thorneycroft ended the call.

There were signs of movement in the house. For an instant a crack of light gleamed at a back window, then a curtain was closed with a jerk. They had moved to Langley's study. Time went by. Half an hour, forty minutes. There was no sound, no noise of a struggle, no gunshots.

Were they arguing, or making plans?

Thorneycroft waited. His breathing was steady, his mind cold and clear, focused on the job in hand.

It was close on an hour before the two men emerged from the house.

They walked together, Moorland gripping his father's arm from behind. The pistol in his right hand was pressed against Langley's spine. His rifle was slung over his left shoulder.

Thorneycroft welcomed that fact. Had Moorland been aware of his presence, he would not have moved so openly, and the rifle would have been in his hands.

There was still a chance to surprise him, take him off balance.

Thorneycroft watched the two men pass, their steps quiet on the paved path. When they were out of hearing, he called Dysart.

'They're out of the house, heading for the hangar. Moorland's holding a gun on Langley. Be calm. Langley can't have told him we're onto him.'

'Or they're faking it,' Dysart said. 'If Langley backs that scum, you're in trouble, John. Best let us take them.'

'No. Better if I can take Moorland myself. I'm going in. Enjoy the fireworks.' He cut the connection.

Moorland and Langley were taking the branch of the path that led to the tarmac in front of the hangar, where the plane was waiting.

Thorneycroft ran down to the ditch, traversed it and crossed to the porch that housed the control board. As he reached it the lights along the airstrip sprang to life. They faced inward, brilliant on the course the plane must take, but less bright on the target areas and the hangar.

Thorneycroft depressed the master switch on the control board. A cacophony of noise erupted; lights flared and vanished; figures ran, leaped and disappeared. Thorneycroft raced along the back of the hangar and its east side. The big door stood ajar and the crack between door and wall allowed him a view of Moorland and Langley.

They stood transfixed on the tarmac apron. Moorland had an arm round Langley's throat, pinning him to his own body. His eyes were on the colonnade. Langley broke into violent struggles, seeking to break the stranglehold on his neck.

Thorneycroft stepped from behind the hangar door and shouted, 'Moorland! Drop the gun!'

Moorland's head jerked round, he saw Thorneycroft and his arm swept up, aiming the pistol, and he fired; but Langley's struggles knocked him sideways, and the shot went wide.

Langley broke free, stumbled and fell. Thorneycroft fired a warning shot over Moorland's head, but he ignored it, he was snatching at the sling of his rifle, tearing it from his shoulder, swinging it into position.

Thorneycroft shot him between the eyes. Moorland's body was flung backwards, fell prone. Thorneycroft approached him with caution, but there was no movement. No pulse.

Langley was struggling to rise. He shivered violently and tears ran down his face. Thorneycroft helped him to his feet and half-lifted him to a bench inside the hangar. He took off his jacket and draped it round Langley's shoulders.

There were men racing towards them from the forest, and up the airstrip. Dysart was one of the first to reach the tarmac apron. He came straight to Thorneycroft.

'You all right?'

Thorneycroft nodded. 'Get someone to turn off that bloody switchboard,' he said. 'It's in the porch, round the side.'

Dysart gave an instruction to a uniformed policeman and turned to Langley.

'Sir, were you intending to fly your son out of England?'

Langley raised his head slowly. He stared at Dysart as if he had difficulty in recognzing him. He said, 'I meant to take the plane out over the Atlantic and ditch it. If you check the fuel you'll see that we couldn't have gone far. I had to stop him somehow. He didn't intend to let me live. I knew he'd come back, get to Sybilla, take her money and then kill her too. He's not my son. My son died eight years ago. This man I had to stop, but you saved me the trouble.'

He leaned his head on his arms, seeming not to notice the activity all round him, the police and soldiers, the dead body, encircled now by police tape.

Dysart looked at Thorneycroft. 'I'll ask the questions later ... when we've finished here.'

Thorneycroft leaned against the hangar wall. He felt tired and empty. He wished that there had been some other man to play avenging angel. He said to Langley,

'Thank you. You saved my life.'

Langley looked up at him. 'As you saved mine.' He glanced at the people on the tarmac, the professionals performing routine tasks round the body. He said, 'Can they deal with this quietly? Can they just leave it that Eric died eight years ago? If Sybilla learns what he did, what he became, it will kill her.'

'The law takes its course, I'm afraid,' Thorneycroft answered. Then he remembered Cousins, and those others who preferred to trust in the tissue of lies they called diplomacy.

'We can try,' he said. A thought occurred to him. 'Did Eric talk to you before he came here?'

'Not until a few hours ago,' Langley said. 'He called me just before you did. Said he was "coming home", as if he'd only been away a couple of weeks. He said he'd come to discuss the money owing to him. He was rambling in his speech. I realized he was mad, and when you phoned, so anxious to get us away from here, I understood he was the one who killed those two good men. I had to come back from Reigate. He was my responsibility, that's what I decided. My responsibility.'

XXIX

DIPLOMACY WON THE DAY.

It was announced that the killer of Trevor Cornwall and Julian Bakstein had been identified. He was, the statement read, a madman who had accessed the property of Jack Langley in an attempt to lay hands on money and weapons. He was known to have been in the employ of renegades manufacturing illicit nuclear arms. He had attempted to take Mr Langley hostage, in the hope that he could be flown to a foreign country. This intention had been thwarted by the courageous intervention of Dr John Thorneycroft, who had tried to arrest the culprit. The man had resisted arrest, and had been shot dead. The shooting was clearly necessary in defence of the lives of Dr Thorneycroft and Mr Langley.

The statement concluded by explaining that in order to safeguard the lives of foreign agents loyal to Britain, names and locations which might identify the guilty man could not be revealed.

The story created a brief sensation. Dysart, Thorneycroft and other members of the team were plagued for comment, which they refused to give. Rosa Hopewell, offered handsome remuneration for her version of the tale, dismissed the inquiries out of hand.

Jack and Sybilla Langley, with companion Jane Blarney were not to be found by the searching press. They were sheltered first by friends, and later they left together on a cruise that lasted six months.

Early on, Superintendent Buxton made it plain to the media that they were wasting their time.

Thorneycroft completed the work he'd contracted for, and went back thankfully to his professional round. Claudia, Luke and Gatsby showed that that was the way they liked things to be.

Three months after the case was closed, Liz Cupar and Iain Dysart were married. Thorneycroft was best man at the wedding.

On their return from honeymoon, the newly-weds invited Thorneycroft's family, and the Greenwich team to attend a race meeting at which French Toast was to make his English debut. Hosts and guests put their money on the horse and watched him win his race with that splendid burst of finishing speed that was to become the hallmark of his champion's career.